Lindall, E., pseud.
Paper Frost

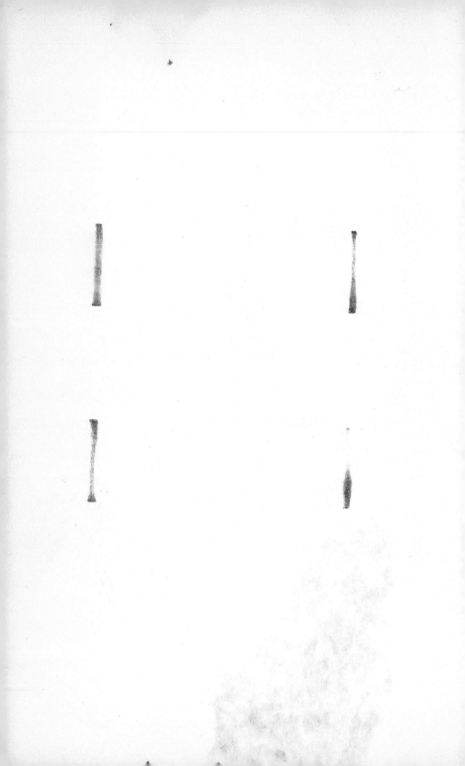

The Paper Ghost

The
Paper Ghost

EDWARD LINDALL, *pseud.*

WILLIAM MORROW & COMPANY New York 1961

The Paper Ghost

1

THE GRASS ON THE LOW, ROUNDED HILL ACROSS THE RIVER CLAY was beginning to turn yellow, and the white patches of the limestone outcrops were growing larger every day. The grass on that hill was always the first to lose its green when summer came shouldering in, for the soil was poor, and thin where it managed to cover the limestone.

I was looking at it through my window, from my desk across the room, remembering how I had loved that mottled look when Clayville and I were thirty years younger. When I was five. It had meant swimming and fishing then, in the bay or in the river, and walking barefoot with the fine, hot, powdery dust puffing up between my toes. It had meant the opening of the joyous season. But it didn't any more.

"It doesn't make sense," Clark said. "A man of your standing coming back to a hick town like this."

He was sitting at the other side of my desk, watching me with sharply patient eyes. He had been there yesterday, too, talking around all this and that for more than an hour without ever getting anywhere; but always with the suggestion of a heavy blackjack somewhere in his verbal armoury. Now, at the outset of his second visit, I recognized the end of skirmishing. The blackjack was bulging through.

"It makes sense to me," I said. "I was born here."

"Sure," Clark said. "But what made you buy a weekly hay-seeds' paper?"

"I have to eat."

"Maybe you got a tip-off," Clark said. "You thought you'd be on the spot for some first-class news."

His voice was gently insistent, his manner tireless. I tried not to let it bother me. It was part of their staff training in the Security Service, the exploratory approach that sometimes turned up a hidden fact.

"I got tired," I said. "I came here for a rest."

"And bought the *Herald* as an excuse to stay."

"You know better than that." I paused, then said evenly: "My story's on the record. You must know all about it."

He shook his head. "Not everything. No matter how much we know, we can't know everything."

I felt a stirring of frustrated anger then, and looked away out the window to the mottled hill again. Ever since the Atomic Research Authority had moved in on Clayville, six months before, I had been expecting that something like this would happen. The wonder was that the Security men had left me alone so long.

I had returned to Clayville because I'd had a gutful of the world and its politics, its hatreds and suspicions, its crass inflexibilities. When I had first got back, Clayville was still the same little outport it had always been, prosperous from the richness of the sheep and wheat lands at its back, stirred to occasional activity by their seasonal demands, subsiding again into its own warm daydreams. I had felt at peace again. But when the atom men had moved in, taking the hill and the plain beyond it, ringing them with a high electric fence, placing out of bounds the northern half of our little bay, I knew that I would have to hold on with both hands to keep what I had gained. I was holding on tightly now. I was determined not to let Clark needle me into spoiling everything.

"You could have got a tip that the Authority was coming," Clark said steadily. "You used to be a bigtime newspaperman. You've got plenty of contacts, haven't you? People who would know?"

I brought my eyes back into the room. Clark was smiling faintly, looking at me from under long, dark lashes. He was just a shade too handsome.

"Listen," I said, biting the word. "I came here for rest and quietness. I want to live my own life and mind my own business. Just that, and nothing more."

"Sure," Clark said blandly. "You've had enough excitement."

"Don't kill me off," I said. "I'm only thirty-five."

He lifted an eyebrow. Interrogative. Without amusement.

I made myself grin at him, and it felt like putting on a mask. "I'm not too old for excitement. I'm just not looking for it."

"Oh, sure," Clark said. "Sure."

He took out a cigarette case and selected a cigarette with vast deliberation. The case was of gold, heavy and expensive. One of those cases that certain types lug around even though they feel like diver's boots in a suit pocket. It bore his initials in a monogram on the outside, and doubtless a message inside from some admiring female. He lit the cigarette, using a gold lighter.

He was purposely building up a silence, so I let him go. I lounged back in the lurching swivel chair that the late Neil Townley had occupied like a throne in his forty years of editorship. And from that position I examined Clark again, trying to assess him, trying to fathom just what it was that he was looking for in me.

William Clark was handsome. He was big, built like a football champion, and his body always seemed relaxed. He was in his late twenties and still possessed the insolent athleticism of the young. He moved smoothly, quietly, but behind his dark eyes there was that watchfulness of repressed energy you see in the eyes of padding animals in a zoo. His hair was black, with a slight wave, pushed straight back from a side parting—well to the right, of course. He had dark, thick brows and long lashes. His face was high cheek-boned and fairly full, sallow-skinned, with the shadow of a subcutaneous beard around the chin. He was a careful dresser. The gray suit he was wearing was the sort of thing you saw generally in advertisements in high-class magazines.

He had smoked half his cigarette before he spoke, and then he rolled it around in his fingers, musingly. "You're an interesting fellow, Scotter."

I watched him carefully. "You flatter me."

He stubbed his cigarette in the tobacco-tin lid that served me for a desk ashtray. "No," he said. "It's not flattery. There's a lot to you that doesn't show on the surface."

"I'm unique, of course," I murmured.

Then he leaned forward, quickly, big chest hard against the desk's edge, dark eyes suddenly intense. "Tell me about Indo-China," he said.

It was an attempt to rattle me. I didn't rattle worth a damn, but I felt a clench of bitterness deep inside. What I had done, and what had happened to me in Indo-China was old stuff. It must have been old for him, too. It was on the official records. Maybe even with my fingerprints, taken from a dirty beer glass on a bar counter. *Dossier: Scotter, Wade; occupation, journalist; nationality, Australian; domestic status, single.*

"What d'you want to know?" I asked.

"Everything."

"The women?" I'm afraid I sneered a little. "Did I take opium, and have a cheroot-smoking mistress?"

Clark grinned tightly. "They tell me you had a lot of Communist contacts up there."

"Who tells you?"

He got another cigarette out of that gold case, and brandished the gold lighter before replying. "We pick this stuff up. Here and there. . . . You know how it is."

"Yes," I said. "I guess I do. Did they also tell you that every other newspaper correspondent worth his salt had Communist contacts, too?"

"No," Clark said blandly. "Tell me about it. I'd hate to go wrong on a thing like this."

There was humbug in every syllable of every word, and I began to wonder if he had thrown Indo-China at me only in preparation for some other goal, to put me on the wrong side of the fence before leading out his ace.

"You know I was up there for a responsible British news-agency?" I said.

"We checked that far."

"It was like this, then," I said patiently. "The French were losing the war. Even then that was fact, and not subversion. And when people are losing wars they're liable to tell you anything to conceal it."

Clark was looking at his hands, which were rather white and with just a hint of pudginess around the fingers. He seemed faintly bored. "I'm listening," he said.

"The French used to tell us tall stories at their press conferences in Saigon," I said, forcing myself into a show of enthusiasm. I hate charades. "They used to tell us how many thousands of the Vietminh they'd killed overnight, how many tanks they'd knocked out, and how many villages and square miles of land they'd recaptured. They weren't really good at it. They laid it on too heavily. The more their troops fell back, the more they said they were winning. It was screwy. So after a briefing we'd look up some Red agents . . . Saigon was full of them . . . high echelon ones, too. By averaging the two versions we reckoned to get somewhere near the truth. . . ." And then I added, fully aware that Clark would be outraged, "The Vietminh, incidentally, were generally the more accurate. They could afford to be. They were winning."

Clark put his hands away. He looked up quickly, his face sharp and stern like a judge in full rebuke. "Why did the French kick you out?"

"Lots of us were kicked out."

"You're the one I'm interested in," Clark said curtly. "Why did they kick you out?"

"For God's sake," I said disgustedly. "Because they didn't like the truth."

"Because you were a security risk," Clark snapped. "Right?"

"That's what they said."

"That's what you were." He thrust out his jaw. "Maybe it's what you are still. A security risk, right here, in Clayville."

I sat there without moving for a long moment. I could feel the muscles knotting in my stomach, and cursed myself for letting it get me that way. It was nearly a year since I had been troubled by that cancelled visa. It had been sunk almost without trace in Clayville's rustic calm. Now it was on the surface again, like a bloated corpse thrown up by a switch tide. And with it came up all the attendant ooze, the stench of suspicion and of accusation, of half-truths and whole lies, the unanswerables that had made my life a misery in Sydney, in London, and the other places where formula and faction were the accepted ways of life. I put my hands flat on the desk and leaned on them, facing Clark squarely.

"And if you'd been a correspondent, what would you have done?"

"Played it straight," he said. "I'd have taken the French communiqués."

The swivel chair squeaked with sympathetic disgust as I flung myself back. "You'd have been a great success," I jeered. "Front-page spreads in the *Civil Service Journal*."

Clark tipped cigarette ash into my tobacco-tin ashtray, and passed his eyes slowly over my battered desk and around my poky, paint-scratched little office.

"You don't seem to have been such a great success yourself," he said deliberately. "Or perhaps I'm deceived by outward signs."

I had tracked his eyes around, touching the things he touched on, pausing where he paused. My desk was battered and untidy, the leather top rolled back at the corners where countless visitors had pushed it with their behinds. The portable typewriter on the pull-out slot at the side was battered, too. It had been through Korea, and Malaya and Indo-China with me, and it had every right to look battered. The walls were a sort of cream, weathered by the hot Clayville summers, with spidery cracks webbing the paint, and, up near the ceiling, a frieze of dust. The floor was covered with brown linoleum, inlaid with green. It must have been bilious new; but now it had sobered down and was, at least, efficient.

To the right of the window was Poldi's desk; a small one dominated by a heavy old organ-grinder of a typewriter. Poldi Lorenz was my sole part-time reporting staff. Her main job was as receptionist-bookkeeper to Dr. Frank Barber, the town's physician. Between times she worked for me. She lived with the Barbers, Frank and Mary. The door leading to the composing and press room out back was also cream, like the walls, but Harry Wells' ink-stained hands had smeared around its handle a square yard of black memorial to his years of coming and going. The street door, more or less clean, was straight ahead of my desk. Behind me was a third one, leading into my living quarters, a fair-sized bed-sittingroom, a bathroom, and a cubicle kitchen.

The office was functional. It had two typewriters, two desks, a telephone and a wastepaper basket. Actually, I had always thought it a dump, but then, with Clark being supercilious on top of everything else, I suddenly changed my mind.

"If there's nothing else you want," I said, "no true confessions, no boyish confidences, d'you think I could get on with my work?"

A small, lopsided smile disfigured Clark's full-lipped mouth. "Very funny," he said softly. "Very, very funny."

13

But he made no move to go, so I knew there was some other maggot thought cavorting in his mind.

"Clark," I said. "I'm taking an early lunch today."

He took out that gold cigarette case again. His fingers rubbed it with slow, unconscious pride before he thumbed the catch. Then, surprisingly, he offered it to me with a slight uplifting of his splendid brows and a little smile that said he really regretted our waspishness and wouldn't I be friends.

"Virginia, this side," he said, pointing. "Turkish, the other."

And I thought the affectation fitted him like a second skin. I hadn't carried two brands of cigarettes myself since my undergraduate days in Sydney. It was then considered smart. I took a Turkish, and on the half-empty Virginia side I saw inscribed, "To darling Bill, from . . ." The inamorata's name was decently concealed by the remaining cigarettes.

"Thanks."

I struck a match, but Clark drew his gold lighter like going for a gun. I snuffed my match and took his proffered light. If he wanted to play at pals I was curious enough to go along. It wouldn't last. I knew it was only a gambit—and a stagey one, at that.

He tucked away his lighter and leaned back. "What gives with you and the Austins?"

His voice was languid, but his eyes were sharp. They were watching me so intently that I knew this was his goal. I wanted to laugh, but a tightness held the laughter back. So this was the big moment. The summit of his carefully built-up questioning. What was between me and the Austins? It was fantastic.

Belle and Clara Austin were the two gentlest, kindest, most unworldly people I had ever known. And I had known them all my life. I had attended the kindergarten they still conducted in their home on Main Street. They had been my parents' lifelong friends. They were my only family now. And Security Officer William Clark was wanting to know what gave with them and me. I didn't mind that so much, despite its stupidity. The thing I minded, that planted uneasiness in me, was the fact that it meant he had got them in his sights.

"What d'you mean, what gives?" My voice was thin.

"Just what I said," he answered softly. "What gives? You call them Aunt Clara and Aunt Belle. And they're no relation."

"They taught me as a kid," I said, trying to sound casual, hoping without conviction that this was something I could pass off. "They were friends of my father . . . and my mother. . . . They changed my pants, for the first time, when I was two weeks old. . . . Why shouldn't I call them aunt?"

Clark held up a hand, limply. "Sure," he said. "But it's strange they should be the only folk in Clayville who fought to stop the Authority buying some of their land. Useless land at that . . . land they had never worked."

"You know why they didn't want to sell."

"I know why they *said* they didn't want to sell," Clark corrected. "And it's just crazy enough to be clever."

My eyes were staring. I could feel them, dry and hot.

"Maybe you just can't understand. Some things must be beyond you."

He shrugged. "I get to understand most things eventually. Just give me time."

He stood up, easily, gracefully, an athletic unfolding of his height and bulk. He looked down at me and I stared back, not getting to my feet. Back of his eyes there was a look I didn't like. I knew, with a terrible certainty, that he was going to start questioning the Austins. And it was somewhere about then, I think, that I started to dislike him thoroughly.

"I'll drop in again some day," he said. "Maybe I'll have some more things about your aunts than we can talk about."

He said it as though he expected to be welcome. I savaged the Turkish cigarette, half-smoked, into my tin ashtray. And when I looked up he was a rear-view silhouette in the doorway, black against the naïve brightness of the street.

2

LUNCH WAS INDIGESTIVE FROM THE FIRST BITE. COLD BEEF from Small's delicatessen, fresh tomatoes and lettuce from Harry Wells' home garden, bread from the Main Street bakery, butter from Wogga Hammond's factory, a can of peaches from Mildura, and a bottle of frosted beer from my own ice box. My favourite hot-weather bachelor lunch, and it all tasted strongly of acid. I couldn't stop thinking about Clark, the things he had stirred up in me with his technique of question and innuendo—and, even more, the implied threat of his suspicions of Clara and Belle Austin.

His sort of loaded questioning would play hell with them. I knew it. He would be able to have them admit anything, from having Martians in the bottom of their garden to being Communist major-generals in disguise. They were so innocent and unworldly they wouldn't know what was happening. Questioned by a Security Officer! It would be, to them, like being flung into the middle of an egg beater. And all because William Clark was too damned tortuous, or dumb, to recognize that truth, even more than untruth, can have it oddities.

The "just crazy enough to be clever" reason why they had wanted to keep their land was because there were rabbits on it. Ordinary, wild, grey, white-tailed rabbits. The government buyers hadn't been able to understand that. Neither could Clark, apparently. But to the Austin sisters it was simple. They loved the wild rabbits, as they loved everything, and the tract across the river was their home. If it were sold and put to use, the rabbits would be driven away. Clark would doubtless have understood their affection if they had kept the rabbits in tiny cages, and poked limp lettuce leaves through to them and given them water in some scum-covered dish. But to reject money for land because it was the home of wild rabbits was so abnormal to him that it could only be the outcropping of some lode of perfidy.

"Just crazy enough to be clever," I murmured, nodding my head in imitation of Clark's judicial weighing, spacing the words the way he had, parading them like exhibits in the tawdry court-room of his mind.

I got up from the table, with its plastic cloth decorated with green fleur-de-lis, and carried the last glass of beer over to the window above the kitchen sink. I wanted to look out because the little room had become claustrophobic, and also, I suppose, because unpleasantness always seems to do with rooms and rarely with the out-of-doors.

I couldn't see the Atomic Research Authority buildings from any of the windows. They were out of sight on the other side of the hill. But I could see the fence, and the yellow timbers of the new jetty they had built in the northern sector of the bay. Clayville itself was largely out of sight from the kitchen. It stretched away to the left, running along the river bank; and behind me, lining the southern shores of the bay. It was shaped roughly like an L, with the *Herald* office and a clump of houses filling the angle where river and ocean met.

Contentment hung like a smog above those houses, with their bright tiled roofs, and tall trees and daubs of flower garden.

They were beautiful the way nature can be so beautiful. But impersonal. And somehow I found myself thinking of a French soldier we had found once in a field in the lush green country out from Saigon. He had had his stomach slit open and filled with sharp stones . . . and he was still alive.

Then something snapped. I whirled around and threw the beer glass with all my weight. It exploded against the wall. Pieces flew upwards and outwards like a grenade in flower. The heavy bottom dropped and smashed the plate I had left on the table. I stared blankly at the wreckage for a moment, then walked slowly into the toilet and got the broom that I kept behind the door. When I swept up the mess my hands were trembling slightly. I felt ashamed and a little bewildered. I had been so certain in recent months that I had everything once more under firm control.

The door opened, and Harry Wells came in with his teapot, small head darting on his long and scrawny neck with all the curiosity of an awakened lizard. His pale-blue eyes were steeped in melancholy, even in the moment of their questing, for Harry had learned not to expect too much of life. Life was a monotony of wife and family, alcohol and work. Life was a marking time between being squeezed out on to a labour bed and being lowered into a hole in the ground.

"Yu drop a glass?" Harry asked, gazing innocently at the mark on the wall.

"Horizontally," I said. "I'm clever that way."

He took his brown china teapot over to the sink and emptied it. He swilled the tea leaves around until they went down the outlet, then switched on the hot-water jug. He dumped four heaped spoons of tea in the pot and stood it ready for the boiling water. Tea was a ritual with Harry during the day. By night he tangled with sterner stuff.

"That Clark been here?" he grunted.

"You know him?"

"Seen him around," Harry said. "Looks a proper pain in the tit."

18

I grinned appreciation. "He's all of that."

"Whyn't yu throw him out then? Yu got no time to spare on Wednesdays."

"We're well up with it."

"Yeah," Harry said sardonically. "I've heard that one before."

Like all printers, Harry was always complaining about copy being late. Our old flat-bed press beat itself into a frenzy every Thursday night, and we distributed the *Herald* on Friday. It was market day, and all the farm and station people came into town for their shopping. By coming out on the street that day, we had only to deliver in the town itself. It saved a lot of mileage.

I sat on the edge of the table, watching Harry make his tea, and wondering how much he knew about Clark, and about me. My guess was plenty, because the good citizens of Clayville talked. They didn't gossip. It was more than idle chatter. They talked They talked with purpose and indefatigable regard for detail. But, even so, just how much did Harry know? He jerked the cord from the jug and poured steaming water into the teapot.

Then, waiting for the tea to draw, he turned, leaning against the sink and looking me in the face, settling his hands under the thick leather braces he wore to keep up his blue workpants, crossing his slippered feet . . . Everything about him proclaimed the simple fact that he wanted to talk with me about the shattered glass and about William Clark.

"This feller Clark," he said. "What's he after?"

"Anything," I said evasively. "And everything."

Harry blinked. "Yu don't say?"

I had intended to keep on being evasive, but then I realized it would gain me nothing. Harry was my compositor and printer, my week-end fishing companion, and my friend. But he was still a Clayvillian. He would find out, anyway.

"He's been frisking me for concealed ideas," I said.

"Strewth," Harry said. "No wonder you blew up."

I let that pass. It was as good an explanation as the truth.

19

"He reckons I'm a security risk because I was chucked out of Indo-China."

"Them bloody frogs," Harry said. His long nose twitched in a monumental sniff. "Man's a fool."

"Maybe," I said. "But he's got power."

"Yeah?"

Harry lifted his eyebrows, and wrinkles made deep contour patterns all over his forehead. He looked something like an old brown pencil, he was so thin and straight up and down. A pencil with the paint scratched and the end of it chewed. His light-brown hair stood up just like that, every way at once and no two hairs the same.

"He's Security," I said. "Anyone in Security has power."

"Strikes me too many bastards've got power," Harry said. "Some of 'em has to be fools."

He reached around for his teapot, lifted it head-high and, opening his mouth, poured a stream of scalding tea straight down to his stomach. It was a habit he'd inherited from his father, who had learned the trick of it as a sergeant in the Indian Army. Harry always took his tea that way, even at home, despite his wife's protests that it wasn't right in front of guests.

"The Frenchman who had me thrown out of Indo-China was a fool," I said sourly. "Everyone was agreed on that. But he had me thrown out. And his report has followed me everywhere. It hasn't helped me that he was a bloody fool."

Harry hit his gullet with another jet of tea. "Now, don't bash my ear with that again. This here's different. You're not a foreigner in Clayville."

"This isn't just Clayville any longer, Harry," I reminded him tersely. "This is Atomville. We're all foreigners nowadays."

He put his head on one side, squinting at me with sleepy eyes. "The Austins, too?"

"You sneaking old swine," I said. "You've been listening."

He grinned, quite unashamed, and poured the rest of the

tea down his yawning gullet, finishing with a flourish of bony wrist and hand.

"Christ," he said disgustedly. "You and Clark were jawing away for more'n two hours. I had to find out what was holdin' up the work."

"Well, don't blab it."

"Me?" Harry looked affronted.

"I mean it, Harry."

He looked at me with contemplative curiosity for a moment, as though I were taking a mildly ridiculous attitude and he wanted to store the memory of it. Then he shrugged his thin shoulders. They reached almost up to his ears. The heavy leather braces appeared to embed themselves in his sparse flesh.

"Okay," he said. "But it wouldn't be news to anyone."

I slid off the table. "What d'you mean?"

Harry gave a snort of disgust, a high snickering noise like a horse with hay fever. "Yu don't think you're the only one Clark's been chasin', do you? He's been all over town."

"He's been to the Austins already, then?"

"Dunno about Clara and Belle." Harry showed his false teeth in a grin. "But he's been makin' up to Lucy."

There wasn't space enough to pace around my kitchen. So I stood quite still. Harry couldn't have told me more unwelcome news if he had tried. Maybe he had tried, at that.

"Blast him," I said, at last. "How long has this been going on?"

Harry swished the last drops of water from his teapot, and grinned again. "Why don't you ask Lucy? I'm the type setter around here, not the reporter." He made it his exit line. A shuffle of slippers, and he was gone. Then I heard the slip-slop coming back. His head poked around the door. "Don't ask her today, though," he said glumly. "I'm two columns light on page three."

Ten minutes or more after he had gone back to his linotype I was still standing in the kitchen, shuffling the problem of Lucy and William Clark around in my mind. It was unpleasant from any angle. Lucy was the Austins' adopted niece. They had brought her up from babyhood after both her parents, old family friends, had been killed in a train accident somewhere in New South Wales. Once Lucy and I had been pals, brother and sister pals; but when I had returned to Clayville she had been a brittle stranger, moody, spiteful, given to sudden tantrums. It was almost a turning of the reason. At times she appeared almost to hate her aunts. I feared to think what crazy information Clark would extract from her, with his leading questions, his patient preparation of the conditioned reflex.

There was no use in seeing her, as Harry had cynically suggested. But I felt a compulsion to go down to Aunt Clara and Aunt Belle and see if there was anything I could do. If Clark had not started quizzing them, I could perhaps prepare them for it. If he had started, I could at least try to rationalize it for them and quiet their twittering unease.

So I shrugged on my jacket and tidied up my mind. I wasn't worried about page three. There was plenty of old cable fill-up in type. The great reading public of Clayville didn't give a damn what was in the *Herald* so long as it had twelve pages each issue. Clayville and its surrounding homesteads still used the pan system of nightsoil disposal. Toilet paper was a rarity, and small boys cut the *Herald* into squares after the family had read it, and threaded them on loops of string. Clayville was one of the few places in the world where a newspaper still fulfilled an entirely useful function in the community.

The afternoon sunlight nearly blinded me as I hit the street. I fished in my top pocket for sunglasses and put them on. I could feel my eyes opening again behind them, and the town came forward in its spindly haphazardness to challenge me once more with its naïve serenity.

I was a native son, it said. My father, Dr. Alec Scotter, and my mother, were dust of its dust, lying in the sprawling little weed-grown cemetery just past the railway yards. I had been a baby and a boy there, a college and a university student back from Sydney on vacation, filled with the growing importance of knowledge, slightly insufferable the way young students are. But I was a different person come back from years of newspaper work in the city, from fighting in and observing wars, from scarring myself with ideologies, moralities and the thinking things that can drive men mad.

I was thinner, harder, and my height seemed more than its exact six feet because somewhere along the line my mind had toughened and my body had lost its puppy fat. Now it was sinew and bone and muscle, and the threaded nerves were closer to the surface. And there were a few grey hairs in the black around my temples. Perhaps they meant nothing more than that thirty-five years was time enough to tire some follicles and not others. Grey hairs can mean a lot, or they can mean nothing. Most people like to read experience and worry, even wisdom, into their grey hairs. Me, I had no idea.

"Hiya, Wade."

I blinked myself back into the street and saw Joe Porter. I had gone to school with Joe. But now he was a fat man in shirt sleeves, squashing his bottom on the wooden bench outside Peltzer's hardware store. People still sat outside shops and pubs in Clayville.

"Hiya, Joe," I didn't stop.

"Warming up," Joe said.

"Well, It's summer," I said, and then I was out of the conversational zone.

The weather was Clayville's most keenly debated subject. And why not, anyway? I thought. At least it was better than the political titbits you had thrown at you elsewhere.

And it *was* warming up. The heat was rising in shaky little waves from the strip of bitumen that ran like a black carpet down the middle of the street, breaking into dust the red-brown earth that lay on either side. The sky was paling to a light and faded blue. When midsummer came it would be bleached still more, its canopy so high and thin that there would seem nothing between Clayville and the stars.

This was Main Street I was walking down, an attenuated street along the south bank of the Clay, stopped at one end by the sea and spearing off into the hinterland at the other. I could see straight down it. And out past the houses, where the bitumen ended, a red dust cloud advertised a mob of sheep on the move.

Main Street was the heart and vitals of the town. Shops and houses were strung along both sides of its arrow-straight half-mile. The shops threw shade on the hard-packed limestone pavements, their high verandas standing up on thin iron poles, decked out with wrought-iron friezes and badly needing paint; the houses sat back, their gardens bright with shrubs and trees and flowers. Most of the houses were of wood, but a few were brick and white stone carted from the south. There was something at once ramshackle and dignified, ugly and graceful, about the place.

On my right as I walked, its back to the river, was old Wogga Hammond's butter and cheese factory, with its unloading ramp of splintered timbers that even now made my buttocks flinch at the memory of my father's pecking forceps. I had tried to slide down it once. There were secret caves beneath the factory's working floor, caves in which we had holed out times without number as Indians, posses and desperadoes hunted us. . . .

There were two pubs in Main Street, the Federal and the Terminus, a police station with a dwelling and two lock-up cells, and a volunteer fire station equipped with a wheezy engine that had been dying for years of a bladder complaint. It could neither hold its water, nor get rid of it without dribbling. The council chambers were also there, alongside the police station, a square, rather ugly freestone building where Collins, the district clerk, and Mayor Hazlegrove guarded their tremendous secrets from the Press. Things like a decision to put in a new culvert, or fill the pot-holes in some avenue or other.

It was a placid street. A few motor cars stood nosing the pavement, like patient horses at a hitching rail. Under each veranda I passed at least one curled dog enjoying the shade, stirring at my footsteps to snap in apathetic and assumed ferocity at the pestering flies. A half-dozen or so men, hatless for the most part and in shirt sleeves, wandered here and there in haphazard animation. They were men like fat Joe Porter, going nowhere much and not caring about anything much, except perhaps a pot of beer, some minor lechery.

Then I heard the whistle of an engine shunting in the railway yards, cutting the silence with its saw edge, crying the song of progress that Mayor Hazelgrove and his business friends enjoyed so much. The railway station was back beyond Main Street, near the bay, and when the sea wind blew you got the whiff of coal smoke all over town. When I was a kid it happened rarely. Clayville was the railhead and there had been only two trains a week. But now the trains came rolling in each day, sometimes twice a day, laden with steel girders, sleepers and rails, dog spikes and fish plates, and great sealed boxes that were swung off by cranes and trucked away to atomland.

They were building an extension of the railway line, from the station through the town (which necessitated knocking down two houses and a shop) to a new steel bridge across the Clay, and thence over the limestone hill to ARA headquarters. The line itself meant little to the town's prosperity, but droves of workmen had been brought in to build the line and the bridge and the wharf, and they all lived in a tented camp strung along the riverbank on each side of the bridge. They were European immigrants, speaking little English, which made them easy prey for Clayville's men of commerce. Mayor Hazlegrove, who owned the town's only department store, loved them like a profiteer. And they, poor devils, respected him like a mayor.

Coming opposite the Austins' I passed my old home, a big, square house with a wide veranda on all sides, and a green-painted iron roof with a fancy wooden gable. My left hand scraped along the white picket fence and my eyes roamed the unruly shrubbery of the garden. It's strange how long the feeling of proprietorship can last. Dr. Frank Barber lived there now.

A nice fellow; a displaced Pole. His real name was Francis Barbasiewicz, but he had anglicized it because his patients didn't like being treated by a foreigner. Frank Barber, duly notarized, was different though. I think my father would have approved Frank Barber. And my father, for all his kindness, had been a hard man to please.

I swung away to the right, slanting diagonally across the street, towards the big, two-storied block of brick and stone in which Clara and Belle Austin lived in their hermetic world within a world. The house stood about a hundred yards back from the street, its blunt angularity softened by the wondering symmetry of ancient gums and the dark uprightness of pines. A botanist's collection of native shrubs flourished among the trees, and as I trod the curving gravelled driveway to the front door I half expected, as always, a kangaroo or emu to start up at my feet. The front garden was urban bushland, carefully designed to shield the house from view. The rear was in complete contrast, a great formal lawn skirted with flowerbeds, running clear down to the river's edge.

Before I had cleared the bushland the clatterbugging of children at play rushed at me. They were on the lawn in front of the house, swarming over playground equipment like so many ants. I paused a moment on the driveway, just inside the line of trees, and looked them over. They were the same, I suppose, as we were in my kindergarten days but, frankly, their energy was almost frightening.

There were about twenty of them, trying to jar their heads off on see-saws, to brain each other on swings, and bury each other alive in a big sandpit. Up near the house, just outside the big open French windows of the kindergarten room—it was the front corner one on the ground floor—two boys were having a tug-o'-war over what appeared to be a dead cat, but was

26

probably a piece of black cloth. By the set of their faces it wouldn't have made much difference. Three little girls were playing with dolls in the shade of a tree, with a grave preoccupation and patience they would lose soon enough when they came up against the real thing.

The whole scene was of furious, leaping activity and ragged noise. Lucy was obviously in charge. She affected the kids that way, somehow communicating to them some of her own thinly held hysteria. With Clara and Belle Austin the children would have been making just as much noise; but it would have been a different sort of noise. More restful and controlled. . . .

I stepped out into the open and looked for Lucy. I didn't see her at first. She was standing under a tree to my right, well away from the kids, staring down past the house towards the river. She turned as I went across to her and watched me silently, without a sign of recognition on her face. I could have been some stranger with a case full of camphor balls for sale. She was a pretty girl, dark-brown hair, dark-brown eyes, and a figure that had more than neatness to it. Her nose was rather long, and tilted slightly at the end. Her wide mouth was full-lipped, with the lower lip rather more full than the upper. In those other days it had given her a rather sexy look, but now it gave the effect of a perpetual pout.

"Hello," I said.

She eyed me coolly. "Not so big. I can't stand it."

"So big?"

"The big hello." She tilted back her head and looked down her nose. "You've come, of course, to see the world's only living dodos."

Her voice was expressionless, her face a blank. But somehow she managed to drip contempt—for me as well as for her aunts. She was in one of her darkest moods. I should have recognized the storm signals in her face as I had come across to her, and walked straight on. But I hadn't, and it was now too late.

"I came to see Aunt Clara and Aunt Belle," I said evenly.

"Dear, dear Wade." A small sneer tugged her lips. "So dutiful . . . so respectful."

"Why not?" I challenged. "They've been good to me."

She gave a tight, high tinkling laugh. "The dear, sweet souls. They've been good to everybody." She stood a hand of straddled fingers on her stomach, while the elbow angled outwards, and her shoulders hunched—the mantis pose of some piece of wire sculpture. "Pardon me while I vomit," she said mincingly.

The incredible bitterness of it shocked me, even though I had come to expect it of her. I felt anger rising in me and did nothing to hold it down. "You ungrateful bitch," I snapped.

"Ungrateful?" She spat the word at me, her face suddenly ablaze. The pose dissolved.

"They've given you a good home," I said, and even to me it sounded inadequate.

She laughed again, but this time there was a hint of hysteria. She threw her head back and brought up her hands to press on her full breasts, tight now against her white shirt-tailored blouse. Then she cut the laugh off, brought her head down and glared at me with wet and stormy eyes.

"That's just what I'd expect you to say," she whispered, with a cutting edge. "What d'you know about this good home. You've never lived in it. You haven't lived in Clayville for years and years. What d'you know about living with them?"

"I know they're good and kind and generous," I said coldly. "That's enough for most people."

"Kind and generous," she said. "And dull. It's like being buried alive."

"You're well past twenty-one," I said harshly. "You're free to leave."

She looked at me with patently assumed amazement, moulding her face like an actress in the silent films. "How silly can you get," she said. "D'you think I'd leave now, after all these years, and spoil my chance of being left their money?"

"People have," I said. "People with principles."

She sneered. "That'd suit you fine, wouldn't it? Leave the field wide open. But I'm going to stick it out. And when they die I'll sell the lot . . . this blasted house . . . the farms . . . the sheep . . . everything . . and get out." She paused, then said deliberately, viciously, "And I hope I won't have long to wait. I can't stand too much more."

I grabbed her by both arms, my fingers digging into her flesh with convulsive tightness as I felt her softness under them. "Lucy," I said hoarsely. "Listen, Lucy. Listen carefully. If you ever speak like that again, I'll take a stick to you."

"For Christ's sake," she said. "Stop being so old-fashioned."

I shook her slowly, stressed with anger, and any feeling I had ever had for her gone flat and stale. "Don't ever speak to *them* like that."

She looked at me with a bland, almost inhuman curiosity. Then bawdy laughter shook her. "Let go," she said. "The kids'll think you're trying to rape me. Y'know what kids are like these days."

The children were still playing as I turned away and headed for the classroom. They didn't stop to look at me. They jumped and ran and pitched their treble voices in that same non-stop fury of activity they were pursuing when first I came in. They had no time to waste.

I crossed the classroom, threading through the desks, smelling the faint smell of chalk dust, seeing the little balls of plasticine, the self-expression paints and easels, the bold wall drawings that Clara and Belle so proudly made, opened the door on the inside wall and went through it to the stairs. The stairs led to the first floor living rooms, and half-way there I suddenly cursed myself for not having thrown William Clark at Lucy, and seen which way she would jump. But it was too late. I couldn't go back and start our talk again. I didn't want to talk with her about anything any more.

3 ——————————— ⟋ ———————————

CLARA AND BELLE AUSTIN WERE AN INSTITUTION IN CLAYVILLE.
Not just because they had the most money, but also because
they were quite unlike anyone else. They were, I suppose,
eccentrics, although I would have preferred a more kindly term.
Aunt Clara and Aunt Belle were the sort of eccentrics who, to
me, made all the other people in the town seem out of step.
They were gentle people who had let time outpace them because they weren't interested in the race. They lived in some
lush, fairy valley of the mind; plateau dwellers, to whom the
industry and commerce of the plain was some remote, antlike
activity seen through the wrong end of a telescope.

The kindergarten was their closest link with the realities
of Clayville, and even that was an expression of their rarefac-
tion. They had started it during the First World War as a free
patriotic service to the community. And somehow they had
never got around to closing down—or to charging a fee. Once,
in my undergraduate brashness, I had asked why they burdened
themselves with it, and Aunt Clara had blinked in mild astonish-
ment and said: "But Wade, there *must* be a kindergarten."

Which, when you come to think about it, is about as complete an answer as you could get.

I was thinking about it as I topped the stairs and padded along the green-carpeted hall towards their sitting room. It was at the back. They had sited it there because, at dusk, they had been able to look out over the lawns to the land across the Clay and watch the rabbits emerge from their siestas and bob around the grass. Aunt Clara and Aunt Belle had loved those rabbits.

They loved all animals, actually, but I think they loved rabbits most because they were so gentle, so quiet and vulnerable, and partly because everyone else in the district shot them, trapped them, poisoned them, ripped their warrens, chased them with ferrets, and reckoned they were the worst God-awful pests the world had ever seen. But no one had ever harmed a rabbit on that strip of land across the river. Before the Atomic Research Authority took it over, there were so many rabbits that Harry Wells reckoned, if you were nimble-footed, you could walk across it without ever touching boot to grass. But after the new landlords had been in two months the rabbits had all gone. Workmen, patrolling guards, the electric boundary fence, and, I suspected, the frantic noise of men thinking, had been too much for them.

The sitting room door was open, so I walked in behind one of those silly "Yoo-hoo" warning calls you give in houses where you don't knock and wait to be shown in.

Aunt Clara and Aunt Belle were sitting at the window in straight-backed wooden chairs and, seen against the light, they looked just like those Degas drawings of nannies watching their charges frisking in the Tuileries. They wore that sort of clothes. Long, ankle-length dresses of a heavy grey material, black lace-up shoes—and hats. They always wore those hats; the same ones, I think, that they wore when I had been in kindergarten. Flat, basin-shaped concoctions, with bunches of imitation fruit, and pearl-capped pins driven through to anchor them against the wind. About every ten years they were in fashion, but not the way Clara and Belle Austin wore them, without make-up and with their hair straggling from beneath.

"Wade, dear." Aunt Clara turned, smiling, in her chair, and the smile chased all the plainness from her weather-beaten face. "How nice of you to visit us."

"I was passing and couldn't resist," I said, bending to present my cheek for her kiss.

"Darling, you look peaked," Aunt Belle said vaguely. She always spoke vaguely and with the volume pitched just above a whisper. There was a fair amount of lip-reading involved in listening to her. "You are working too hard on that paper."

The idea of anyone working too hard on the *Herald* was pathetically funny. But she always made that same comment. And I always made the same reply. It was like a game, only she was serious.

"Editors don't work hard. I leave all the work to my staff."

They nodded their heads in unison. They really believed I had a staff. In fact, they believed almost anything that was told them. Travelling salesmen and swagmen did wonderfully well at their door. I'm sure, if they had ever read newspapers, that they would even have believed the denials of politicians.

"Bring up a chair, my dear," Aunt Clara said. She slid a quick glance at Belle. "We're trying to make a big decision, Wade. Perhaps you can help us."

Then they both looked at each other again, consulting with that effortless telepathy that comes of long companionship.

"Yes, perhaps you can," Aunt Belle whispered, turning her gentle grey eyes on me.

I dragged up the least uncomfortable chair in the room, an old rocker, mounted on a stand and held to it by powerful spiral springs. They were worried about something and I gave it two guesses—William Clark or Lucy. I settled myself in the chair, started it in motion, and lit a cigarette. I coughed on the first draw. I was on edge, a state I'd never known before in that cloistered room.

Aunt Clara and Aunt Belle were staring out the window again, over the closely shaven lawn and the sun-polished river to the empty rabbit pastures, now sealed off by that pulsing fence. The silence didn't help me. It enabled me to think too much about Clark's declared intention, and the bitching hate that had taken hold of Lucy. I couldn't think what I should say about either of them. The sort of simple goodness possessed by the sisters Austin made it almost impossible to explain human bastardy of any kind. I sat in a noisy inward quiet, puffing at my cigarette, waiting for them to launch their trouble at me. It was no use trying to hurry.

Clara, I should explain, was the elder. She was sixty-five. Belle was sixty-three. They were physically, mentally and emotionally alike, but Clara was the stronger. Or, perhaps it would be more accurate to say, she was the less vague. They were both tall women, square and big-boned, with a fair covering of flesh. Facial wrinkles they had, but not many, and mainly around the corners of the mouth and the neck. They both had their own teeth, the bottom incisors worn down the way they are in most elderly people, and the gums receding a little. Their hair was the chief difference. Clara's was thick, grey and black, but mostly grey; Belle's was pure white, soft and fluffy. They both had grey eyes.

Why they had never married I didn't know. I don't think I'd ever thought about it much. No one in Clayville did. Everyone accepted the Austin sisters as pre-ordained spinsters and left it at that. And even later, when I knew so much more about them, I still didn't know about Belle—and I was far from sure about Clara. It is so difficult to be sure about people, and about their motivations. I knew a bachelor once, a man past seventy, who confessed the reason for a lifelong celibacy was the fact that he could never reconcile himself to the indignity of the sexual positions.

33

"Clara, you explain it," Aunt Belle said suddenly, in her curious whisper.

I turned my head and she was leaning forward, hands clasped in her lap, peering at Clara with that funny nervous intensity she brought to everything. She pressed her rimless spectacles back against her nose with her right forefinger. It was a nervous trick. She did it with a lift of the eyebrows, as though she were trying to test whether she was looking through the lenses or not.

Aunt Clara cleared her throat, delicately, and one brown, pigment-spotted hand went up to touch that poignantly ugly hat. I stopped rocking my chair, and began carefully stubbing my cigarette in a big silver ashtray because I wanted to be looking somewhere else when she started. I was certain she was going to open up about Lucy.

"We're thinking of moving this sitting room to the front of the house," she said with vast solemnity. "It is dreadful here now, with the rabbits gone. . . . Quite dreadful."

I wrecked the cigarette because my hand jumped suddenly as I controlled the laughter that tried to burst out of me. I should have known better than to have expected any other crisis.

"We find it depressing to look out now that our darling rabbits have all fled," Aunt Clara flowed on, nodding quietly in agreement with her own words, the artificial fruit on her hat brim clacking a castanet accompaniment. "It was so wonderful. . . . Now it is so lonely, so empty. . . so sad."

"But if we move it will be like deserting them," Aunt Belle whispered. "Perhaps they will come back."

"Then so could we," Aunt Clara said, with a sudden firmness. Then, as though regretting her assertiveness, added: "We could, couldn't we, dear?"

I lit another cigarette, and their preoccupation with this vital issue was so great that neither of them remonstrated with me for smoking too much.

"What do you think, Wade dear?" Aunt Clara was smiling at me, with confidence because I was a travelled man but with

34

slight trepidation because, knowing me, she feared I might answer with a "yes" or a "no" and thus enforce decision.

I smiled at her, feeling a rush of fondness, the sort of fondness you feel for children when they put their hands in yours in simple trust. "Whatever you decide would be just right."

Aunt Clara said: "You look so like your dear father when you smile like that. . . . Only he had a beard."

"I wore a beard once," I said. "In Korea. We couldn't get razor blades."

"That frightful war," Aunt Clara said, shuddering as though I'd just given her a camera's eye picture of the murder lust that had rolled down from north of the Yalu.

"We were out of toothpaste, too, for nearly five days," I said gravely.

"Dear boy. . . ."

"I used salt for a while, but it set my teeth on edge. Then I tried wood ashes. It was much better."

Aunt Belle stood up. Or rather, she became standing up. You could never detect any actual body movement, any activation, under that long grey dress. At one moment it was broken by the two right angles of sitting; at the next it was a straight line from neck to toe. She glided off behind us somewhere.

"You really think we should stay here?" Aunt Clara said.

I knew then what she wanted. "Yes," I said. "Stay here."

Aunt Belle came back, became sitting, her tall body jointed again in those two right angles at hip and knee. Her right hand held a pair of binoculars, so powerful they looked like two black bottles taped together. She lifted them and stared across the river, her lips working as though some small prayer were on them. Aunt Clara groped beneath her skirt-shrouded chair, and came up with another pair.

She smiled at me and nodded proudly. "Our rabbit glasses. So wonderful. We could even see the expressions on their sweet faces, the way their whiskers twitched when they were eating. . . ."

Her voice trailed off as her expectant eyes roved the rabbit pleasance across the river, hovering over deserted burrows with an air of benediction, raking the greener patches near the river bank with the hopefulness of a lover defying her better judgment. And once at least, I am sure, she paused over a pile of black pellet droppings, examining them closely, clinically, for the dew of freshness and turning away disheartened at the evidence of their sun-dried age.

Then Aunt Belle lowered her binoculars, with a *moue* and a whispered petulance. "There is that young man with the dog again, Clara."

I swung my head around, and there, behind the fence, a uniformed guard was pacing, rifle slung across his back and a great, black Doberman straining at its leash ahead of him.

"The rabbits will never come back with those dreadful dogs about," Aunt Clara said. "So savage . . . I've never seen such dogs before. It's almost . . . almost as though they want to hurt someone. They frighten me."

"And he is such a handsome young man," Aunt Belle said.

"Aunt Clara," I said quietly. I think you ought to move this room."

"But, Wade dear . . ." Her hands made eccentric dance patterns in the air.

"The rabbits have gone for good," I said, knowing I was being cruel, but knowing also it was the best thing to do. I had a feeling, born of experience, that it wasn't wise to watch security zones through binoculars, even though there was nothing to see. The hill quite hid the research buildings. "The rabbits won't come back," I said. "There are too many dogs. Too many men."

The sisters looked at me as though I had struck them, as though I had uttered some shuddersome blasphemy, and I grew red with annoyance at myself for having done this to them.

Aunt Belle was the first to speak. "But surely, Wade. . . ." Her voice faded. She prodded her spectacles more firmly against her nose with a forefinger that trembled. The sagging hopelessness of old age facing defeat, and too tired to resist was showing in her face. "Surely the rabbits will come again. . . ."

"Certainly they will," Aunt Clara said, and her voice had taken on a firmness I had never heard in my life before. Such a firmness as I imagine the Christian martyrs suddenly acquired a fang's length from the lion's mouth. "The rabbits will come back, Belle. And we will be here to greet them."

"Oh, Clara! Are you sure?"

"Perfectly sure."

"As sure as Christian charity," I muttered.

"Oh, Wade," Aunt Clara said eagerly. "Do you really think so?"

That quite demolished my resistance. What could I do against such wide-eyed innocence? I had forgotten they believed in things like Christian charity. Things like that are easy to forget.

"Maybe the rabbits have only been scared away temporarily," I said lamely. "When they get used to the presence of the people, and the dogs . . . maybe then they'll come back."

Aunt Clara beamed. "I'm sure they will."

"I *know* they will," Aunt Belle said.

She backed the declaration of her faith with a quick sweep of her binoculars. I waited until she had lowered them into her lap.

"Have you ever," I said, and paused a moment before committing the question. "Have you ever met a man named William Clark?"

"Why, yes." They admitted it in chorus, their eyes lighting up with pleasant recollections. "Such a pleasant young man."

I rode that on the chin. I should have known they'd take to him like that. "A friend of Lucy's, I believe?"

A shadow flitted across Aunt Clara's face and I was sure it was thrown by the mention of Lucy, and not by her friendship with Clark. I glanced quickly at Aunt Belle, but she was again conning the rabbit land across the river. When I turned back to Aunt Clara she was looking at me with a worried seriousness, and pain was muddying her clear eyes. I knew then she was distressed about Lucy. She had no gift for dissembling. But I also knew her loyalty would never permit her to mention it to anyone.

"Such a nice young man," she said, whispering the words with a queer intensity. "They seem very happy together."

For a moment I hung on the brink of warning them against Clark, but I drew back, aware that nothing I could say would rupture the sweet pastel dream of him that they had conjured up. He had met them and done nothing to disturb their equanimity. This meant, I realized, one of three things. Firstly, he had not questioned them; secondly, he had questioned them so subtly they had not been aware of it; or thirdly, he had never meant to question them, but had thrown their names in merely to needle me. The more I thought about it, the more I favoured the third, and I began to wonder if Mr. William Clark were not more subtle than he seemed.

I rose abruptly. "I must go."

Aunt Clara glanced at the large filigreed gold watch she wore pinned to her dress, riding at an angle on her bosom. "Oh, dear, we are late for class." She got to her feet, smoothing her dress of imagined wrinkles. "Belle. . . ." Then louder as Aunt Belle continued her scrutiny of that yellow and lifeless rabbit land: "Belle. Come, dear, we are late."

I watched them place the binoculars on a carved cedar sideboard standing against the far wall, decked out with lace cloths, a cut-glass drinking set (for lime juice) and some pyramidal fruit in a mulga wood bowl. I nearly suggested they should put the binoculars in one of the sideboard's cupboards, but decided that Clark had probably seen them in action already. Even if he hadn't, I no longer thought it mattered.

Downstairs, the schoolroom was empty. The noise of children tumbled through the windows and danced among the desks

38

and chairs. The noise was pitched higher than before, shot through with treble quarrels, rebel yells and squeals of ecstasy. The sort of noise you hear when twenty or more kids are left alone to make their own carousel. Lucy wasn't anywhere in sight.

I was not surprised. Neither was Aunt Clara. I saw her dart a glance at Belle, saw their eyes hold for an instant and their lips tighten almost imperceptibly. Then Aunt Clara crossed to the open french windows and blew a whistle. The noise dropped, small figures slackened speed and stopped.

"Come to your desks, darlings all," Aunt Clara called, singing it with the rise and fall of a muezzin calling the faithful to prayer. It was an invitation, not a command.

The darlings clattered in, sweating, panting and dishevelled. Aunt Belle moved forward and disarmed a red-headed boy in the act of clouting a small girl over the head with a lump of wood. "Christopher, *darling*, don't be so violent." She patted his head and dropped the weapon in the floor. Christopher looked aggrieved.

"Good-bye, now," I said, grinning, because suddenly I remembered having declared my love for a small girl with a lump of wood just that same way. I couldn't remember her name, but she had freckles. "Good-bye. I'll see you soon."

Aunt Clara and Aunt Belle turned towards me, shepherding the last of their flock inside, and beamed. "You will come to lunch on Sunday, of course," they said in a quiet, treble chorus.

"Of course," I said.

"Don't be late, dear boy."

"I wouldn't dare."

We laughed at that. We always did. Sunday lunch was a fixture and so was the conversation about it. After mother had died, my father and I always had Sunday lunch with the Austins. Then it had been father's place to say "I wouldn't dare." Now it was mine, and the words warmed me. I went off down the curving driveway with a pleasantness inside me.

39

Then I heard voices, just ahead to the right. Clark and Lucy were standing there, within the line of trees, standing close together, talking spiritedly and with just enough covertness to match their trysting place. Clark was facing me. He saw me, quickly. He placed a hand on Lucy's arm, a restraining hand, and with the other waved to me.

"Colonel Astor, I presume," he called, and his eyes were mocking.

"Heil, Himmler," I threw back, and the bastard grinned as though it were a compliment.

I walked straight on, angry with myself for having sunk to attempted repartee with him. Poor repartee, at that. The white picket gate clicked shut behind me. I marched across the road, and Frank Barber said: "You are trying to have yourself run over, it is clear."

4 ———————— ʒ —————————

FRANK BARBER WAS SITTING BEHIND THE WHEEL OF HIS CAR, stopped at his front gate, watching me. His mouth was laughing, but his eyes, behind thick rimless spectacles, were deadly serious. They were light blue, with a ring of brown about the iris. It gave them a birdlike, peering quality.

"You look as though you have seen a ghost," he said.

The only emotion I could feel was a residue of anger against Clark and Lucy Austin. Maybe some by-product of it was showing on my face. But it wasn't supernatural. I grinned. "No one I knew."

"Strange ghosts are sometimes the worst."

"Frank," I said. "Please, no Freud."

"Poor Sigmund Freud." He shook his head. "Everybody is afraid of him. And he has done so much good. It could even be that he could save you from walking right under the wheels of motor cars."

His voice, as ever, was cool and pedantic. He had learned his English from books and linguaphone records. It was unspattered by the impurities an Australian picked up, the short cuts, and the slang. He gave his words a slight upward inflection and, at the same time, clipped them, so they came out strung together like a scale passage from Bach, each word separate, given its full value.

He climbed from the car, reaching back to drag out his black calling bag. "Will you come in? I can offer you a fine, cold beer, and then, perhaps we can have a little talk."

"Beer and a little talk, yes," I said. "But no consultation. Not even for free."

"You are afraid of something?"

His eyes, peering at me, had a diagnostic look. He was short, with the beginnings of fleshiness on his bones, and standing beside him made me feel taller and thinner than I knew myself to be. But it still didn't make me feel in need of a doctor.

"I'm not sick, Frank," I said. "One day I might get ulcers. But not yet."

He lifted his shoulders in a heavy shrug. "You are showing on your face some of the things that were there when you first came back to Clayville. They were not good things."

Frank had helped me in those early days, not so much as a doctor as a philosophic friend. My nerves had been badly frayed by the unending arguments of the world of "isms," and I had needed help. He knew a lot about me. But if Frank Barber had a fault it was that he took his profession far too seriously. He seemed always about to test your pulse, flick back your eyelids, or ask you for a bottle of urine. He was taking it too seriously now. Clark's pawing of the old dirt fretted me deep down, and I was still uneasy about his presence at the Austins. But I was sure if anything were showing on my face it was no more than a scratch mark. These feelings were minute, mere shadows, when considered against my former state.

"There's nothing I can't handle for myself, Frank," I said quietly. "But thanks."

He looked serious. "The time to treat a sore toe is before it turns to gangrene."

His tone was so solemn is sounded like a parody. I wanted to laugh, but held it back because I knew it would only hurt his feelings. I hoped like hell there was no amusement showing in my eyes.

"There are some things a man must work out for himself, Frank," I said evenly.

"Sometimes a friend can help."

"I know," I said. "I'm grateful."

He nodded gravely, pleased with my awareness. Then he lifted his head quickly and gave me one of his rare smiles. "I will still offer you the beer. We will drink it and not talk about our health."

I took him up on that because, firstly, I needed a beer, and, secondly, it occurred to me he might know something about what had caused the change in Lucy Austin. And if those two reasons were not enough, I liked talking with him. Unlike so many medicos, he had a good mind for things other than the general messiness of the human body.

We walked along the slate path towards the front door, between the green buffalo-grass lawns my father had planted some forty or more years before. The house was square and ugly, yet comfortable. The iron roof came shooting down from a high gable, extending twenty feet beyond the walls to form verandas on all sides. It looked something like a too-large hat. The roof was green, the walls dark blue, and shade lay on them all day. It was the shade that made the house so comfortable. Deep shade in an Australian summer landscape is a luxury.

"I sometimes wonder how you feel about having a foreigner living in your old home," Frank said, spreading the proposition out for my inspection with a sweeping gesture of one white hand.

Naturalization and the adoption of an Anglo-Saxon name hadn't lessened his sensitivity, his Polish belief in the sacredness of home. He had hinted around the subject before, but this was the first time he had made the point explicitly.

"Psychoanalyze me," I said. "I don't feel anything about it."

"You don't?" His face was almost comical with query as he turned, one hand on the front door knob, to stare at me.

"Of course, I retain some affection," I said. "But I don't want the place. It's too big. So why should I resent someone else living in it?"

"It is your father's house."

"He would've liked to think a doctor would succeed him in it."

Frank Barber beamed. "Everyone speaks so well of him. He must have been a fine doctor."

"He could have been better," I said. "But he was too fond of fishing and shooting to be bothered with much study. That's why he stayed here all those years. . . ."

Frank Barber nodded gravely. "Ah, yes. The good life. You also would be much better for being fond of the fishing and shooting, Wade."

"I go fishing."

"And think about politics."

"No," I said. "About fish."

He turned to look at me, one hand still resting lightly on the polished brass knob of the front door. His eyes were quizzical, as though he disbelieved me, and I guessed that somehow or other he had heard about my two visits from William Clark. That would account for his insistence that I had been seeing ghosts. I thought for a moment he was going to abandon the oblique approach and tackle me straight out, but he must have sensed my opposition. Instead, he put on his bedside manner, opened the door and held it for me.

"Let us have that beer together."

The hall was dark after the glare of sunlight, the air was cool, and the whole house hushed with that remote silence you meet in houses where there are no children. You never get that same sort of silence in family houses, even when the children are away. I suppose it is an atmosphere rather than a silence, as though air once disturbed by children never quite settles back into its same ordered way again.

44

Frank led down the hall to the kitchen, a big room bright with sunlight, and aseptic with white paint and tiles. I dropped on a chair drawn up to the table, while Frank went to the refrigerator and took out a bottle of beer and a siphon of soda water. He held them up with a grimace.

"You do not mind? I would join you, but I have calls to make this afternoon. Old ladies do not like their doctors to smell of beer."

I held out a glass. "You should've been a newspaperman. Everyone expects them to smell of beer, or worse."

He poured and then we drank. The beer was icy cold, and I didn't taste its pleasant bitterness until half a glass of it was in my stomach. I watched Frank drink, his long white fingers delicately around the glass, eyes half-closed against the exploding soda bubbles. Then he put the glass down, pushed it an inch or two with his fingertips, and leaned across the table.

I knew he was going to probe me again, and I didn't want any part of it. He would get too damned serious. "Mary not home?" I asked.

A faint annoyance pinched in the nostrils of his long nose. "She is in the office with Poldi. They are going through my accounts."

"Perhaps they'd like a beer," I said. "Accounts are dry work."

"They will come in later." He swept my suggestion aside with a gesture of the hand, as though clearing the table between us. "Wade, is there something you want to tell me?"

Well, there it was, the big question. I suppose I should have felt grateful for his concern. But I didn't. It irritated me, possibly because it gave the Clark episode an importance I would not admit. Maybe because I was afraid to let it grow too big in my mind.

"Tell me about it, Wade."

His voice was softly compelling, his blue eyes sharply observant, and there was a waiting tension in his body. His hands, resting on the table, were still. I was surprised at his intensity, until I remembered that Frank Barber was Francis Barbasiewicz, a Pole. Security officers' inquiries in Poland were a matter of life and death. I owed it to his peace of mind to minimize my troubles.

"There's nothing much to tell, Frank," I said quietly. "You've probably heard that a security officer has called on me. It doesn't mean anything. A routine inquiry, more or less checking the records. Nothing to worry about."

He inclined his head. "I had heard about it, and it worried me. Perhaps, deep down, it worries you also."

I shook my head. "It annoys me a little. That's all. What worries me is the change in Lucy Austin."

"So?"

"Perhaps I shouldn't ask."

He sat back slowly in his chair, dragging his hands across the table, disappointment showing in a slight softening of his face. He was an extraordinarily sensitive man. He had fancied a rebuff in my off-handedness. I had the feeling that he was hurt.

"Ask all you want," he said evenly. "She has not consulted me."

"She's been acting strangely," I said, rather defensively. "I thought something may have happened. Something medical."

He drained his soda water before replying. "I do not know," he said precisely. "She is rather too young for menopause. More likely it is an unhappy love affair."

"Perhaps you're right."

I agreed, although I was sure he was wrong because love affairs in Clayville were public property. I could sense his disinterest, and behind it a suggestion of tit for tat. He had offered to help me and I had rejected him. Now he was unwilling to be drawn into discussion on a secondary target. A coolness, fancied or otherwise, sprang up between us. I was relieved when the sound of women's voices approached us down the hall.

Mary Barber and Poldi came in, as women so often do,

46

squeezing together through the door in a fixed intentness of conversation. They saw us without surprise, and ignored us after a quick appraisal that took in my beer, Frank's soda water, and our physical attitudes, without deducting so much as a breath from their discussion. It was something about grilling eggs on a waffle iron . . . or perhaps I don't remember it exactly. But I do remember that it had all the appearances of a dead heat.

They were complete opposites, both physically and temperamentally. Mary, a Hungarian, whose name originally had been Magda, was a dark-haired, comfortable woman of forty, with creamy skin and high slavic cheekbones. She had a wide, thin mouth, and a short, rather big nose. She spoke excellent English, like Frank, and she spoke it slowly, not because of any uncertainty but because she was an unhurried person. She liked good food and good wine, and her figure was beginning to show the effects.

Poldi was twenty-seven. I knew that precisely because, as her employer, I had filled out her group insurance forms. She was Viennese and her name was short for Leopoldina. Leopoldina Lorenz. But Poldi suited her better; she could never have been a Leopoldina. She was fair and laughing, like a Strauss waltz, and yet there was enough basic seriousness to remind you that Beethoven and Brahms had also worked in Vienna.

She was of medium height, long of leg and slender of body, with a full bosom carried high. Her hair was blonde almost to whiteness, and with a tendency to curl. She wore it cut close to her head, and nature, with a little coaxing, had turned it into a close-fitting cap of ringlets. Her eyebrows were a shade darker than her hair, eyes a deep blue, and her face was oval-shaped and glowing with a golden tan.

All of which would prompt anyone to ask why she should have been working for me, the editor of a two-bit country newspaper? And all I can say is that I had often asked myself the same question without getting any sort of answer. When she had first asked me for a part-time job, as a multi-lingual reporter among the growing immigrant population, I had started out to refuse because I was afraid of having anyone like her working with me in such a small office. But somehow I had changed my mind in midsentence, without knowing that I had done it, and within five minutes I was showing her over the plant, explaining the set-up and enjoying the bewilderment that was running around on Harry Wells' face. From that time onward, Harry started to wear a clean flannel shirt each day.

"Are you trying to mesmerize, or ogle me?"

Poldi's voice was laughing at me and I realized, at second try, that she and Mary had finished their discussion. Mary was looking at me with that placid shrewdness that married women employ so much at the expense of the unmarried. I sipped my beer with elaborate unconcern.

"Ogle," I said. "I didn't think you'd care."

"I don't," Poldi said, showing small, white teeth. "But you didn't have your mind on it."

I put down my glass. "I was wondering if Frank would offer me another beer."

"Australian men are so romantic," Mary sighed. "They prefer beer to a pretty girl."

"Beer, of course, is very much safer," Frank said carefully. "It might make you sick, but there is always the good reason for such an effect."

Mary threw up her hands, rolling her big brown eyes in mock dismay. "I knew I should never have let you become naturalized. As a lover, you are now a cabbage."

Poldi had a cigarette out, and I leaned forward to light it. Her eyes laughed at me. "I'd like a beer, too," she said softly. "As a doctor's wife, Mary should know there is something very nourishing about a cabbage."

So I went over to the refrigerator and took out a bottle of beer and opened it without even thinking to ask Frank or Mary for permission. I poured for Poldi and had another for myself. Mary got herself a bottle of sweet red wine, and Frank frowned slightly. It was a sign, and, reading it, I saw that it wasn't the day's first drink for Mary. She was flushed, and her hand-movements on glass and bottle had the clumsy deliberation of someone trying too hard to be casual. Frank drank some more of his soda water and belched delicately into his left hand.

We all sat around the table, three of us in light summer clothes and Frank in his doctor's visiting uniform, a dark lounge suit. There was a lot of sunlight. The early afternoon sun was slanting through the windows and splashing on the floor. It created a picnic atmosphere—we only needed ants—and a feeling of well-being bubbled up in me. Poldi gave her glass a slight lift towards me, then let her eyes slant down her short, straight nose to watch me as she drank. She was wearing a red and white candy-stripe blouse that set off her golden colouring and showed her long, firm arms. Mary Barber didn't know what she was talking about when she said Australian men preferred their beer.

"Frank," I said. "There's one thing you've done to my ancestral home that my father would never have approved."

"Please?" Frank peered at me, head on one side, and eyes opaque with uncertainty.

"All this." I gestured around the table. "Alcohol. He hated it . . . wouldn't have it in the house."

"And you?"

"When I discovered beer, it was the disappointment of his life."

Frank made wet rings on the table with his glass. "It is a strange thing for an educated man," he said thoughtfully. "Usually it is the ignorant who condemn something they cannot understand."

"The pub-keepers hated him," I grinned. "He used to order all his patients to give up drink."

"That's the trouble with democracy," Mary said noisily. "It

gives freedom to the strong to make everyone else do what they want."

She had been sitting with the fingers of one hand playing in her hair. Now, with the fingers abruptly withdrawn, the hair stood up, giving her a crazy, lopsided look. The wine bottle in front of her was a quarter empty.

I laughed. "No one took any notice of him. They reckoned he was entitled to one fault."

"His son, too," Poldi said.

I made her a little bow. "Thank you."

She gave me a slow smile, and her dark-blue eyes twinkled like sunlight on deep water. "I mean you will soon have to make a selection," she said tauntingly. "You have so many faults, and you are entitled to only one."

"It is not democratic to ration faults," Mary said. She stood up, her ample breasts tight with energy against her dress, her face flushed. She raised her glass. "There is only one true democracy—"

"Sit down," Frank said harshly. The hard, cutting tone slapped Mary back into her chair. "We know you are only making a joke, Mary," he said, in a softer tone incongruous with the stern rigidity of his face. "We know, just the four of us in this room. But others might not understand so well."

"Stop being so serious, Frank," Poldi said.

I grinned. "Comes of drinking soda water."

"I was just making a little joke," Mary said. She said it defensively and all the happiness of the wine had gone out of her.

"Politics are not a subject for joking," Frank said firmly. "Particularly not for immigrants." Then he snapped a quick, shrewd glance at me. "Nor for some people who have lived here a long time, either."

And with that the don't care, relaxed pleasantness of my few beers went out of me, too. I looked at Frank's serious face, with the straight black hair fallen over the forehead, his white hands fixed and still on the table top, and I wondered had the security men been pestering him? There was only one answer. Of course they had. Frank, to them, was a man from the wrong side of the Iron Curtain. And I became certain then that Frank Barber no longer enjoyed the complete freedom of mind he had come so far to find. The poor devil, I thought. No wonder he was so touchy about jokes concerning democracy. Silence wrapped all of us. We had lost the brief, easeful spontaneity of the time before politics had erupted. Then Poldi stood up, trying to do it naturally, but unable quite to carry it off.

"It's late," she said, then remembered to look at her watch. "Are you coming, Wade?"

"Why, yes." I grasped her exit line like a tired swimmer in an undertow. "Harry will be chewing the spout off his teapot, waiting for copy."

Frank came awake as I got up, shaking his head slightly. "Don't go." He held out restraining hands to both of us. "I must go on my rounds. But you stay. Stay here with Mary and have a little party. Maybe I will finish early and can join you." He gave a short, self-conscious laugh. "Then I will not have to drink soda water and spoil everybody's fun."

"Some other time, Frank," I said. "Some time when we're all free to carry it off."

I cursed myself for saying that. It was the sort of thing you used to fob off someone who bored you stiff, or to placate some alcoholic with his finger in your buttonhole and his methylated breath scorching the skin right off your face. But there wasn't a damned thing else I could think of to say that would have sounded any better.

"So long, Mary," I said. She looked so crumpled that I had to say something. I reached out and touched her shoulder. "I liked your joke, anyway. It wasn't nearly so bad as Frank made out."

But out in the street, walking with Poldi in the hot, seductive sun, I felt again the sharp, barbed probe that Clark had twisted in me, remembered the Austins with their big binoculars searching the forbidden land for absent friends, while William Clark and Lucy kept their tryst.

The clatter of steam hammers on the new bridge bruised the air. Far away, out of sight beyond the yellow hill, the scream of a jet engine stripped the day down to its bones. Unconsciously, seeking comfort, something tangible to hold, I slipped my hand through Poldi's arm and held it tight. She didn't try to move away.

5

SATURDAY MORNING. THE MORNING OF MY DAY WITHOUT A
conscience. The day of ragged pants, and sandwiches, a boat
and a fishing line. My day of rest, with the week's *Herald* behind me and forty-eight hours before I should have again to
assess the newsworthiness of Clayville's multicackle. It is a
part of weekly journalism, this vast exhalation after the rat race
has been run, this expunging of a slate that wipes none too clean.

I swung out of bed and sat on its edge, enjoying the cool strike
of the iron frame through my thin pyjamas, letting the day seep
into me. The rectangle of it framed by the bedroom window
had a quality of unworldliness, as though someone had taken
all the separate perfections of a summer's day and bought them
together on one canvas.

The air still had a caressing coolness, the sun a clarity that
freshened rooftops and drew green fire from the avenue of
Norfolk pines some apostle of civic pride had planted along
the river mouth some sixty years before. The bay—I could see
the northern segment of it arcing over the right of the canvas
—was turquoise, looking like one of those incredible northern

Italian lakes, where you can see the bottom through your own reflections and everything is so lovely you wonder why Italians ever want to emigrate. It was going to be good out there in the boat.

I sauntered through some cereals, a couple of fried eggs and some toast. And over coffee one of my hands reached out, without instruction, and propped the *Herald* against the sugar bowl. It wasn't bad, as country journals go. It wasn't good. It had a sort of cornbelt probity, elevating trivia to forty-eight point type, conniving at the local supposition that Clayville was the world.

It's smugness irritated me, but I knew if it were better the local public wouldn't buy it any more. The important things of life, the efforts of men to make the world a better place, the struggles against great wrongs, the strivings to enshrine the fundamental rights. . . . These were nothing. Nobody's business. The efforts of writers to write better, of musicians to express the soul of things, of painters to find new ways of recording the moods and emotions of their times. . . . These were mere intellectual snobberies. . . . none of them could supplant, even for a moment, the importance of three square meals, a pot of beer, and a woman to warm, and enliven, the nightly bed.

Sometimes I thought the readers were right; at others I knew they were wrong. This was one of the latter times.

I got up from the table feeling annoyed for having let my thoughts take hold of me. Some of the day's brightness had been smudged. I pitched the *Herald* into a wastebasket, and the office phone squealed as though it were a crime. It was Bert Thompson, sergeant of our two-man police force and third member of our regular fishing party.

"Can't make it today, Wade," he said. "Sorry. But something's come up."

He didn't sound sorry, which was strange, because Bert Thompson loved his fishing. He sounded brusque and just the tiniest bit nervous.

"We'll wait," I said. "When can you get finished?"

"No idea," he said. "You go without me."

I took another look at the day. It was too good out there for a man to miss. "Harry's down at the boat now," I said. "We'll go out and come back for you at lunchtime. How'd it be then?"

"Look, Wade," he said. "I don't know."

Again there was that little touch of nervousness in his voice. It could only mean that Bert Thompson was holding something back. And when a policeman holds something back from a newspaperman it is always something that a newspaperman wants most of all.

"Bert," I said. "This was my day off until you rang. Now it isn't. What's cooking that smells so much?"

Silence sang along the line and I could almost hear Bert ponderously thinking. The bay was sparkling, and far out I could see a flock of gulls making low-level passes at a school of fish. I could have spat in Bert Thompson's honest eye.

"Nothing," he said. "It's nothing, Wade. I just can't come. That's all."

"Okay," I said, watching the gulls. "We'll bring you some fish."

"Thanks," he said.

I went over to the window, the better to confuse myself. Down on the beach, just back from the river's mouth, I could see Harry fussing about the boat, and any time he was going to start muttering about bloody young fools who wasted the best part of the day. I began to curse Bert Thompson for his inability to act a lie, for his having thrown a complexity into my day without a conscience.

Getting dressed, I didn't choose my fishing clothes, but grey flannels and a light sports jacket. I was going round to see Bert Thompson and I was being stupid. Whatever he had could wait the week end out and still be four days early for publication. But his evasiveness had riled me. I was still too much of a newspaperman to let a country cop sell me a line of bull. And I liked Bert Thompson. That riled me, too. If he had come out in the open, told me he had something but couldn't release it, I'd have let it go. I'd done it before with him. There was no such thing as a scoop in Clayville. We worked together. Or, we had.

Sergeant Albert Thompson was sitting at his old-fashioned roll-top desk when I walked into his office five minutes later. He was writing something of tremendous importance. It must have been, because he couldn't tear his attention away from it. I stood just inside the doorway, watching him, and I could feel the hair at the back of my neck bristle like the hackles of a hunting dog that had scented something it didn't like. Bert Thompson had never ignored me before. I watched his big ham fist move up and down and across the paper with painstaking care, and I could see a muscle in his neck standing out like a hawser it was working so hard to keep his head from turning.

At last, I said: "What goes on, Bert?"

He put down the pen and looked around, slowly. His big, sunburned face was like cast-iron. His light-brown eyes were unnaturally steady, as though being held on target by an effort of will.

"I told you, Wade," he said, spacing the words out and giving them a flat, impersonal emphasis. "Nothing. You're wasting your time. You're wasting my time, too."

I stared at him until he looked away. "Something's eating you, Bert," I said softly.

A touch of red crept up above his collar. "I got work to do. Will you get out and let me do it?"

"Someone after a dog licence, Bert?"

"Yeah. Me. I'm getting a dog to keep newspapermen outa my office."

I moved around and faced him at close quarters, leaning over the tired pigeon-holes of his desk. "That's very funny, Bert. Keep that up and you'll be on television."

He half rose from his chair, then settled back on the edge, crouching slightly at the knees. "I told you to get the hell outa here," he grated. "D'you walk, or do I throw you?"

I still kept my eyes on him. "Are you coming with us next Saturday, Bert?"

"No," he said flatly. "Not next Saturday. Or any other Saturday. We've got to give up this fishing and old pals together stuff. It's not good enough. . . ."

Suddenly that bare office, with its battered furnishings and the sun-warped files festooned along the walls, closed in on me. I felt cold. I fancied I could smell the stale manure stench of a Turkish cigarette.

"Bert," I said quietly. "Have you been listening to a man named William Clark?"

Bert Thompson's eyes opened quickly, like camera shutters, then stopped down to zero. And he was wearing a poker face. It is standard equipment for cops in charge of stations, but when a man who is your friend starts looking at you through slits in a mask, you know as much as if he'd written the message in words a yard high.

"You don't want to be seen with me in public, Bert," I said insistently. "Clark's put the finger on me, and you accept it."

Bert Thompson picked up his pen and threw it down again. He rubbed one big hand across his chin, and it was so quiet, so expectantly quiet, in there that I could hear the scrape of whiskers against the hard skin of his palm.

"You've got it wrong, Wade," he said slowly. "It's just that we've been getting too friendly. Don't you see it? I'm the head policeman around here. You're a newspaperman. It doesn't pay to be seeing so much of you. People are starting to talk, Wade. I get a lot of confidential stuff in here . . . private stuff . . . family affairs and that . . . you know. . . . People will start to think I blab it. You know how it is, Wade . . . in a little place like this."

I looked at him with a sick emptiness inside me. "You're lying, Bert."

He flopped back in his chair and the squeak of its ancient springs was like a scream. He waved his hands in a gesture of hopelessness. "Yeah. I'm lying."

I walked around the desk, my heels like drumsticks on the bare board floor. "What did he say about me, Bert?"

He looked away. "I can't answer that."

"What d'you think about what he said about me, then, Bert?"

"What does it matter what I think?"

"It matters to me. I want to know."

He shrugged. "I'm playin' safe. That's all. I've got a job to hold down and a family depending on it."

Anger burst up and out of me then. Anger against Clark, but more against the dreadful cowardice of respectability that Bert Thompson was confessing. The sort of cowardice that makes people stand by a street fight and watch a man get kicked to death without attempting to intervene. I was gripping his desk fit to overturn it, stretching across it in a hard, brittle tenseness.

"So now you think I'm a security risk. Is that it?" I fairly speared the words at him.

"I didn't say that."

"You mean it."

"You're putting words in my mouth."

"All right. I'm putting words in your mouth. Am I a security risk?"

He got up suddenly, knocking his chair to the floor as he swung away. He stamped across the office to the window that looked out on Main Street, the window with "Police" half-mooned across it, then turned to face me. His big body in its dark-blue uniform pants and light-blue shirt without a tie, its black regulation boots, looked strangely puny beneath the red shame that was showing on his face. There was no longer any mask.

58

"Look, Wade. See it my way." He held out a hand, palm uppermost, like begging for alms. "There's a bit of a smell hanging around you now. I don't know about security risks. That's not police business. But there's this smell. And I've been in the force long enough to be sensitive about smells. I'm due for retirement in another ten years, Wade. I can't afford no trouble . . . I can't risk my pension now, after all this time."

I looked at him, and my hot anger had matured into bitterness. "Sure," I said. "How can friendship compete with a great big police pension?"

Harry was a snapping turtle when I got down to the beach. He had rolled the dinghy down to the water on its jinker, rigged the outboard, stowed the bait, our rods and half a dozen beers. He had been ready to go for the better part of an hour. His face, as he watched me approach, was sour with disapproval. His long, thin neck stretched forward as though he were reaching out to bite me.

"Where'n hell yu been?"

"Business," I said. "I'm sorry, Harry."

He sniffed. "For Chrissake. Business . . . on a Saturday."

Harry would have made a magnificent clown, he was so lugubrious through the gamut of emotions. Now he was comic in uttermost disgust. I felt a grin crack through the ice that Bert Thompson had frozen on my face.

"You'll be pleased I didn't make anything on the deal," I said.

"Good," Harry snarled. "And where'n hell's Bert got to?"

I kicked off my old tennis shoes, rolled my pants and started for the boat. "Bert's not coming."

"More business?"

"That's what he said."

"Well, flog me," Harry said disgustedly. "Business . . . on a day like this."

The little outboard phut-phutted us out into the bay, and I got that wonderful seaborne feeling right up through my buttocks. The bay was calm and the dinghy slid along with a soft lifting motion that had the rhythm of poetry in it. The sort of poetry Keats used to write . . . about seasons of mist and mellow fruitfulness. There was no mist, only the warm, clear sunlight, but there was mellowness. That was something that always got me out in the bay. From the land, the water would look bright and sparkling, with a hard clean brillance borrowed from the sun. But when you got out and looked back on the shining roofs, the geometry of the town, you found soft colour all around your boat and an easeful soaking warmth inside it.

We anchored on the whiting ground in the south arm of the bay, about half a mile from shore. It was a big patch of white sand and seaweed, shaped like a leg of mutton, and when you looked down through the green opalescent water you could see the white blur of the sand, and the dark-green weed plots all set out like some botanic garden. It was so beautiful you'd expect to find mermaids there. I remembered them telling, when I was a kid, how a crusty citizen called "Dong" Bell had seen one once, at the end of a day's fishing, and had dived in after her. He came up with a gutful of salt water, and sober. After which, he had taken up golf.

It was a magical place, but only the second best whiting ground in the bay. The best was up in the north arm, close in by the red earth cliffs, and off limits to everyone but Atomic Research Authority personnel, who didn't have the sense to fish it anyway. The way I was feeling then, with Bert Thompson still trolling through my mind, it was another thing I had against the atom jugglers. At the end of an hour I had even more against them. We hadn't got a single bite between us.

"Maybe they've got business somewhere else," Harry growled. "Like you and Bert."

"Harry," I said tersely. "I wasn't having fun."

"Me neither," Harry said. He jerked his rod impatiently. "Too bad we can't go up near the cliffs. Those bastards never fish there anyway."

"Shut up, Harry," I said.

"The fish must be lyin' there head to tail."

"So what good does that do us?"

Harry slide a thumb under his braces and snapped them, letting his arm and hand arc out in a gesture of triumphant decision. "So we go in there and get us a few dozen."

I frowned at him, but deep inside me there was the beginning of rebellion. I could feel it working like a purgative. "The regulations forbid it—"

"Bugger the regulations," Harry said. "If we tack well out t'sea and then slant back, we'll get in under the cliff. We'd be dead unlucky if they saw us."

I started to reel in my line, slowly, giving myself time to think about something I didn't need to think about any more. "I don't like it," I said, and I was lying because thumbing my nose at Security was just what I needed. I'd been on the receiving end too long.

"Even if they caught us they wouldn't do much," Harry said, stowing his rod inboard and reaching for the starter string. "First time'd only be a warnin'."

"Well, what are we waiting for?" I said.

Harry flipped the starter and the little outboard burst awake. "If we get a haul I'll take some up t'Bert," Harry said. "He's a man that likes his fish."

"Oh, sure," I said, and my belly started to have convulsions at the thought of that righteous cop eating the forbidden flesh, the non-kosher, the unclean. And if I had needed anything more to persuade me to go on, the thought of that delicate revenge would have tipped the scales. "A Christian gesture, Harry," I said. "And Christian gestures are their own reward."

Harry swung the rudder and we headed out to sea through the wide neck of the bay. We steered north for a while, and I could see down the reverse side of the limestone hill that hid everything from the town. In the immediate foreground was the new wharf, with its bright timbers and a big, black mobile crane. Beyond, in the middeground, was a great sprawl of buildings, brilliantly white in the sun and very ordinary. I think I'd half expected to see them shaped like retorts, all connected with vast network patterns of pipes.

I could see straight up the Clay, the glint of the hot fence on one bank and the little white town peering through trees and bushes on the other. I could see the black figures of men moving about the garish framework of the new road and railway bridge, repulsively painted in a salmon undercoat. Alongside it, strung across the river, was the black streak of a temporary pontoon bridge; and, on the town end, the neat white pyramids of the immigrant worker's camp. The sound of some pneumatic tool came hollowly across the water.

Then everything was sheared off by the line of marching cliffs. We came about and sneaked in past the northern spit. Five minutes later we were gliding into the shadow of the cliffs, and under our keel I could see the white and silver gleam of fish.

Harry pulled in the first one so soon it seemed to come up as a counterbalance to the anchor. It was a good eighteen inches long, sleek and beautiful, and clean, with that delicate white and silver cleanness that belongs to whiting. He had another threshing on the floor of the dinghy before I'd had so much as a nibble. And I knew my luck was out. Whiting are like that. They'll bite like hungry travellers at one end of a boat, and utterly ignore a hook at the other end, ten feet away.

"Cover up your face," Harry grinned. "You're scaring 'em away." His left hand struck again and his right hand reeled in. "Man, oh, man," he crowed. "Why haven't we come 'ere before?"

"Because Bert Thompson wouldn't have let us, for one thing," I said sourly. "And because—" I stopped as a motor launch roared around the corner of the cliffs. I looked at Harry. "And because we haven't been so bloody silly before."

Harry grabbed his third whiting expertly as it broke the

surface, brought it inboard and freed it from the hook. "Ah, tell 'em we're taxpayers," he said. "We got rights."

Harry was a man who didn't care much about anything but late copy. But I felt a sinking in my stomach as the launch raced up, spray flying from its grey bows, and a white-clad seaman aiming a Vickers machine gun at us. I wasn't afraid of the gun, we weren't dealing with that sort of people, but I knew being caught in a prohibited area wasn't going to look healthy in my record. William Clark was going to lap it up. And Bert Thompson.

The launch rocked us with its bow wave, slid alongside and stopped. A young, fair man, with square shoulders and a strong, square face, stepped from the glassed-in wheelhouse. He was dressed in white shorts and shirt, with a black service pistol at his hip.

"You're in a prohibited area," he said. His voice was pleasant, yet with a touch of steel. "Don't you know that?"

"First time I heard whiting were protected fish," Harry drawled.

"We made a mistake in navigation," I said, challenging him transparently because I had been stupid and was stuck with it.

The launch skipper gave me a searching look. "You're Scotter, aren't you?"

I collapsed my fishing rod and stacked it away. "Yes," I said tersely. "And would you mind asking that character to turn that gun somewhere else?"

He gave an order and the machine gunner straightened up, grinning, to lean against the rail. He was a thin, dark-skinned kid, with an Italian look about him.

"You ought to know all about the regulations," the skipper said. "A newspaperman. A war correspondent. ... You ought to know better than this."

"I should," I said harshly. "But I don't."

His eyes gave out a hard stare and his mouth tightened a notch. He was a pleasant sort of kid and I was a fool to be needling him, but I couldn't stop myself.

63

"We'll have to search you," he said coldly. "You got any cameras, binoculars . . . anything like that?"

"We've got three whiting," I snapped back. "Confiscate them for the officers' mess, why don't you? There's a telescopic camera in that fishing basket, and a special reconnaissance rocket built into my rod. . . ."

"Look," the skipper said, and this time his voice was all steel. "Don't fill me up with the funny stuff. I've got a job to do. There's the regulations and I stick to 'em." He paused and bent towards me. "You mightn't find it such a bad idea yourself one of these days."

I gave him a tight, wry grin. "Yeah. One of these days."

"Come aboard," he ordered. "We'll get this searching over." He turned his head. "Jones . . . Carslake . . . get into that dinghy and check it."

For a moment I was tempted to tell him to go to hell. But what was the use? His boat was faster, he had a machine gun and a pistol . . . and. . . . Oh, Christ . . . I climbed aboard his launch and Harry followed. We stood with our arms up while he frisked us, then stood watching his men go through our little dinghy.

"All right," I said, at the end of it. "What now? You going to arrest us?"

"No," he said coldly. "We know where to find you any time."

They escorted us out of the area, our little outboard phut-phutting in a frenzy above the murmur of their powerful diesel. They shoved us right down into the south arm of the bay before they opened throttle and turned away. The young skipper stood near the machine gun, balancing neatly against the deep heeling turn, and when they straightened up I'm damned if he didn't salute us.

Harry said, "That's nice and proper. After all, he's only a servant of the taxpayers. An' that's us."

We opened our sandwiches and knocked off some beer. Then

we moved back to our original whiting grounds. We dropped our hooks into the cool green water again and, just for irony's sake, the whiting started biting for us. We took about three dozen, but there was no fun in it any more. We hadn't been arrested and probably nothing was going to happen, not even a fine. But the memory of the whole affair was in my mind like the dirty taste of a bad dream. I'd been a fool, a blind, stupid, peevish fool. But that, of course, is the way that pressure and resentment gets you. I told myself I was going to start all over again learning how to relax. I meant it.

We up-anchored and beat homeward somewhere about mid-afternoon. As we left the beach, carrying the heavy fish basket between us, Harry said: "I must take some to Bert. He's a man that likes his fish."

"Oh, sure," I said sourly. "Good old Bert. Give him the three you caught first. They ought to suit him fine."

Harry looked across at me with the mournful eyes of a dog that has been kicked. "Sorry about talkin' you into that, Wade," he mumbled. "Yu want to cuss me out, go right ahead."

I grinned. I didn't feel like grinning about anything, but he was so contrite that I had to make the effort. "Don't think about it, Harry. I'm grown up. I went along."

"Buy yu a beer," he offered, brightening. "Then come home and we'll have the missus cook some fish."

It was a kindness in him, an attempted final expiation of his fancied guilt, but I couldn't take it up. I felt too disjointed. I went back to my bed-sitting room and put some records on the phonograph. The first few were little more than surface anodynes against the residual poisons of the day. But when I started Schubert's second trio, the record they made with old "Pau" Casals, playing with Horzowski and Schneider at the Prades festival, somehow I began thinking about Poldi. The music was like her, quiet and gay and sad, and beautiful.

It was the first time I'd thought about her in such a way. I played the record twice.

6

IF SATURDAY WAS THE DAY WITHOUT A CONSCIENCE, SUNDAY WAS the day of compromise, the transition period from the hedonism of Saturday to the hard practicality of Monday. Sundays I was like a timpanist in an orchestra, screwing the pegs up here and there in preparation for a good, hard smack at the drum first thing Monday.

Sunday mornings I did the chores and let my mind graze on sundry things that sometimes mattered, but mostly didn't. I bundled the week's laundry, tidied my rooms, picked up on my letter writing, browsed through the latest copies of the *Economist* and *New Statesman* and marked passages for the basis of some powerful editorial. Then I went to lunch at the Austins, and listened to their weekly lecture on why I should go to church. And I always explained that some people got up and went to church and others just stayed in bed. Perhaps if I had lived so close to a church that I couldn't relax for the sound of bells I'd have got up too, but the *Herald* was only in the faintest earshot, and the bells barely hinted at the wrath to come.

Normally, I enjoyed my Sunday mornings, but this one was

66

being roughened by the memory of my damned silliness over the fishing grounds. The day had started off all right, with sunlight and a light breeze stirring up those summer scents that make you think it's good to be alive.

But then I grilled some whiting for breakfast, and every mouthful accused me of stupidity. If anyone needed to keep his nose clean it was I; and yet I had embraced temptation like Lady Chatterley's gamekeeper with much less reason. Some garrulous birds began tweeting outside my window and I thought, "For God's sake go away, before someone thinks you're carrier pigeons."

I realized then that I was getting away from my resolution to relax, so I switched on the phonograph. The Schubert trio was still on the turntable. I started it on the second side, where the scherzo picks you up and whirls you around, and soon I was thinking that nothing of real importance had changed since Franz Schubert wrote his melodies . . . I moved from there into thinking about Poldi again. She seemed to go with Schubert.

It's funny how you can see a girl every day for months and never think of her in any particular way. Then suddenly, you can't stop thinking about her except in a particular way. I wasn't leering. Neither was I being platonic. But there are things you can think about a girl, about the way she looks, turns her head, or the way she walks, the way a line of beauty is disclosed at certain moments, in certain attitudes or actions. These things don't mean an urgent necessity to go to bed, although sometimes they can lead to it. There are conditions of thought, qualities that scanctify emotions that could otherwise be lewdness. I could see Poldi in the clean singing of the violin and in old Pau's cello.

Then the scherzo ended, and in the little needle-hissing silence before the *allegro moderato,* the door swung open and William Clark stepped into the room. I stopped the record.

"Don't you ever knock?"

67

Clark grinned. "I knocked," he said. "Maybe the music was too loud."

He was dressed like an advertisement for what the smart young executive wears on Sunday mornings. Brown golf shoes, grey flannel slacks and a tan lightweight sports jacket. A silk paisley scarf bloomed at his throat and disappeared beneath a pale-green shirt. I felt, for a moment, absurdly self-conscious in my old blue dressing gown and scuffed leather slippers. I hadn't shaved and my hair was roughly done.

"Why don't you take a day off," I said.

Clark grinned again. "What were you trying to do yesterday? Prove something? Or find something out?"

I could see he was going to play cat-and-mouse questioning again. I took off the record and stacked it away. "What are you going to do about it?"

Clark lowered himself into a chair, crossed his legs with due care for his pants' knife-edge creases, and got out his gold cigarette case. "Nothing, I guess. We can afford to wait until you do something big." He lit a cigarette. "It'll be so much more fun."

"Clark," I said patiently. "You'd save yourself a lot of time if you'd try to believe that spies aren't hiding behind every bush . . . that everyone isn't in the business."

"But I *do* believe it," Clark said, and puffed out a cloud of smoke. He was using Turkish. "I'm like Maupassant. I believe a virgin is a girl of six, sometimes seven. I'm even more liberal. I'm not checking on anyone under ten."

"Then why," I asked, "are you hanging around the Austins' kindergarten?"

Clark's lips straightened slightly in annoyance. "I'm taking Lucy Austin out. D'you mind?"

"No," I said coldly. "It's nothing to me. Even as a kid she had a strong stomach."

He didn't like that. He measured me with his eyes as though storing a memory for future use. I gave him what I hoped

68

he would construe as an insulting grin, and I saw the expression in his eyes change, become assessive. It puzzled me for an instant, but I had no time to think about it. He threw his cigarette down on the floor, stamped his foot on it and jerked forward, big body straining against his hands on the chair arm. It was his prosecuting pose.

"You know a man named Curthoys, don't you?"

"In Clayville?"

"In Sydney."

"I also know a man named Carthew in Sydney," I said levelly. "He's a Liberal Party official."

"I'm asking about Curthoys," Clark snapped. "He's a Communist, isn't he?"

I walked over to the open window and leaned against the sill. The sun struck warm and friendly on my back. Yet it didn't ease the sudden tension in the room, because I knew it was not the question that I had to answer, but its implications. And how could I answer them?

"You came to ask me about the fishing," I said.

Clark laughed shortly. "I know all about the fishing. What I want to know now is all about Curthoys. He's a Commie, isn't he?"

"As far as I know he's a Communist," I said. "Unless he's an undercover security agent. I wouldn't know about that."

"Skipping the humour," Clark said. "You've been around with him a fair bit, haven't you?"

"I've never been around with him."

Clark sat back and lifted his eyebrows in assumed surprise. "But you've been to parties with him. Used to drink with him regularly at one time."

"Let's get this straight," I said. "If you're interested, I've been to parties at which he was also present. I used to drink at the same pub he patronized."

"You knew all the time he was a Communist?"

"Everyone knew. He made no secret of it."

Clark lit himself another cigarette, using that shiny gold lighter with the engraved initials. He had the smug look of a man sitting in the box seat.

I said, "Use the ashtray when you butt that cigarette."

He grinned crookedly and I knew I had made a mistake in saying that. It was a straw to beat him with, and he knew I had nothing stronger. He reached out with one foot and kicked the butt on the floor towards me. His grin became derisive.

"You appreciate how difficult you make things for yourself? Mixing with the Commies in Indo-China. Chumming up with them in Sydney?"

"I knew a man who got the clap once," I snapped. "I didn't catch it, though."

"That supposed to prove something?"

"Only that infection isn't automatic."

"Y'know," Clark said smoothly. "Sometimes you get just a bit too smart."

"Is that suspicious, too?"

"Everything's suspicious," Clark said silkily. "But not about you any longer. I've got you all wrapped up, Scotter."

He threw his half-smoked cigarette on the floor and stamped on it, watching me for reactions. He must have read my first one accurately, because his eyes sharpened. He half-rose from his chair, getting his weight back on his feet. But I stopped myself in time. Hitting him wasn't going to get me anything but a beating, or a spell in jail. Maybe both, because firstly he was bigger and in training, secondly he was on official business and protected by the law.

I knew I'd gauged it right when I saw the disappointment in his face. He leaned back and crossed his legs, showing some inches of jazzy socks and some more of black-haired leg. He stretched his arms and clasped hands behind his neck, as though in invitation to king-hit him. He grinned, and his mouth was lopsided with contempt.

"You were going to say something, Scotter?"

70

"Yes," I said coldly. "Is your chief on duty today?"

Clark took his hands down. "Why?"

"Because this has gone far enough. I'm going to ask him to call you to heel."

"You think he'll listen?"

"I don't know." I paused to choose my words, wanting each one to hit the mark. "But there's something I do know, Clark. Something that's an axiom with pressmen. . . . Don't argue with the bumboys. Get to the top man. I should have done it days ago."

"Well, ring him," Clark said icily. "Tell him how pure you are. He enjoys a joke."

I went through into my office with Clark padding at my heels. I dialled the number. A girl's voice said, "Atomic Research."

I said, "Connect me with Colonel Tucker, please."

"Your name?" Her voice was precise, devoid of interest.

"Wade Scotter. Editor of the Clayville *Herald*."

A pause, and I didn't need Clark's smirking grin to know I'd lost. When a switchboard girl, or a secretary, pauses at her end of the phone you can turn it in.

"The colonel doesn't receive phone calls," she said primly. "You will have to write for an appointment, stating your reasons."

"How long does that take?"

"I'm not authorized to say," she reprimanded, using number one quotation from the phrase book.

I felt like shouting at her. Minor officials always get me that way when they start parroting their lessons. But I gave her the benefit of her regulations. "Okay," I said. "Thanks. I'll write."

I put down the phone with slow deliberation because Clark was watching me, grinning, and I didn't want to show him I was nettled. I walked across the office, not looking at him, and sat down behind my typewriter. Clark didn't say anything until I was feeding paper into the machine.

Then he said, "Would you like to know what will happen, Scotter?"

I started to type, trying to ignore him, but irritatingly conscious of his smug amusement and my own poor show of nonchalance: "Colonel R. G. Tucker, Security Branch. . . ."

"He'll ask me for a report," Clark said. "A verbal one. I'll tell him how it is, and he'll write telling you the matter is being looked into and he is sure you will appreciate that the nature of his officer's duties entails private inquiries which can sometimes prove embarrassing. . . ."

I looked up, my nerves jangling at his persistence and the drawning suspicion that he was talking sense. I kept my voice down only with an effort. "Are you trying to prevent me writing this letter?"

"I'm trying to save you from disappointment," Clark said, and grinned. "But we will endeavour, as far as is possible in the circumstances, to minimize any inconvenience that our officers' inquiries might occasion . . ."

"Would you mind getting the hell out of here?" I asked. My voice was thin, and hardly above a whisper.

"Sure," Clark said easily. "Never intrude on the privacy of a citizen."

"Why don't you go home and have a nice mouth wash?" I said. "Your breath smells."

"Enjoy your jokes while you can," Clark said blandly. "There's a certain smell to the name of Scotter that I must tell you about some day."

He went out with that peculiar padding walk of his that reminded me of a big cat, and I noticed for the first time that his back hair was shaped and brushed around like a cruiser stern. It was another touch of his dandyism, a little thing, but it gave me the empty pleasure of a sneer.

When the outside door had banged and I had seen him pass the window on his way up-town, I finished my letter to Colonel Tucker. But my enthusiasm had gone. Tucker had set him on me. He wasn't likely now to take my side.

7 ——————————z——————————————

THE DAY'S TEMPERATURE LEAPT FROM THE MID-NINETIES TO past boiling point when I walked into the Austins' upstairs sitting room for lunch. Clark was there, sitting on the sofa with Lucy, smiling around as graciously as a curate on a free lunch ticket. His dark eyes mocked me, inviting me to take note of his assured position in the family circle. I couldn't miss it. He was the personification of the Sunday suitor.

"So there you are, Wade dear," Aunt Clara started up from her chair and made a little swooping run at me. "We've been waiting."

"I'm sorry, Aunt."

I bent forward and kissed her. My eyes were hot and dry on William Clark.

Clark made a little smirk and patted Lucy's hand. "He's been home catching up on his *Pravda*."

"So you're friends," Aunt Clara said. "How nice."

Lucy giggled. Her dark-brown eyes were gleaming with that curious light you see in women's eyes at ringside seats when some poor punchy is being butchered—and she was looking at me. I went across to Aunt Belle and kissed her on the cheek.

73

"Lucy, dear," Aunt Clara said. "Go in with Mr. Clark and Wade. We'll serve up now."

We went into the dining room, the three of us, and sat at the table, a big heavy cedar piece from the days of monumental furnishing, covered with a white tablecloth whose pale flowers and lace frills had taken Aunt Belle some two years of work. It was a magnificent thing and it always made me nervous. I was scared of spilling so much as a bread crumb on it.

The room, like the others in the house, was sombre and over-filled with dark red cedar furniture. The chairs on which we sat were plain and high-backed, built not so much for comfort as to ensure that their users sat up straight. A small bowl of red roses occupied the centre of the table, and a fallen petal on the white cloth looked like a pool of blood. I picked it up and dropped it back into the middle of the bowl.

Lucy said, "That's a dear, kind, thoughtful boy."

She said it in a mocking imitation of her aunts' manner, but the way she looked at me along her eyes was all her own.

"Be nice to him, my dear," Clark said. "He's had some nasty shocks lately."

"Clark," I said tautly. "Drop that line of talk while you're lunching here."

"Well, well." He raised his eyebrows. "Mr. Scotter giving orders." He smiled thinly. "Tell me. Did you post your letter to Colonel Tucker?"

"Yes," I said, "and marked the flap so he can tell if you steam it open."

Clark looked across at Lucy, and indicated me with a sideways, contemptuous, jerk of the head. "Wonderful to see him in such high spirits, isn't it?"

"Always was a brash little devil," Lucy said.

"I can believe that," Clark said. He turned to me, and his voice became feline soft. "You won't be nearly as brash soon, though, will you, Scotter?"

I didn't look at him. My hands were vices on the table's edge.

I hated his guts, not only for pushing me, but also because he had brought his vileness into that quiet room. And then Aunt Clara and Aunt Belle came in with a big tray piled with food.

Clara said grace, and then we were pushing salt and pepper and things around to improve the basic course that God had just provided. It became a meal on two levels. The Austins up on their pink fleecy cloud, passing food and comments with that vague, and somewhat terrible, assurance of theirs that everything was for the best in this best of all possible worlds. And Clark, Lucy and I down on sub-basement level, rasping swords of bitterness in an endless thrust and parry.

Time and courses passed. I was spooning sweets, prunes and custard, wondering about the strange communion of bitchery that existed between Clark and Lucy, when I picked up Aunt Belle's intense whispering.

"It sounds so much worse," she was saying. "With all those queer vowels and consonants mixed up. . . ."

"But so much more imaginative," Aunt Clara said. "So much better than the monotonous vulgarity of our men's swearing."

"Hey," I said. "What sort of talk is this?"

Aunt Clara looked at me severely. "Wade," she said sternly. "You've been woolgathering again."

"I'll write it out a thousand times, darling," I smiled. "I must not gather wool."

"Nor doubtful friends," Clark said.

"We were discussing the problem of Christopher and Sergei," Aunt Belle said. "Sergei is a little immigrant boy, and he is teaching Christopher to swear in Russian. Sergei already swears quite remarkably in English."

"He picked it up from Aunt Belle," Lucy said maliciously. "You should hear her cursing sometimes . . . when she thinks she's alone.

"Lucy! . . ." Aunt Belle dropped her spoon and spattered custard on the tablecloth.

Aunt Clara looked around, quietly and remotely. "If you

have finished, Belle, shall we take our coffee in the sitting-room? Mr. Clarke, would you take Lucy in? Wade, give Belle your hand."

If the sitting room had not had that big window spanning the back wall, it would have been a deadly repetition of the dining room. There was the same staid Wilton carpet, the same dark red cedar furniture, and three of Aunt Belle's teacherish land-scape oils to fill the wall space. I saw Clark's eyes pecking around the moment we debouched through the doorway. They halted at the binoculars standing on the sideboard, moved across to the big window, and then returned.

"Binoculars," I said. "Lots of people have them."

"All sorts of people," he agreed smoothly. "All sorts indeed."

"Do sit down, Mr. Clarke," Aunt Belle whispered. "Here, by the window. It's our very loveliest view."

Clark held her chair, smiling and looking out over the lawns of the back garden, down to the river and over it to the yellow grasslands of the Atomic Research Authority's territory. And I could see from the way he smiled that he was going to make something out of the binoculars.

Sitting, he hauled out his gold cigarette case and offered it to Lucy, moving it away as she reached for a cigarette and looking down her dress as she leaned forward. I had seen the manœuvre before often enough, carried out by other men, in other places, and had never liked it. I hated it now because, firstly, it was so out of place in that setting and, secondly, Lucy was enjoying it, leaning forward further than was necessary, wriggling her shoulders slightly as she looked into his eyes, smiling with lips just parted and the pink tip of her tongue showing. I had seen that done before, too, but only publicly by prostitutes and patho-logically enthusiastic amateurs.

"Lucy and Mr. Clark might prefer something iced," I told Aunt Clara, who had walked in with the coffee things.

Lucy leaned back in her chair, twisting a little sideways to look me in the face. She smiled a sleepy cat smile that was supposed to tell me I didn't count for anything. It wasn't entirely a success. Gleams of hatred shone in her eyes.

"Wade," she said. "Why don't you shut up?"

Aunt Clara made a quick, sucking noise of displeasure. "Lucy. Don't be unpleasant dear."

"All right," Lucy said. "*You* tell him to shut up, then."

I winced for the Austins, but I need not have worried. Aunt Clara was calmly pouring coffee. Belle was staring out over the river, grazing in those remote pastures of her mind, rocking gently in her chair to the beat of some celestial metronome.

"Why d'you have the binoculars, Miss Clara?" Clark asked bluntly, stirring sugar into his black coffee.

Aunt Clara looked puzzled. Her fingers plucked uncertainly at the gold watch riding on her bosom. "Why . . . for rabbits . . . of course."

"Of course," Aunt Belle echoed.

"Rabbits?"

Clark flicked a speck of cigarette ash from his impeccable suit, a grey, worn with dark-green accessories and a white, triangular fin of handkerchief peeping from the breast pocket.

Aunt Belle pushed her spectacles more firmly on her nose. She shook her head gently. "We watch them. . . . They are our friends."

"Oh, sure," Clark said. He levered himself up and went back to the sideboard, picked up a pair of binoculars, and returned to the window. "Good glasses, these." He traversed them across the river. "But I don't see any rabbits."

"They have gone away for just a little while," Aunt Clara said eagerly. "But they will soon be coming back. Maybe in the autumn. You must come here then, of an evening, just before sunset . . . and see them . . . so, so beautiful. . . ."

"There's one we call Wade," Aunt Belle said, giving me a skittish and tender smile. "Just like our dear boy . . . a little bit cheeky, then scared and hurt . . . then he becomes bold again. . . ."

77

"That's our boy," Clark said, and sniggered.

I didn't look at him. I shifted buttocks on my chair, kept my eyes on the back garden and cursed myself because there was nothing I could do to break up this preposterous situation.

"We'll call one after you, Mr. Clark, if you'd like that," Aunt Belle said, in her twittering birdlike way.

"Ah, knock it off," Lucy snapped. She sprang up and whirled around the room. "You'll have me crazy too, if you don't stop talking about those damned rabbits. They've gone and good riddance to them. You'll never set eyes on them again, so forget them. Stop talking about them . . . for Christ's sake!"

I looked quickly, and anxiously, at the Austins. They seemed stunned, carved in stillness, as well they might for Lucy's outburst was, to them, as blasphemous as it was vindictive.

I turned on Lucy and she was waiting for me, her eyes defiant, and every hard, taut line of her face and body daring me to pick a fight. I couldn't do it. Anything I said, or did, would only make things worse.

"Would you like more coffee, Mr. Clark?" Aunt Clara asked.

She sat so upright in her chair that she appeared propped within her clothes. Belle watched her fixidly, trying to borrow strength. There was hurt resignation in her eyes.

"Thanks. No." Clark smiled easily at her. Then he grinned towards the rest of us, seeming pleased at his little playmate's performance. He turned and put the binoculars back on the sideboard, among the bowls of fruit, the cut-glass drinking set and the lace mats. "What else can you see with these?" he asked. "Besides rabbits?"

"There is so little else to see now," Aunt Clara said.

"With a periscope you could see over the hill," I said. "Surely you've got a periscope."

Aunt Clara looked confused. "What an odd thing to say, my dear."

"I'm the odd man out." I leaned forward and patted her shoulder.

"We often see that young man with the dog," Aunt Belle

said, with a whispering rush of eagerness. "Such a handsome young man. But I am afraid it is a cruel, savage dog."

"Now that's interesting," Clark said.

"Even more interesting if some of those damned rabbits came back for the dog to chase," Lucy said spitefully.

I glared at her. She stared back at me with eyes that had a bright, hard surface sheen, and a hot fire behind. I felt that she was working herself up to an explosive rage. Why, I didn't know. She was taut to breaking point.

"A really fine young man," Aunt Belle murmured.

"He is, indeed," Aunt Clara nodded.

Lucy whirled on Aunt Clara, face white, and the corners of her mouth pulled down. "Like T. P. Moody, perhaps," she shrilled. "D'you remember T. P. Moody?"

I felt, rather than saw, the quick stiffening of Clark's body. I swung my head in time to see him shoot her a venomous, warning glare. She glared back, and for a moment their eyes locked in a soundless battle. Then Lucy looked away, out the window but not seeing anything of the bright warm day outside. She was so still, so stiff, that I could see she was balanced on the edge of letting go completely.

Aunt Clara craned forward and I had an absurd urge to call out, "Don't ask it . . . don't . . . don't." But, of course, I didn't.

And Aunt Clara said, "Whom did you say, dear?"

"Lucy, be quiet," Clark snapped.

Lucy licked her lips. She didn't move her head. "Thomas Patrick Moody," she said in a thin, brittle voice. "Dr. Thomas Bloody Moody."

The name hit and ricocheted around the room. There was a moment's silence. An oppressive, weighted silence that pressed against my temples and caved my eardrums. Aunt Belle gave a little whimpering cry and toppled off her chair.

I jumped forward, but Aunt Clara beat me to her. The others didn't move. She looked up at me fiercely, as a stranger, or as someone hurt too badly to recognize a friend.

"Take her shoulders," she said curtly.

79

I did as I was told, not stopping to wonder at Aunt Clara's newly found efficiency. She took the legs. And neither Clark nor Lucy moved a hand. We went out through the dining room and across the hall to the bedrooms. We laid Aunt Belle carefully upon her bed. She was waxen, her breathing was ragged, and there was a dribble of saliva from her mouth. Suddenly I had time to be scared.

"I'll get Frank Barber." I turned towards the door.

"No." Aunt Clara stopped me. "She has only fainted. The heat, you know. . . ."

Aunt Clara was composed, almost implacably composed. It was something I had never seen in her before. It was the sort of change you see sometimes in a mental patient sitting up after the dreadful shock of electrotherapy. Calm and assured on the surface, but stressed with fear below it. Aunt Clara's composure affected me more strongly even than Aunt Belle's fainting fit. Belle had always been the weaker one. To faint was perfectly in character. But it wasn't like Aunt Clara to be exhibiting such a hard efficiency.

I hesitated, looking for some way to say "What happened?" without accusing her of lying about the heat. But all I could think of was the thing I didnt want to badly say. I said it. "Who is Dr. Moody?"

Aunt Clara looked as though she hadn't heard me, as though she never would hear me when I asked that question. "Just leave us, Wade dear," she said gently. "Please. We will be all right."

I went out, on tiptoe, far from convinced that I should leave them, but knowing I would only embarrass Aunt Clara by staying on, or by calling up Frank Barber. Something dreadful had been recalled by the mention of Thomas Moody. That much was obvious, but whether I should do anything about it, if there was, indeed, anything I could do, was far from clear. I stood in the hall turning these things in my mind, confused and irresolute, barely conscious of the jagged stream of talk that buzzed from the open dining room door. Then I heard Lucy laugh. Sharp, acrid, scornful. And rage against her choked me. I blazed in through the door.

They were standing, Clark and Lucy, just by the window, their faces dark, their voices brittle, with dispute. Clark was pounding his right fist into the palm of his left hand. Lucy was spitting sibilants of defiance. . . .

"You little bitch," I shouted. "You did that deliberately."

They spun around, cutting off their words, but the quarrel was still in the stressed expressions on their faces, the stiff unnatural poses of their bodies.

"And what'n hell is it to you?" Lucy snapped, her face contorted into ugliness.

I grabbed her shoulders, shook her until her head jerked and her mouth flew open. "I love those two old women. That's what it means to me. I love them."

"Take your hands off or I'll drop you," Clark said harshly.

He had moved around and was standing beside me. His right fist was drawn back. I let her go and stood away. I hadn't meant to hurt her, anyway, and I was wide open there to Clark's right hand. But face to face with him I had an urge to lash out, to hit him on the jaw and knee him in the groin. I had the joyous mind's eye picture of him crashing through the glass into the spiked rose bushes in the garden bed below.

Instead, I said: "Who is Thomas Moody?"

"King-bloody-Kong's first cousin," Lucy said. "Why don't you go away?"

"I can find out."

"Well, go," she flared. "Go and find out."

"No, don't find out," Clark rasped. "Thomas Moody is my affair, not yours."

I looked at him bulking large against the backdrop of sunlit garden, staring at me with that smug arrogance that identified him as surely as a fingerprint. If anyone ever made out a Bertillon index on him, that intimations-of-godhead look would be the first thing recorded.

"Pretty soon we're going to be asking you for permission to go to the can," I said thinly. "Thomas Moody seems to be very much Lucy's affair, too."

Lucy lit a cigarette and sat down, crossing her legs and adjusting her composure. Clark flicked his eyes at her, pushed out his chest until the room seemed full of white shirt and grey tailored suiting.

"You agree with me, Lucy, I think?" He turned suave with her, like a great chameleon chasing its mate. "We can't have Scotter poking his dirty nose in where it isn't wanted."

Lucy shrugged. "Throw him out. I don't care."

"I can do better," Clark said. "I can shut him up."

"The gangster and his moll," I said bitterly, sickened with them, hating them for what he was, and for what she had done. "You won't shut me up," I said deliberately. "I'll find what this is all about. And if there's any way I can hit you with it, I'll hit you until you yell for mercy."

A cold grin twisted Clark's wide mouth. "Scotter," he said quietly, his voice drawn out theatrically to a whisper. "Before you go any further I'd like to tell you some things you ought to know. You remember I told you this morning there's a certain stench about the name of Scotter?"

"Make it quick," I said. "I want to throw up."

He took out his cigarette case. He was acting. I could almost see the mummer's smock slide over him, erasing the grin from his face, making his hands and body move and pose in the attitudes of dramatic ham. He selected a cigarette, then gave me a quick, upward look.

"D'you know why your father came to this dump instead of staying in Sydney?"

A swift, hot prickling itched up my spine. "He liked the simple life." My mouth was dry.

Clark lit a cigarette with his gold lighter, jetted a stream of smoke into my face, and grinned. "That's not true, you know. He left Sydney just hanging on to his right to practice. He was nearly struck off the lists by the Medical Board and had to get out. He chose this place because he thought no one would know him."

His voice was tasting the words, enjoying each syllable, but I was too shocked to hate him for it. I was too shocked to react in any way. I was numb, and through the numbness all I could hear was a church bell tolling in the distance, or perhaps it was something, some thought, some memory, hammering at my mind to be let in. Then I knew it was a lie, a monstrous, wicked lie to suit his purposes.

"You bastard," I whispered. "You rotten, lying bastard."

Clark's grin widened. "He operated on a man stinking drunk, and killed him. He was a great drinker in those days."

If there had been a knife, or a gun, in that room, I think I would have killed Clark then. The whole room was blackness, with Clark a target in silhouette against the window. Then he moved and I came back from the edge of madness. I was trembling.

"You filthy, lying swine."

"You could write to the Medical Board," Clark said. "Or, if you like, I've got photostat copies of their finding. Any time you want to see them just let me know.

"My father hated liquor."

"Sure," Clark said. "It fits, doesn't it? I didn't say he didn't have a conscience. Of course he hated liquor, after he'd killed a man because of it."

I knew he was telling the truth. Damn and blast him. I couldn't look at him any longer, at the triumph in his face. Lucy had turned away. I could only see her back. I forced my voice out through the stiff numbness of my lips. "And what's this got to do with Dr. Moody?"

Clark waved nonchalantly, cascading cigarette ash on the carpet. "Why, everything," he said. "Moody was once your father's partner, for one thing. For another, you mind your own business about Moody, and I'll keep those photostats in my files. Meddle, and I'll circulate them all over Clayville and beyond."

"Clark," I said tonelessly. "One of these day someone is going to kill you."

"Splendid," he said. "I'll make a note of that, too."

I turned and found my way along the hall, and down the horrendous darkness of the stairs. I was drunk. I was drugged. I couldn't think. But later the hangover would arrive. It was going to be a bad time.

8

THE MONDAY SKY WAS ONE VAST BRUISE OF DARK CLOUDS. IT pressed down almost to the rooftops, saturated with moisture and electricity. The air was stifling with soggy heat.

We always got those days at intervals during summer. I re-remembered them as a kid. They used to scare me then with their prickling expectancy; and I was released from fear only when the storm broke, the storm that should have terrified me with its violence of lightning and thunder, its tearing winds and water that fell so solidly you'd think the ocean had been up-ended.

This morning there was only the withheld violence, but I felt as though its pressures were pushing me out of shape. I felt sort of rhomboid, an animated Picasso figure. My fingers turned papers on my desk, were being fussy and I couldn't stop them. My mind, that had been trained to work under pressure and all conditions, refused to settle down to any sort of orderliness. It kept revolving about two doctors—Doctor Alec Scotter, my father, and Doctor Thomas Moody, whatever he might be or might have been.

It was a hell of a way to start a week. It was a hell of a way to be at any time.

Aunt Belle had quite recovered from her indisposition, Clara had told me when I had phoned on Sunday night. She hinted, delicately, that it had been a sudden gastric attack, and I could almost hear her blushing at the mention of such a thing. I knew it was a lie. I had heard the whimper with which Aunt Belle had met the name of Thomas Moody. I had seen the tense, hushed undershadow of torment in Aunt Clara, and, thinking about it, I was certain that she had been more deeply affected than her sister. The name had been, to both of them, a knock in the night. And that, in itself, was bad enough. The obsessive interest of William Clark made it sinister.

I looked out the window at the bay. It was flat and leaden, offering no comfort. I turned back to my desk again, and shuffled through some memos I had left myself of stories to be followed. But I couldn't concentrate.

I had not yet adjusted myself to Clark's story about my father. I had gathered fragments of memory together all night through, fitted them together, tested them, and arranged them in a pattern. His hermitry here in the medical backwater of Clayville . . . his fanatical hatred of alcohol . . . a devotion to his patients that amounted to self-punishment . . . I knew that Clark was right and the knowledge was an added bitterness. It poisoned me. And yet I felt a greater tenderness towards my father than I had ever known before. I went back over, and regretted, the careless, perfunctory affection I had shown as a youth. I regretted, as I had heard men regret in dying, the neglects that now could never be repaired.

Out in the composing room I could hear the metallic clanging of Harry Wells throwing forms about, clearing his decks for the new week. Silence, and then the shuffle of his slippers coming my way. He came in with a handful of type metal, held in that peculiar vice grip of old printers' hands. His washed-out blue eyes looked at me with Monday melancholy, mixed with the printers' conviction that all editorial men are fools.

86

"Here. D'you want this kept?" He thrust out the handful of type. "We didn't use it last week."

"What is it?"

He read the first few lines quickly, reading the type upside down and back to front as though it were meant to be that way. It was a three-inch item about someone's dog that miaowed like a cat, one of those three-inch overseas fillers we kept around to block out the odd corners.

"Change the date line and hold it," I said. "It'll still be good six months from now."

Harry didn't usually bother me with things like that, and when he didn't go away I realized there was more to come. He looked ill at ease.

"What's on your mind, Harry?"

He ran a thumb up and down under his leather braces. The Adam's apple jumped in his scrawny neck. The wrinkles on his forehead rippled agonizingly.

"Come on," I said. "Out with it. Don't stand there like you've wet your pants."

Harry grinned a little. He liked even mild vulgarity. "Some things are hard t'say, Wade."

"You can't stop now."

"I know why Bert Thompson didn't come with us," he said.

"He told you?"

"No." Harry scratched his seat. "Ella's been talking to his old woman."

A coldness fingered its way along my spine. "So now everybody knows."

Harry shook his head. "Not from Ella."

"That's fine," I said bitterly. "Only from Ethel Thompson, a human bloody megaphone or I've never met one."

"Ella said last night I oughta get a job some place else," Harry said quietly. "On the new bridge . . . in a shop . . . anywhere but here with you."

I sat quite still, incapable of movement because the blood had frozen in my veins. I looked at him, and I could feel the bones of my face pushing through the stretched skin until it was near to bursting.

"I told her to shut her great pie sump of a mouth," Harry said evenly. "I told her if I ever heard her talkin' that way again I'd knock her down and wash out her mouth with soap and water. An' she knows I mean it."

Something inside me grinned. Perhaps it showed on the surface. "Thanks, Harry."

"Your ol' man saved our eldest kid's life. Slit her windpipe when she was dyin' of bronchitis. Right on our kitchen table. . . ."

"That doesn't prove I'm not subversive," I said woodenly.

"We didn't even pay your ol' man," Harry said. "We were broke and he wouldn't take anything then or after. That's the sorta bloke he was."

"So now you're paying me?"

There was faint reproach in Harry's eyes. "I'm tellin' you because I reckon people like that don't raise spies."

"Tell Clark," I said sourly.

"Clark," Harry said. "Is a shit—in spades."

"Thanks, Harry. Thanks a lot." I grinned up at him, warmed by his championship. But behind the grin I was wondering if he would be saying the same things if he had known that Dr. Alec Scotter had once killed a man in a drunken operation.

"There's not an old-timer in this town that don't owe somethin' to your father," Harry said. "But they'll all forget. Even Ella did. They'll forget because rememberin' a man like that makes 'em all feel mean."

"It's not the same town," I said evenly.

"It's goin' clean to hell," Harry snorted. "An' if I wasn't a cantankerous old cuss I'd get the blazes out of it. . . ."

He glared at me with such heat that, if it had been sustained, his watery eyes must surely have boiled. Then he swung away, muttering some masterly obscenities. At the door of his com-

88

posing room he turned, shook his handful of type at me, snarled, "An' if I was editor of this here paper I'd write an article saying this place is goin' to hell—and who's to blame. I'd buy into 'em about the fishing, too."

I got up and switched on the electric fan clamped halfway up the far wall. It moved the heavy air around, but scarcely made it better. It was so thick you could almost see it move. I opened another button of my shirt. I had already shed my tie. I was feeling the delayed effects of Harry's talk; not the staunchness he had shown, but the evidence that Clark's poison was spreading everywhere under the respectable skin of Clayville. I was now Exhibit A—without a trial.

I wanted to lash out at something. I had an unreasoning urge to punish someone. I wanted to attack, like some self-interested Quixote, any windmill, any citadel. I was tired of taking punishment. If ever a man needed an emotional laxative, I needed one that morning. I dragged my typewriter around, fed in a copy slip, and tapped out the catchline "Atom."

Even as I wrote it, I knew that such a piece as I planned was not going to get me anywhere. There was nothing conclusive that I could say about the intangibles of suspicion, the omnipresence of Orwellian "Big Brothers." I had an inkling that Frank Barber had been questioned, but by whom I did not know. Maybe other townsfolk had been questioned, too. It was extremely likely, but again I did not know. I knew only Clark, with his genius for building undigested trivia into muckheaps. But what sort of case could I develop from the doings of one man—developed, at that, by an interested party, as the majority of readers would be aware?

I thought, perhaps, I could bang away at the curtailment of land and water rights, speculate on the possible pollution of air and water by atomic waste, congratulate Clayville on being promoted from a flyspeck on the map to the full dignity of a priority hydrogen bomb target. . . . But what would that achieve? The making of new enemies, the hardening against me of undecided minds, an increased pressure from Security. . . . Nothing more. I pulled the copy slip out of the machine and pitched it in my wastepaper basket. I was being wise. I was still feeling lousy when Poldi walked in, half an hour later.

"Good morning, Wade." She shook her blonde hair at me. "What filthy weather."

"Execrable," I grunted.

"I know what that means, too," she said, and smiled with a slow curving of her mouth that took me with it. "And if you're going to keep making me prove how big my vocabulary has grown, I'm going to have to ask for more money."

"For more money," I said. "You'd have to work back nights."

"Wade," she said softly. "You must not joke about things that terrify you."

God, she was beautiful. And she knew that she was beautiful, without it hurting her. She was wearing a pale-blue dress of some soft material, and the blue picked up the colour of her eyes. Its short sleeves gave me golden arms to look at, and when she turned towards her desk I could see her body turn against the cloth. Quick creases ran down from her bosom, then disappeared as she sat down. A lot of the old tension went out of me.

"You're mixed up again." I said. "Terrify isn't the right word."

She shuffled some papers out of her handbag. "Terrified," she said. "It is the right word, and mixed up are two words you could also have for your own."

"Please," I said. "It's too early for psychiatry."

She looked around and smiled. "I cannot help it. I am from Vienna."

"So's schnitzel," I said. "And it's early for schnitzel, too."

She still smiled. "Are you not going to ask me why I am here so early . . . before afternoon."

"No," I said." Psychoanalysts are crazy enough for anything."

"I have a big story. For myself, and for your paper."

"Oh, fine," I said. "That's fine."

Then I was thinking I had to find out something about Thomas Moody, if only because Clark had warned me off. Where did he fit in with the Austins? Why was Clark so concerned? He had glared at Lucy for mentioning the name, and they had quarrelled about it afterwards. Not, I was sure, because he was worried about Clara and Belle Austins' feelings. It could only have been because he didn't want me to know. And then, confronted with my knowledge, he had sought to muzzle me with a threatened smearing of my father's memory. Clark, I thought, was playing a deep game, and probably a very dirty one. . . .

"I have this story," Poldi said. "That is, if you are thinking about stories this week."

Her voice cut through my thoughts with the blitheness of a song. I brought my eyes back into focus, and she was still smiling at me. A touch of excitement pinked her face. The long, shapely fingers of her right hand tapped a pencil on her desk blotter.

"Good," I said. "I could do with something for the early pages. Sooner Harry gets them away the better."

She shook her head. "This is not for your early pages, Wade. This is for page one."

"Splendid," I said. "Perhaps we can get the paper to bed by tomorrow night, then take five days off."

"Sometimes you are funny," she said severely. "Mostly you are not."

"Mostly I don't even feel funny."

"It is a pity," she said, "because when you smile you do not look much more than middle-aged."

I thought: Could Moody have been some informer who had given Clark, or if not specifically him, the Security Service, some sort of information about the Austins? Clark said he had once been my father's partner, but even if that were true it didn't purify him in any way. If anything, it would have given him a greater opportunity for delving into the Austins' family cupboard. Or could Moody have been someone, now proscribed, whom the Austins had once helped and now regretted? It was Lucy who had thrown up the name, but it was Clark who had tried to gag her. As though Moody were his property. He was probably some ace that Clark had been holding up his sleeve against the appropriate occasion. The more I considered that, the more feasible it appeared. Maybe he had told Lucy more about his business than he should. It wouldn't have been the first time a man had done it.

"Here is the story," Poldi said, dropping a typed sheet of paper on my blotter. She leaned across until her face was only inches from mine. "You are not well?" Her voice was soft. "You are worried about something?"

I could feel her breath on my face. It was sweet and warm. I could see her teeth, white and small and regular, each one glistening with the moisture of her mouth. I could see her lips, no more than touched with lipstick, but red and soft and scented with something more subtle than ever came out of a twist-propelling tube. I could see each separate hair of her brows, a deeper gold than her blonde hair, delicate, and the clean, smooth skin between them. Her eyes were looking into mine, resting on me while her mind was searching for what there was to find. My hands moved upwards, slightly, wanting to touch her, but somewhere in the beginnings of that movement some frightful rectitude took hold of me and told me this was not the time, the place, the anything . . . I was marked for trouble and she had had enough of trouble in her own homeland. . . .

I picked up the sheet of paper. "What is it? Apart from a list of names."

She stood up, drawing her hands across the desk, clasping them across her thighs. Her face showed nothing, but her eyes were bright.

"Clayville's first naturalization ceremony," she said steadily. "Ten new citizens to be born on Wednesday night."

"It had to come," I said. "Everyone's doing it this year."

"I also had a copy of Mayor Hazelgrove's speech."

"Have," I said.

Her lips tightened. Some of the brightness left her eyes. "Shall I go on? Do you want this story?"

"Why, sure," I said. "We're a newspaper. We record the facts. The moral hardly matters."

"You are being hateful," she said coldly.

"I feel hateful."

"Well, do not visit it on me."

I looked at her for a long moment and she was so wonderful that I was nearly perverse enough to go on snapping like a dingo bitch with pups. Then I felt ashamed. "I'm sorry. I'll get Tomkins, down in the town, to photograph all these people."

"That is better," Poldi said.

"We'll run single-column head and shoulder pics of them across the top of page one," I went on. "Hazelgrove's speech and any others can swing in under them. It's the best we can do with this hayseed set-up of ours. Couldn't get a block of the ceremony made in time."

"That is good," Poldi said. "If a little disinterested."

I shrugged. "What's it to me?"

"Look again at the names."

She had lost her coolness. The earlier excitement was back in her eyes. I ran down the list of names and found the one I'd missed. Leopoldina Lorenz. Poldi. I looked up.

"You?"

She smiled, deeply, without gaiety. "It will be nice to belong somewhere again. To be someone."

"The way things are?"

She looked at me soberly. "How are things, Wade?"

I glanced down at my wastebasket, where the "Atom" catchlined copy slip was lying. "You ought to know," I said. "All these atomland restrictions . . . the Security people . . . men like Clark. . . . You must know Clark."

She nodded. "I know him. He has asked me questions. He

has asked Frank and Mary questions, too. But that is, after all, only . . . how is it? . . . routine . . . what you could expect."

"It is less than I expect," I flared. I lit a cigarette, suddenly feeling the need of it. "I expect freedom in a democracy . . . freedom of thought, of speech, of action. . . ."

She shook her head. "Wade, you cannot have everything."

Her acceptance grated on me. "The creeping death of compromise." Bitterness welled up in me. "That's how they felt in Austria before the Nazis seized power, wasn't it?"

I shouldn't have said that. It was a rotten thing. She had suffered from the Nazis. It was why she was in Australia. Her whole family had been sent to a concentration camp because her father refused to stop playing Mendelssohn on the violin. Poldi had been the only one to emerge.

She turned away from me, not sharply, but with controlled reproof. And I thought for a moment she was going to walk out. I held my breath. She walked slowly to her desk. She sat there stiffly for a moment, then swung around to face me. The clench of pain in her blue eyes stabbed me.

"Wade, you are not thinking straight." Her voice was careful, choosing its words. "The way things are is not ideal. But if I cannot have all of democracy, I am happy to have as much as there is left. As much as there is possible to have. The fault, you must realize, does not lie with democracy."

My mind flashed back over the things I had thought about, the things I had intended to write but hadn't, not because I disbelieved them but because they didn't make sense any more. Not with the sound of her conviction in my ears, the look of hope that was on her face.

"You could write the mayor's speech now," I said quietly. "He won't change it. But check it when he speaks on Wednesday night."

"I had hoped that perhaps you would come."

She spoke softly, with the intentness almost of a communicant, and I realized for the first time that I was faced with something beyond my capacity to comprehend. The civic platitudes, the adjurations of some plump politician to be "good Australians," the intoned oaths of loyalty to the new and the renunciation of the old, were to her a personal nativity.

"Of course I'll come," I said. "I've only been waiting to be asked."

She laughed, and all the strain of the preceding moments dissolved away. "That is what I want to believe, so it is true."

I grinned back at her. "Freud or schnitzel?"

"Neither," she said. "Just the wise logic of a woman."

9

JUST AFTER LUNCH, WITH THE LAST DISH LAID DECENTLY IN THE sink and the last crumb tossed out the window for the birds, an idea wriggled up to the surface and stared me in the face. I was alone. Just me and this idea. It was so obvious, I should have thought of it before. But that's how ideas behave. They hide away in case the world should get spoiled by everyone thinking of the right thing at the right time, leaving no misery for joyous comparison.

My idea was to go out and buy a packet of aspirin from Wilberforce Sunter. If there was anyone who could tell me about Dr. Thomas Moody, it was Wilb Sunter, a seventy-plus gnome who had been Clayville's chemist since before the pill had been invented. And, as he had been my father's closest friend, there was a good chance that Clark would not hear about my inquiry.

I went out through the office to the composing room to tell Harry I was going downtown. He was setting type, hunched over the keyboard of our sole linotype. He sat back when I walked in, took his old brown teapot from the empty fruit case that served him for a table, held it at arm's length above his head, and poured a jet of tea down his throat. The technique always fascinated me. He finished with a quick upward flick of the wrist, and snapped his mouth shut on the last drop. He put the teapot down.

"Nice about young Poldi." He jerked his head towards the story propped on the linotype copy tray.

"Yes," I said. "She'll be allowed to vote."

He looked at me solemnly. "You're a joyless young bastard, aren't you."

"I was just trying to make you laugh."

"Don't," Harry snapped. "I got work to do." He reached again for the teapot, stopped himself, and looked up testily. "If you're feelin' so Goddam frisky, go out and get me some more copy. Unless you're plannin' on half a dozen blank pages this week."

"I'm on my way round to the council chambers," I lied soothingly. "They've got some new road works starting next week."

"What about them cable stories on yu desk?"

"When I come back."

"When," Harry grunted.

"Harry," I said solemnly. "You must trust me."

"I do," he said sourly. "It's just that yu habits let me down."

Main Street was the same street, but toneless under the grey-black sky. The flies were bad. They clung about my face, feeding on the sweat. There was no breeze to blow them off. And every time I swiped at them with my hand, they merely rose on the wind of it and settled down again. Joe Porter was still splaying his fat bottom on the wooden bench in front of Peltzer's hardware store.

"Storm coming up," he said.

"Looks like it," I didn't stop.

"Gonna be a hot summer," he called after me.

Conversations came easy to Joe. He put no effort into them. If ever a ship were named after Clayville, I thought, it would need to have a figurehead like Joe, a paunchy, sleepy merman with ever watchful eyes.

Now, he was almost the only sign of life along the street.

Shop doorways gaped like black, open mouths, and down in the gullets of some of them electric lights glowed yellow. The strip of bitumen down the middle of the street was dull and marked with dusty car tracks. The red-brown earth that lay on either side of it was hard and dry, yet looked as though it could put up no dust, because the air was pressing down too heavily. The houses were glum. And the hammering from the new bridge was so loud it sounded like artillery. By the time I had reached Wilb Sunter's chemist shop, asking for aspirin had almost ceased to be a front.

"Afternoon, Wade," Wilb Sunter's face wriggled with a thousand wrinkles. He was sitting on a high stool behind a gorged display counter, looking, with his white hair, big head and thin small body, for all the world like something sitting on a mushroom.

"Hello, Mr. Sunter." I leaned against the counter, and I noticed that his eyes, peering over half-moon spectacles, were without expression. "Could I have some aspirin?"

"At your age, boy?"

"I'm getting old," I grinned. "Gone thirty-five."

"Puppy." He reached under the counter and tossed a packet across to me.

I dropped some money on the little rubber mat that advertised a brand of toothpaste and was supposed to prevent the glass counter from getting scratched. Wilb Sunter picked it up and dropped it in the till. He frowned when I didn't move.

"Yon want to take that aspirin now?"

"It might just stop me from dying."

He sniffed. "I'll get some water."

I sent my eyes and memory around the shop while he was out back in the dispensary. It was just what a chemist's shop used to be before chemists got hungry for the retail trade. An apothecary's cave, stocked high with boxes, walls tiered with bottle-packed shelves. In the window were huge bottles of coloured fluid, bilious green, purple and violent red, a shelf of patent cough medicines, a mound or two of pastilles, and a tasteful array of toothpaste and brushes.

"Here, young Scotter."

I took the glass of water and washed down two aspirin. "Thanks," I said. "I needed that."

He stared up at me, his lips bulging with contained displeasure. It was in his eyes, too. "You want something else?" he asked curtly.

Wilberforce Sunter had never been curt with me before. He was a fussy old man, a bachelor, and he didn't approve of much, but he had always suffered me gladly as being my father's son. I stared back at him until he looked away. I guessed then what was sticking in his gizzard. He was acting just like a small, shrivelled-up Bert Thompson. He had heard the talk about me.

"Who was Thomas Moody?" I asked bluntly.

"Thomas Moody?"

He picked the glass up from where I had put it on the counter. His hand was shaking slightly, but that didn't necessarily mean anything. He had nerve-control trouble, something that went with the arthritic thickening of his knuckles. But an odd, furtive look was in his eyes; and that meant something.

"Doctor Thomas Moody," I said tersely.

"Ah, yes, I remember him now," Wilb Sunter said, pursing his lips in a spurious agony of recall. "He came here once as a locum for your father. One of his rare vacations. Tall, thin chap. Stayed on for a while as a partner."

"Where is he now?"

"He's dead." Wilb Sunter's thin old voice became defiant, not at me, I think, but at death. He was at that age when death becomes so personal that every whiff of it presents a challenge. "Died up in Queensland. . . . Scrub typhus, so I heard."

I leaned a little over the counter. "Was he a friend of the Austins?"

"Everyone's a friend of the Austins." His fingers did crab legs on the counter. He watched them, unhappily. "Wade, I can't remember things back that far. It's what? Thirty or so years ago. I just remember he was here once, for a few months. Then he went away."

"Mr. Sunter," I said levelly. "This is serious. I want you to try hard to remember everything."

He looked past me. "I don't remember any more."

He was lying. It was written in every line of his face, in every nervous movement of his body. But it was also obvious that he wasn't going to tell me any more. I switched my attack.

"Why did my father come here, to this one-horse town, to practice?"

Wilb Sunter's eyes opened wide. He nibbled at his lower lip. "Who wouldn't leave the city for a quiet place like this?"

"A good doctor, who wanted to be better, for one," I said.

"Your father was a sincere, Christian man."

"He could still have been a Christian in the city," I said. "He didn't have to become a country hack."

Wilb Sunter pressed his lips together. "He saw his duty here."

A woman came in, middle-aged, dressed in the floral cotton that was summer uniform in Clayville. She glared at me as though I had no right to live. I stepped back from the counter and she leaned over and whispered to Wilb Sunter. He handed her a neat, pre-wrapped package. She walked past me with her nose in the air and disapproval frozen on her face.

"Mr. Sunter," I said. "I want to ask you something about my father. Something I was told. It's important. Terribly important."

Wilb Sunter touched his wrinkled, old man's lips with the tip of his tongue, then rubbed the back of his hand across them. He shifted on his stool, as though the bones of his thin buttocks were cutting into him: "What is it?"

"That he left Sydney to hush up a scandal. That he killed a man operating when drunk, and the Medical Board gave him the choice of leaving the city or being struck off the rolls."

I could feel sweat running down my sides from my armpits. Thunder, somewhere out to sea, grumbled about the God-awful weather, and Wilberforce Sunter flicked his eyes nervously around the shop. The deep wrinkles of his face were set and still, except for the left corner of his mouth which twitched and sent little shock waves radiating out along the flaccid skin.

"Who told you this?"

He asked the question with a slight breathlessness, an inward sucking tenseness, as though listening for some answer he didn't want to hear. A sudden prescience swept over me. I answered slowly. "A Mr. William Clark."

I saw it all in his eyes then. Just for a moment the hostile, curtained front rolled back back and I caught a glimpse of shame. The sweat still rolled down my sides, but inside I was cold.

"How long have you known about this, Mr. Sunter?"

He waved a hand in an ineffective, troubled way. "For many years." His voice was a whisper. "Your father confided in me once, many years ago. I have never mentioned it to a soul."

The lying old devil couldn't look at me. I started forward, wanting to grab him by the clothes and shake him. Then, in the middle of the movement, I drew back, appalled that I should even have thought of touching so old a man.

"Never mentioned it to anyone except William Clark, you mean," I said tensely.

He stared miserably at the rubber change mat on his counter.

"You told him, didn't you?"

He nodded slowly. Then he looked up, and I'm damned if there wasn't a challenge in his eyes. "He is a security officer, Wade. It is for the good of the country that we co-operate with such men."

"Balls," I snapped. "How did you co-operate? Did you volunteer this information? Or did he ask for it?"

"He asked for everything I knew about you and your family." Now Sunter was defiant, like a man using a defense mechanism. "It was my duty to answer truthfully. To inform him of everything I knew."

He sounded so righteous, so wrongly righteous, I wanted to throw up.

Duty, I thought. Oh, Christ! The world's bastard child.

"All right," I said roughly. "It was your duty. What else did you tell him?"

"That is all."

"What about Thomas Moody?" I grated. "Did he ask you about him, too?"

"No."

"Mr. Sunter," I said harshly. "You're a liar! . . ."

He jumped off his stool as though I'd struck him, his face red with anger, eyes shrill over the half-moon spectacles. "Get out!" he shouted. "You can't speak to me like that!"

I felt my mouth twist. He should have been grateful that I had called him a liar. It gave him a chance to bluster and restore himself.

"Look, Mr. Sunter," I said sharply. "You were an old friend of my father. A close friend. You've known me all my life! . . ."

"Not all your life," he interrupted. "Only up to the time you went away from Clayville and got into trouble for being a Communist."

I felt like tipping his display counter over onto the floor, like smashing down the cluttered windows of his shop and letting in some light. Somehow I reached down inside of me, and got control.

"So Clark told you that? And you believe it?"

"I hate Communists," he snarled. "Now, will you get out? Or do I call Sergeant Thompson?"

I walked out stiffly, filled with rage against the social straight-jacket that Clark was pulling tight around me. Now, as far as gossip was concerned, I had become a party member. My feet were on the hard, baked white limestone of the footpath. I was on Main Street. Or rather, Main Street was underneath my feet. I was walking in the centre of a whirlwind. The air was still inside, quite still, and the spinning funnel of my thoughts obscured the sight of shops and house. I was alone. Isolated in Main Street, throbbing with the savage twist of things beyond my control.

Wilberforce Sunter was only a stooge, like Bert Thompson, and Ella Wells, and God only knew how many others. They angered me, they hurt me, but I knew they were only the symptoms of the disease that Clark was carrying, like some water bird with a dirty bill. But why? Why? Why? If I was a security risk, why not set a careful watch and crack hard at the first sign of an offence? Or had Security considered I was not obvious enough for drastic action and decided, instead, to freeze me out? Or was Clark merely a bully, a sadist, who enjoyed his power to hurt?

I didn't know. All I knew was that he really did have a power to hurt. It was hurting me to have people shun me. Maybe I had made a mistake. But, I thought, who hadn't in some sphere or other? Who could say he had never taken the wrong woman to bed, or backed a wrong horse, or bought a house with a cracked wall, or a car with a flaw in its chassis? Who hadn't made some mistake of judgment in the course of years? Nothing, I thought, had ever been achieved without mistakes. And yet now, because I had made one miserable slip, had had a petty visa withdrawn, I was being tarred and feathered. . . .

Then I saw William Clark turn out of the Austin's gate and disappear down a side street leading to the river, on his way home to Atomland. Sight of him jolted me back to earth. The whirlwind of my thoughts fell away exhausted, collapsed around my feet, and the clammy heat of the day stuck to me. Flies sucked the sweath beneath my eyes. I considered running after

Clark, without any real purpose, but just because I was hating him so much. Then a vivid lightning flash jagged the sky wide open, thunder burst out of it, and the rain poured down. Like that, without warning, without preliminary drops. There was no wind. Just this solid sheet of rain.

I sprinted for the Austins. Their house was the nearest shelter. In seconds the rain had made the limestone footpath treacherous. I slithered through the gate, pounded up the driveway through the leaking trees and crashed into the school-room. The children were flat-nosed at the windows, watching the storm. They didn't hear my puny noise. But Lucy was looking straight at me across the room, from her desk near the big blackboard. She was smoking a cigarette, and above it her eyes were mocking me. The twisted smile on her lips made it a hateful mockery. I walked carefully across the room.

"Where are your aunts?"

"Upstairs," she said. "Drinking gin out of the bottle."

There was an air of reckless cruelty about her; that kind of exalted instability you find in reefer smokers. It frightened me.

"I saw Clark leaving here," I said. "Has he been bothering them?"

She blew smoke through her nostrils and shrugged her breasts at me. "Christ," she sneered. "You sound more like the Ancient Mariner every time you come."

I turned away and went upstairs. Everything was silent inside the clamour of the rain, the crescendos of thunder. There was no one in the sitting room. The binoculars stood at ease on the cedar sideboard, alongside the bowl of fruit. The cedar chairs were ranged before the window. The back garden and the empty rabbit lands were shrouded in a water curtain. The effect was of utter desolation, and a nameless fear chittered in me. I tried to calm it, tried to blame the weather and my fraying nerves, but when I stood outside Aunt Clara's bedroom door I had to force my hand to knock. I knocked three times before the door moved. And then Aunt Belle's face appeared. She opened the door only a few inches. Her face was ravaged. Her eyes were red.

I pushed open the door and took her in my arms. She put her head down on my chest. She was trembling inwardly, the worst sort of trembling, and I knew her tears were tears that could not be wiped away. Aunt Clara lay on her bed, motionless, with her eyes staring at the ceiling and her lips moving wordlessly.

"What is it?" My voice was hoarse in my ears. "Aunt Belle. What's happened?"

She didn't answer. She didn't move. I asked her again, then several times, but she was beyond my questioning. I led her to a chair and sat her down, then crossed to Aunt Clara, lying in that traumatic half-life on the bed. I knelt beside her, rubbing her hands, trying to make her hear, to make her see me, but there was no response. Her staring eyes still stared, and her moving lips still moved, bloodless, soundless. Her hat, that old-world concoction of straw and imitation fruit, lay crushed beneath her head. I withdrew it gently, straightened it, and laid it on the bedside table. I walked out steadily, forcing this discipline upon myself for some remote, unreasoned reason. They would not have noticed if I had run. But I held steady until outside the door, perhaps for my own sake. Then I ran.

I grabbed Lucy by an arm. "Get upstairs. Your aunts need help."

She tried to pull away. "Help them yourself," she spat. "I'm busy."

I bundled her past the gaping children, out into the corridor, and slammed the door.

"Get upstairs," I barked. "And quick."

She laughed tightly. "Who d'you think I am? Florence Nightingale?"

I hit her then. Right across the face with the flat of my hand. She staggered and almost fell. I walked in after her, my hand upraised for another one. But it wasn't needed. She scrambled away and started, sobbing, up the stairs. I ran for the phone, and Frank Barber's precise English was strange to hear.

He would come at once. I turned away, and a lightning flash fizzed on every raw nerve in my body. In the hushed, expectant interval between the flash and its thunder, a chorus of giggling came from beyond the closed door of the schoolroom. The children were enjoying the best storm of their lives.

"Clark," I whispered. I sat on the bottom stair to wait for Frank Barber. "Clark."

10———⌇——————

FRANK BARBER STAYED IN THE BEDROOM SO LONG THAT WHEN he came into the sitting room the rain had stopped, and the thunder was a mutter of exhaust gas on the inland horizon. The interval of time had also given me the breathing space I needed to compose myself. That is, if a man can be said to be really composed when every nerve and sinew is tense with hatred for another man, and every instinct clamorous with the need to deal with him.

"Your aunts have had a severe shock," Frank Barber said, and put his leather bag gently on the table. He was self-contained, wrapped in that mental plumpness of the consulting medico. "I have given them sedatives, by injection. Lucy and I have put them to bed. They will not wake until the morning."

"Aunt Clara?" I grasped his arm.

"She is much worse than her sister," Frank said carefully. "But that is not unusual. Stronger people often suffer most from shock. They try to fight it. They do not give in. Also, for that same reason, they invariably recover faster."

I let go his arm. "They'll be all right, Frank?"

He nodded. "Of course. Shock, this sort of shock, does not have so many problems now with our new drugs."

"What sort of shock is it, Frank?"

He shook his head slowly. "We will not know that until we can talk with them."

"Of course."

I agreed, even though aware that the statement was not completely accurate. Lucy knew. It was something Clark had said to them, some bullying about the binoculars, some blundering officiousness. Or, more likely still, something about Thomas Moody, who had once been my father's partner, and about whom I was forbidden, by Clark, to make inquiries.

"They'll need a nurse," I said. "Can you get one from the hospital?"

Frank Barber smiled, with just a hint of superiority. "Lucy will handle it quite well. There is nothing anyone can do now until they wake." He picked up his bag. "Let us go, Wade. I shall come in again this evening. I will ring you if there is any change."

"You go on," I said, forcing nonchalance. "There's something I want to do."

"We can send the children home on our way out," he said blandly. "If that is what worries you."

I looked at him. "I want to talk to Lucy."

He smiled again, and his light-blue eyes glinted hugely behind the thick rimless spectacles. "No, Wade. Lucy will stay with them in the bedroom. She will sleep there tonight. Talk with her tomorrow, when she has nothing on her mind." He put a hand under my elbow, urging me along. "She will be all right with them," he said quietly. "I have instructed her. Tomorrow, if they are not much better, we can think of having a nurse."

"Tomorrow," I grunted. "Why do doctors always talk about tomorrow?"

"Not always," he said. "But in the meantime they must

have perfect quietness. No sounds of arguments." He glanced at me keenly. "You know what I mean?"

"All right," I yielded. "I know what you mean."

I knew what he meant all right, but back in my office I wasn't sure that I should have given in to him. By the next day Lucy would have had time to concoct a waterproof story and to have practiced sticking to it. But I couldn't go back and start in on her. Not in the face of precise medical advice. I cursed bitterly, and that mild catharsis must have allowed some logic to come through, because I realized for the first time that finding out what had hurt the Austins wasn't going to do any real good. I had to remove the cause. I had to get at Clark. I had to muzzle him. And the first move was to lay it on the line to his chief. He could be excused, perhaps, for doubting me. But surely, this Colonel Tucker wasn't such a fool that he would think two old women were a security danger.

I sat down at my desk, and felt something scrape my thigh from inside my trouser pocket. I pulled it out. The empty packet of aspirin. I had bought from Wilberforce Sunter, and I heard again the carking, mean old voice spitting at me: "I hate Communists . . . I hate Communists. . . ."

I placed the packet on my blotting pad, quietly and deliberately. Then smashed my fist down on it . . . three, four, five times . . . but still the voice went on. . . . And it sounded like the collective voice of Clayville, not just of Wilberforce Sunter. I dropped my elbows to the desk, and covered my face with my hands. Inside the darkness there was no escape. The voice persisted. The day's events came rampaging in, and I had to meet them. I stripped my hands away and Poldi was walking towards me through the composing room door, trailing a handful of proofs. I had quite forgotten there was anyone else in the building.

"There is something wrong?" she said.

I dropped the battered aspirin packet in my waste basket. "Aunt Clara's sick," I said flatly. "Belle, too."

She came and stood beside me, put a hand on my shoulder. "Are they so very sick?"

A lump came in my throat. "They're old. . . . They can't stand too much."

"If there's anything I can do—"

"There is," I cried harshly. "Shoot that bastard Clark."

Even as I spoke I was sorry for meeting her concern in such a manner. But she understood. Her hand increased its pressure on my shoulder before she moved away. I reached out and dialled ARA. My hand gripped the phone so tightly that it hurt my palm, and I welcomed it. While it rang I kept telling myself I must keep my temper. Tucker, if I reached him, would not accept. . . .

"Colonel Tucker, please," I said. "It's urgent." I hoped that boldness might carry me through. It didn't.

"Who is speaking?" The voice was female, cool and nasal.

"Scotter. Wade Scotter, editor of the *Herald*."

"Have you an appointment with Colonel Tucker?"

"I've written to him," I said.

"Hold the line," the cool voice said. Then it was back. Cold now. "The colonel cannot see you."

The line went dead. I put the phone up slowly, frustrated beyond endurance at the impossibility of doing anything with Colonel Tucker. He held himself inviolate, while his hatchet-men ran amok. Then and there I resolved that I would see Tucker, even if it meant sending Clark's head in on a salver to attract attention.

"You had better write another letter," Poldi said quietly.

"He doesn't want to know anything," I told her bitterly.

She was sitting at her desk, twisted around in her chair to watch me. He lovely face was grave, her blue eyes thoughtful. "Maybe there is a good reason why this colonel does not wish to see you," she said slowly. "You are not pleasant about his friends."

"He is not pleasant about my friends," I mimicked savagely. "Why should I care about his?"

"He is a high authority," she said quietly. "In any country it pays to be polite to such a man."

That hit me right on the sorest spot of all. I leaned forward over my desk, and I could feel my face go taut against the jutting belligerence of my chin. "Look, Poldi," I said tersely. "A man's still got rights in this country. One of them is justice. The fundamental one is justice."

"There seems to be justice," she said. "I do not hear of people being shot, or being put in concentration camps."

"Keep listening," I snapped. "It won't be long."

She pushed her chair back, scraping its legs across my nerve endings, and stood up. The softness had left the gravity of her expression; the thoughtfulness had left her eyes. Her mouth was resolute and her eyes were on high beam. She still clutched that handful of proofs she had brought in from the composing room. She threw them backwards on the desk with a swift, angry motion. Then she advanced on me, and aimed her anger across my desk.

"Wade, you are talking like a fool." Her voice was clipped and brittle with intensity. "You have got a fixation on this man Clark. I do not know all the facts about him. I do not like him . . . what I have seen. But you must not let him poison your mind. He is not justice. He is only a little man. Do not fight with him. Tell him the things he would wish to know . . . and then forget him."

"I don't like him, and you don't know all the facts," I said. "We agree there." I crashed my fist down on the desk. "But I'll fight him now, and tomorrow, and every time I get near him . . . and in between as well."

"You will only destroy yourself," she said, and her voice suddenly rang with a high, trumpet clarity. She was standing straight, with shoulders and head thrown back. Lighting from the window turned her cropped, ringlet hair into a golden helmet. "Wade, you do Mr. William Clark too high an honour. If you had met him anywhere but here, in your own home town, you would not consider him so important. But you came running back here as an escape, and it has thrown you off balance to find that what you were trying to escape has followed you home."

"Poldi," I said tautly. "What you are saying might have meant something to me a few days ago. But not now. What you don't know is that Clark, in some swinish way, is to blame for the Austins' illness. . . ."

"I had guessed that," she said quietly. "I am only half a reporter, but that half is not so absolutely dumb."

I dropped back in my old protesting swivel chair, and threw up my hands in a gesture of despair. "In that case, how'n blazes can you say Clark isn't important?"

"He is important in this one respect only," she said steadily. "In the big pattern he is insignificant."

"Jesus," I whispered.

"One thing else, and I have finished." Her soft lips were set in grim determination. "Understand this, Wade. . . . Conditions have to be right for democracy to grow properly, or even to exist. The conditions are not right now. Maybe they will be in time. Until they are we have to do the best we can. We have to give up some little liberties so we can keep the others . . . the bigger ones."

"You've been reading that booklet they gave you for the naturalization ceremony," I said brutally. "The Ten Commandments, with the new, enlarged appendix by courtesy of the Government."

I rose abruptly to my feet, confused and angry, not looking at her because I knew I had been unfair and, like a schoolboy, didn't know how to make amends. The right words, the right gestures, are never easy; sometimes they are impossible. I felt wretched. Too much had happened, and too much had been frustrated from happening. I took a fresh pack of cigarettes from my drawer, unnecessarily, but it gave my hands something to do, my eyes somewhere to look. I was painfully conscious of her gaze. And then, as I shut the drawer, I knew what I had to do. I did not know how I hadn't thought of it before.

"I'm going out," I said harshly. "Can you wait on and watch the phone?"

"All right." And as I reached the door, she said: "Do not try to climb it. It is electrified, remember!"

I looked back and she was watching me with a funny expression, almost of wistfulness, on her face. Looking back at women is never a good thing. When you turn again you always seem to have lost step a little. As I went down Main Street, and swung right for the pontoon bridge, I could feel the look in her eyes right down inside me, and it felt like the touch of her hand on my shoulder. I wished I hadn't made that crack about the Ten Commandments.

The Clay was running strongly after the rain. There must have been heavy falls inland, too, in the catchment hills. The bridge bellied like a sail, and the river made soft bubbling noises around the big black steel pontoons. The water was white and milky, the way it always was after rain, from all the eroded limestone that had sifted into it along the winding miles. That is how it got its name. All through the winter it had that white clay look, and you could see it push out right across the bay, like a white tongue, until the seas broke it up and absorbed it in the blue-green common denominator of the ocean.

Workers on the steel bridge watched me as I walked across the pontoon. I should have driven my car. It would have been less conspicuous. A welder waved his face shield. Jan Czarnecki, a chunky Pole about whom Poldi had done a story for the *Herald*. He had been a professor of political economy back in Warsaw. Farther on there was Luigi Panozzo, a blond Italian with a voice like a bullfrog, and a vastly mistaken belief that he could sing tenor because he was Italian. Hell! I remember the time he came into the *Herald* office and drowned out the old flatbed press with an aria from *Tosca*. We published his picture under the heading "Man Against Machine," and from that time on he had greeted me wherever we met with a frightening burst of song. He brayed it at me now, "Butterfly," I think, with this crazy Pinkerton high in the rigging of the new bridge. I waved to him.

Across the bridge there was a two-hundred-yard walk to the ARA gateway. I was going through there. Some way. Any way. To more pairs of eyes joined the workers on the bridge. Different eyes. The workers watched me because men on a vantage point will watch anyone going by; but the new eyes belonged to men who stepped away from a sentry box on one side of the gate and stood right in the middle of the road, looking down it and at me. Professional eyes. They were about the same size, these men, tall, wide and tough-looking. They wore khaki battle dress, khaki berets, and black tommy-guns. They weren't overdressed. They were just about right for any occasion.

The iron-barred gate behind them was closed. The fence, on either side of them, ran away in bright, evil lines of death, glinting in the hot and steaming sun. The ground was slippery with mud beneath my feet. I stopped six feet away from the gate. One of the guards wore corporal's stripes.

"My name's Scotter," I told him. "I'm editor of the Clayville *Herald*. Can you take me to Colonel Tucker?"

"Sure," he said. "You gotta pass?"

I shook my head. "No."

The corporal stared. "Then whose tit you pulling?"

"Surely," I said, "if I have an escort—"

"Listen," the corporal said. "You can't even urinate out here without a pass."

The corporal had a hatchet face, with deep weathered lines in it, and a big hooked nose. His steady light-brown eyes were intelligent, and his big square fingers around the tommy-gun's stock looked competent. His companion, a buck private, packed more flesh and had a slight ruddiness in his face. He was tough, though. He displayed banks of ribbons on his left chest, one of them a really good one.

"Can't you ring through and tell him I'm here?" I moved a couple of steps closer.

"No." The corporal grinned. "Go back to your newspaper and ring from there. *You* tell him."

The private grunted. "No pass. No dice."

Well, I wasn't going to bluff my way anywhere with those boys. I hadn't really expected to, so there was nothing for it but to go ahead the hard way.

I paused a moment to make my dispositions, and decided on the corporal. I would hit him on the jaw, close with him and mix it for all I was worth. We were about the same height, but he was broader and a whole lot fitter. It didn't matter; I didn't want to beat him.

From where I was standing I couldn't see if they had their safety catches on or off. But I was prepared to take a chance on that, a fairly safe calculated risk. They didn't look the types who'd hose a man down with a gun, but to play it safe I decided to get into a wrestle as soon as I'd landed my first punch. That way the second man wouldn't dare fire for fear of cutting up his companion. My guess was they'd belt hell out of me with their fists just for satisfaction before taking me inside to their headquarters. It would be worth more than a beating, though, if I could get to Tucker.

"You don't seem to realize this is urgent," I said carefully. "I *must* see Colonel Tucker."

The corporal grinned. "It'd be urgent for me, too, if I let you in without a pass." He made a slight impatient shooing motion with his left hand. "On your way, George. You're only wasting your time and ours."

I moved in closer. "Okay. I'll stop wasting time."

I loosed a decent sort of right hook for his jaw. But he moved, and my arm went around his neck. I clung and drove a short left into his belly. He grunted. "You bastard." His voice was hard in my ear. Then I got my left leg behind his and toppled him. He was skilled and tough. I felt his body twist in my grip as we went down, and as we hit the muddy ground an iron-clad fist slammed into my side. It hurt. Hurt with that dull thudding hurt you know is going to be a lot worse later on when the numbness goes. I tried to jab a left into his face, but, holding him so close I couldn't get any power. He heaved, throwing me upwards, and as I started to come down he swung right over me and a hard knee rammed my groin. Then something heavy crashed on my skull. I didn't see what it was, and I didn't have time to think about it. I just felt it hit and then there was nothing.

I woke to the dual discomforts of a splitting headache and a bouncing motion that kept opening and shutting my skull like a portcullis. I forced my eyes open, and above me was a brown canvas sky. I shut them again. I could both smell and hear an engine. I was in a truck.

Then someone said, "How's the head?"

I groaned.

"Serves you bloody well right," the voice said. "You're lucky my mate's a tender-hearted bastard."

I opened my eyes again and looked up into the corporal's hatchet face. He was squatting on a metal bench running along the tray of the truck, leaning over me, elbows on his knees and a vague puzzlement in his light-brown eyes. I fingered my head gingerly and felt a lump the size of a small football.

"What did he hit me with?"

He touched the tommy-gun resting across his thighs. "This. And you're damned lucky he did. He could've shot you, and no questions asked."

"Well, thanks," I said. "Thanks for the headache."

He grinned. "Any time. Any time at all."

Then the truck stopped.

"Can you walk?" he asked.

I grimaced. "I've got a sore head. But I can try."

"Well, don't start any more of that crazy business," he said sternly. "I've got a sore belly . . . an' it's not making me any happier."

He dropped neatly over the tailboard and swung it down for me. Then he stood back a few paces. And standing there in the hot, bright sun, in the khaki battle dress with the big black gun, with his tough good-humoured face, and the look of competence on him like a second uniform, he was the embodiment of all the Australian soldiers I had ever seen . . . in North Africa, the Pacific, Korea. He made me feel guilty.

"Sorry I hit you," I said sincerely. "But I had to do it."

"Yeah," he said. "An' we had to hit you. So we're quits."

My head spurted pain when I got up and began to lower myself over the back of the truck. The sunlight was speckled with black. But I was fortified by the thought that it would all be worth while if it meant a meeting with Tucker, and an opportunity of telling him about his bloodhound Clark and what he was doing to the Austins.

I looked around, narrowing my eyes to focus them against the pain in my head. The black specks came again. I felt myself falling, and a strong hand grabbed my arm. I opened my eyes again and sent them incredulously around. I was standing just outside the barred doors of the town lock-up, in the police station's backyard.

"What the hell?" My voice sounded ragged in my ears.

"What'd you expect?" the corporal said. "There's a law about bashing people. Even soldiers."

I started to say something, then realized there was nothing to say. I had wanted so badly to see Tucker that I had disregarded all possibilities other than the one that suited me. My spirits sagged, and I began silently to curse myself for the silliest damned episode of my career. Then I saw Bert Thompson come stumping from the house. Sergeant Bert Thompson in full uniform, plumping his big feet down on the narrow path between his cabbage and lettuce and silver beet and carrot patches. His big, sunburned face was as red as one of his glass-house tomatoes. His tunic collar threatened either to burst or throttle him.

He looked straight past me and nodded jerkily to the corporal. He unlocked one of the cells with a great jangling of keys. And then he had to look at me. He motioned me inside with a sideways jerk of the head, and when he turned to lock the door I was standing up against it, facing him through the bars. He had the look in his eyes of a man seeing a two-headed hyena for the first time.

"You've made a proper mess of things this time, haven't you?" he said.

"Spare me the sermons," I said coldly. "Will you phone my office? Tell Harry Wells where I am?"

"Still wanting to make phone calls," the corporal said.

He tapped Bert Thompson on the shoulder and they moved off behind the truck. Then the truck rolled away and Bert Thompson stood scratching the back of his neck. He stood there for a good half-minute, scratching, then came over to me.

"Can't make you out," he said. "Isn't this country good enough for you? What yu trying to do?"

"I'll tell you one day, Bert," I said. "Right now I wouldn't want you to risk your pension."

His face went a deeper shade of red. "Sergeant Thompson to you," he grated. "From that side of the bars I'm Sergeant Thompson."

Then he executed a stiff about-turn and marched off back to the house. I was alone with my headache and my failure. I was in jail.

11 ————— ⌇——————

I STOOD AT THE CELL DOOR FOR A LONG TIME, GRIPPING THE IRON
bars in my hands like some ape in a zoo cage. Only a police
cell is more than a cage to a man experiencing it for the first
time. It is a trap. A psychological trap that closes on the
mind, confusing the power of thought, stimulating the latent
desperation that exists in all men. My head ached savagely and
I felt beaten up; beaten up in depth, not just on the surface
from the blows of the corporal and his buddy.

I watched the westing sun spread gold on the leaves of a
big jacaranda tree beside the police station, and its beauty was
not for me. Bert Thompson's kids came out on the back
veranda of the house, stared down at me and giggled, then
chased each other around the side of the house in a shouted
game of police and robbers. And I knew that was for me.

I let go the bars, or rather, my hands came unstuck, and I
shuffled over to the bare wooden bunk at the back of the cell. It
was hard, but softer on my behind than the air was on my head.
I lay back, gently, until my head was pillowed on some army
blankets piled at one end of the bunk. Then I closed my eyes

and really got down to the business of making myself think. It wasn't easy, but eventually things came jumping up in some sort of order. I kept my eyes closed so I couldn't see the bars.

I had not just balled things up. I had wrecked them. I was in line for at least six months in jail for assault and battery, attempted trespass, and whatever else they could hang on me. And there was little doubt that they could make it stick. The Security men had me in their black book, the local police, led by Sergeant Bert Thompson, sniffed me like carrion, and at least half the influential burghers of Clayville, thanks to Clark, regarded me as the gut content of some ideological Trojan horse. Together, maybe they would manage to get me more than six months. I couldn't think what the maximum sentence was for assault plus—and a nasty subversive little snigger inside me kept whispering it was just as well.

The ponderous voice of Bert Thompson came back to goad me with sententious truth. "You've made a proper mess of things this time, haven't you?" he had said. And, blast him, he was right.

But he was not entirely right, because he had been thinking about my personal situation, which didn't really matter. The true importance of the "proper mess" was in its relation to the Austin sisters. Six months, even one month, even a week away from Clayville would give Clark an open season on them, and God only knew what bastardy he could achieve in that time.

A groan that started deep in my chest rumbled up and shuddered around my head. I opened my eyes and the sunlight outside the cell had paled. The gold had left the jacaranda and its leaves were a dull grey-green. A dark, cold shadow angled out from the police station house and lay across the cell. I sat up suddenly, and almost welcomed the spurt of pain the movement livened in my head. The frustration, the obsessive fear, the powerlessness of being locked up, flooded in on me and I cursed aloud, cursed everything that came into my head. It was the only thing that stopped me from screaming, and tearing at the cell bars the way I'd seen so many poor devils do in police lock-ups around the world. It takes a very old lag to be philosophic in the first few hours.

And then I started cursing Harry Wells for not having come to bail me out. It was therapeutic cursing still. Arranging bail wasn't going to be easy, and I knew it. Maybe it would be impossible. But I cursed Harry, and I knew he wouldn't mind. Goddam his leathery hide, why didn't he get cracking? Blast him . . . and again . . . again . . .

The footsteps were right up against the door before I really heard them, or classified them as a footsteps rather than as some extraneous background noises in a bad dream. Two men stood silently at the cell door, looking in at me. Gravely, perhaps a little curiously, the way free men look in at other men behind bars. One was Sergeant Bert Thompson. The other I did not know. But from the way his steel-grey eyes were ticking off my points, itemizing me, I guessed he knew plenty about me.

He was as tall as Bert Thompson, but seemed much taller because he was so spare of build. A rectangular man, of straight sides and sharp angles. His body was a long rectangle and his head a smaller one joined to it by a leathery column of a neck. His hair, dark and shot with grey, was worn in a near crew cut. He had a quiet presence; not the quietness of humility, but of a man contained within himself, sure of his strength, sure of everything. He wore a lightweight sports jacket, some sort of tan colour, a white shirt that looked startling against his sunburned face and neck, grey slacks and a pair of stout golf shoes. In other circumstances I might have liked him, if only a little; but from my side of the bars he was too obviously on the other side.

I focused on Bert Thompson. "What about my bail?"

Bert looked uncomfortable. "I'll give Harry Wells another ring."

He slid a querying look across to leather neck. The man nodded, almost imperceptibly. And suddenly, seeing that master-servant relationship, I knew him. This was Colonel Tucker, Public Eye Number One, the man whose electrified citadel I had been trying to crash, the man who wouldn't see me, who granted interviews only by appointment and wouldn't make appointments.

"I'll go and ring Harry," Bert Thompson said awkwardly.

I didn't watch him go. Tucker was still watching me and I could feel his mind probing around and jotting notes like some bloodless electronic computer. He had the bunch of cell keys in his right hand.

"I'm Colonel Tucker," he said. "You must want to see me pretty badly."

His voice was metallic, neither cold nor warm. The words were clipped, the way young men are taught English at the Royal Military College, Duntroon.

"Only by appointment," I said coldly. "Have you made one with Sergeant Thompson?"

A slight movement of his thin mouth might have been amusement. He lifted the keys. "Am I invited in?"

"Sure," I said. "But watch the door. It's electrified."

He came in on a big, medieval key and left the door ajar. He sat like a straight-backed wooden chair on my bunk, his legs, thighs and body all tidily bestowed. It was a drill movement, this sitting down of his, and when he produced a pack of cigarettes he offered them with a gesture come straight from the senior officers' mess. Pukka as all hell. But at least it was a pack and matches, not an inscribed gold case and lighter.

"Thanks." I took a cigarette and sat down beside him because there was nowhere else to sit. "And you, I suppose, are why I haven't been bailed out yet?'"

"I had to know where to find you."

"I have an office in town. I live there. . . . Or didn't you know?"

"I thought we'd be more private here."

I didn't know just how to take him, or how I felt towards him, which was probably part of his intention, his military technique of keeping the enemy off balance. He had the whip hand and we both knew it, but he wasn't brandishing it about. He was being almost friendly, in a cold, emasculated way. It puzzled me, and an animal wariness took hold of all my senses. I sniffed for danger, listened for nuance signals in his voice, tried to feel the texture of his manner. And suspicion, peering from my eyes, kept looking for the basic explanation. Why had he come to see me in this cell? Why had he now descended from his top-secret hideaway? He wasn't the type of man to indulge in whims. Something had changed the balance, disturbed the *status quo*.

It gave me a strange, uncanny feeling, to be sitting there together in the cell, at the weary sore-head end of day. On the surface it seemed that things might be at last moving a little my way; but it was the things below the surface, the cross-currents, the unseen things, that chivvied me. What was the why?

"Are you opposing bail?"

"No."

"What charges are you going to lay?"

"Tell me what you want with me," he said. "Then I'll let you know."

I threw my half-smoked cigarette through the cell bars. The acceptance of and the smoking were a part of phase one. The friendly get-together phase. Now I was starting out afresh.

"I want you to call your man Clark to heel," I said evenly.

"Why?"

"He's exceeding his duty."

Tucker's eyebrows rose. He blew some ash from the tip of his cigarette. "You know what his duty is, then?"

"No," I said harshly. "But I know for certain what it isn't. It's not his duty to bully old women out of their wits on some trumped-up security nonsense."

Tucker crossed his legs, pulling up some trouser slack over

the top knee to preserve the precise crease that stood to attention from top to bottom of the trouser leg. "There is no nonsense about security," he said quietly. "And, to the best of my knowledge, there is nothing trumped up."

"You know the Austin sisters, Belle and Clara?"

"By reputation."

"D'you think they'd be a security risk? D'you think they'd be spies? Saboteurs?"

Tucker walked over to the door and stepped his cigarette butt into the ground outside. Then he stood near the door, looking down at me, his lean, angular face impassive. He crossed his arms, at right angles, horizontal to the floor.

"On the face of it, I'd say no. But security men have said that before and been wrong." He shrugged slightly, not with gallic one-shoulder eloquence, but with a stiff, mannered two-shoulder movement reminiscent of chinning the bar in a gymnasium. "Clark has been giving them a routine check. Nothing more. If they are as worried as you claim, it must be of their own making."

"Crap."

I exploded to my feet, exasperated by his absurd red tape construction of a human problem. Two quick steps placed me in front of him. We were about the same height, something of the same figure except that his angularity was precise and geometric, mine in the nature of free drawing. Our eyes locked in contest, and once again I had the feeling he was measuring me.

"I tell you he's bullying these old women. This morning, after he had called on them, I found Clara Austin ill . . . very ill . . . and her sister wasn't much better. I had to call Doctor Barber."

Tucker's lips tightened until they looked like a sharp crease in a piece of brown paper. "They must be hypersensitive. Clark is a first-rate operative. He knows our drill and sticks to it."

"He's a goddam bully," I snapped.

"And you?" Tucker said flatly. "He has been bullying you, too?"

I caught his meaning and thought a little less of him for the blatancy of the manœuvre. "I'm not complaining for myself," I said harshly. "I can look after myself with someone like Clark."

Tucker stepped around me and went back to the bunk. He took out his cigarettes, but didn't offer them. He frowned. "I can understand your dislike of Clark," he said evenly. "He has uncovered some very interesting things about you."

I nearly bought in on that, but stopped myself. My own affairs were secondary. I sunk my hands deep in my pockets, and leaned against the cell wall. At that moment I wanted to be as different as possible from Colonel Public Eye Number One Tucker.

"And what interesting things has he reported about Clara and Belle Austin?" My mouth was twisted, revolting against the sudden taste of something sour and bitter. "That they watch rabbits through binoculars? That they're running a spy ring through their kindergarten?"

"You are a sentimentalist," Tucker said shortly. "I deal in logic."

"Is it logical for a first-rate operative to waste time investigating old women?"

"Detection is a wasteful business, Mr. Scotter. It is essentially non-productive."

"Cutting the clever talk, and the side-stepping," I said, "does all this mean that Clark is free to go on bullying the Austins as far as you're concerned?"

Tucker gave a little dry cough, smothering it with a square and bony fist. "In war it is accepted that some people must get hurt, for the good of the majority. You must realize that, Mr. Scotter. You have seen war. It is the same in peace sometimes . . . particularly in this odd sort of peace we have today."

The words were as cold and implacable as a chapter from some military text book. Tucker's dry, clipped voice conveyed them with no hint of human feeling, no appreciation that they applied to human beings. His face, composed and still, gave no hint of deeper meaning. And yet, as I watched it, trying to read its poker mask, I felt that he was sparring with me. Dusk had fallen while we talked, I had not noticed it, but now his face was blurred. Only the sharp outlines were discernible; the details were obscured. And suddenly I realized that there was more to this than mere word passing. Colonel Tucker would not have stayed so long, so patiently, if something important to him were not involved. It had to be Clark. It could only be Clark. And these words, these official rote words of his, were so much window-dressing.

I said, carefully, "And to protect this odd sort of peace, you assume everyone is guilty until proved innocent?"

"In a way, yes. But not in the way you mean it." He leaned forward, from the hips, making an acute angle as precisely as though his body were engineered. "Put it this way. Everyone is a potential murderer. Everyone has the emotions necessary to become a murderer. Love, hatred, jealousy . . . only a few people ever actually commit a murder, but everyone has the capability."

"And everyone's capable of being a spy?"

"But of course." Tucker sat back again, upright, sitting at attention. "Even a bigger likelihood than being a murderer. Spying is much more refined than pushing a knife between someone's ribs, or shooting them. And the motives are harder to discover. Sometimes they are even noble . . . but not often. You can never say for certain that any man, or any woman, will never turn out to be a spy."

"I am prepared to say, for certain, that neither Clara nor Belle Austin will ever turn out to be a spy." I pushed away from the wall and moved closer, two or three steps, so I could see his face and so that he could see mine. I wanted him to see its seriousness, its resolution. "Furthermore, Colonel Tucker,

I am prepared also to say that if Clark keeps up his pressure he is going to find himself in trouble." I paused. "It might hurt you, too."

Tucker looked stern, so stern that I think I could have seen it from the other side of the cell, even with the dusk between us. "You have already assaulted one of my men. I would not advise you to repeat the offence."

"I'm not stupid enough to strike him," I said. "But there is still a Government at the head of this country. Not a Secret Service bureau."

"Go on," Tucker said.

"I'll approach the highest people in the country on this thing," I warned bleakly. "Questions can still be asked in Parliament. Awkward questions. A Royal Commission of Inquiry could even be set up."

"Excellent," Tucker said cuttingly. "Just what I would have expected. And when they call for a report on you, what d'you think we will have to say? A man with known contacts with Communists . . . in Indo-China . . . this man Curthoys in Sydney. . . . Trespassing on out-of-bounds areas here. . . . Assaulting security guards. . . . Do you really think anyone will listen to you?"

"You bastard," I said, deliberately.

Tucker jumped to his feet as though jabbed by a bayonet. "Mr. Scotter. . . ."

"You're calling me dirty names, too," I blazed. "It's fair for both sides."

He locked his eyes on mine for a long moment, standing very squarely, his face carved in old mahogany. There was something going on behind his eyes, but I couldn't read it. I doubt whether I could have read it even at high noon.

"Mr. Scotter," he said slowly. "I am going to ask you to do something. I am going to ask you to put up with us, with Clark and the rest of us, for just a little while longer.

"While Clark continues to hound the Austins?"

"I'll instruct him to leave them entirely alone."

"He's been spreading dirt about me, all over town. He's threatening me with more."

"I know," Tucker said, a trifle stiffly. "I am not entirely without sources of information. He will leave you alone, too."

"No publicity from me, no persecution from you," I said.

"Put it any way you like," he said. "You know, Scotter, I'm not in this game because I want to spy on people. I am in it because I believe it is important. . . . Important to all of us."

"I'm objecting to the means," I said. "Not the end."

"I appreciate that," he said quietly. "Will you help us, help me, to achieve that end?"

"I thought I was a security risk."

He shrugged. "I don't think so, myself. But officially it is different. That visa, you know. Officially, it's very, very difficult to go back to being a virgin."

I grinned wryly. "I can see your point."

"I thought you would," he said. "It's a hell of a thing. But I'm asking you to take it quietly. Clark has been . . . well . . . perhaps a little too zealous. He will not bother you, or the Austins, again."

I balanced on indecision for a strained moment, but it was only indecision born of habit. "All right," I said. "I'll play along."

"Good man." Tucker voice was almost warm. He found my hand in the darkness and shook it, his hard, dry fingers squeezing like a vice. "If you have any worries, phone me."

"I've tried before."

"That was before," he said. "Not now."

"It'll be even harder now," I said. "I'm in jail."

Tucker laughed. It wasn't much of a laugh. A short, hard bark that sounded like the crump of a bursting grenade. But it was something.

"As of now, you're out of jail," he said. He took my arm. "Let's go up and talk to Sergeant Thompson. All charges are withdrawn."

128

12————

ONE OF THE BEST THINGS ABOUT LIVING ALONE IS THAT YOU
don't have to weather a barrage of questions when you come
home tattered. One of the worst things is that there's no one
around who gives a damn about anything except yourself. That
evening, when I got in from the police station, my head was a
roaring ache from being clouted with gun butts and ideas. I
wanted more than stale cigarette ends, strewn magazines and
dishes in the sink. Harry had a mania for shutting windows,
and the air was hot with the summer, prickling with dust,
cloying with the oily smell of warm machinery from the printing
room. I opened all the windows and a faint breeze came drifting
from the bay. It chased out everything with its sea smells. But
there was still an awful lot of allergy left inside me.

I went into the bathroom and swallowed some aspirin. Then
I took a look at my scalp in the mirror. The hair just back from
the centre of my forehead was matted with dried blood. A
black crust of it ran down almost to my eyes. I sponged it off,
explored my scalp and cleaned a two-inch cut with antiseptic.
It looked ugly, with a lump on either side. I cropped the hair

around it with a pair of nail scissors and slapped on an adhesive bandage.

Then I couldn't help wondering whether Colonel Tucker had been dealing from a stacked pack. He had come to sound me out. He had been prepared to act tough until I threatened to cry stinking fish to Parliament. Then he had almost fallen over himself to shut me up, promising immunity for the Austins and myself. It was what I had set out to achieve, but to gain it I had promised to play along with him—and Clark. Somehow I had the feeling that I had compromised with my own ideals, that I had sold myself. Tucker, I could accept. But could it possibly be that Clark was important to anything worth while?

I stared accusingly at myself in the mirror until my mouth grew bitter. My head was still hurting, despite the aspirin. I shook it and was almost glad of the pain that stabbed me. Then I told myself, roughly, to stop being so damned silly. Idealism was a luxury I could not afford. No one could. The whole world lived in compromise, and upheavals occurred only when the idealists could no longer be restrained from their paths of frightful righteousness.

I went out into the sitting room and poured a whisky. I snapped on the phonograph and started Serkin and Ormandy off on the Brahms Second. But neither the whisky nor the music really helped. I was alone. And in my aloneness, through the brave sweep of the music, I had time to consider the inexorable simplicity of Colonel Tucker's summation of my future. It was, as he had said, very difficult indeed to go back to being a virgin. Off-hand, I couldn't think of a single case where it had been achieved. And right then, more than anything, I wanted company. Needed it.

The theory is that books, and music, the pursuit of studies, are enough for any intelligent adult. But it isn't true. The world is just as crammed with loneliness as it is with books and music. No book has yet been written, no music composed, that can take the place of a human body and a human voice, the pressures of a hand, the softness of an eye.

I wanted like hell to ring up Poldi and ask her to come over. Not from any sudden, overwhelming rush of hormones, nor for the comforting of Oedipus. . . . But, oh hell, how can you know these things? How can you dissect and enumerate urges and their reasons? Maybe I did want to take her to bed, to end my separateness. I didn't know. All I knew was that I wanted her there in that room with me, fully lighted, and fully dressed, listening to that Goddamned lonely music of Johannes Brahms. I got up and went into my office to call her, but phones are mechanical affairs, stiff with common sense. I didn't call. What could I have said that would have sounded right? "Poldi, I'm lonely, come and hold my hand? Poldi, come and talk with me?"

I called Frank Barber instead, "How are they, Frank?"

A pause, then Frank's precise words came stringing along the line. "Wade! They are not well. Particularly Clara is not well. But I will be able to tell you more tomorrow. Perhaps you will call to see me after dinner."

"Sure, Frank. Sure."

"It would be better if you did not go to see them during the day," he said. "I have them under sedation. They must be kept very quiet."

He was talking in that calm, professionally reassuring way adopted by all doctors, and quite a few of the better-type undertakers. No matter how well you know a doctor, when he starts talking patients, he remembers his strict union vows and hands out the prescribed treatment for inquiring friends and relatives.

"What's the prognosis, Frank?"

I used the medical term because I knew doctors never liked laymen speaking their patois. I think I was feeling bloody-minded because I was talking to him and not to Poldi, who would be reading, or hanging up her stockings, or doing something no more than twenty paces from that phone.

"The future?" He avoided repeating the word prognosis. "It is not easy to be sure, but I think they will be all right. I will know better when I can examine them more thoroughly."

"Well, thanks," I said. "I'll see you tomorrow night."

He cleared his throat. "I thought perhaps you might want me to look at your head."

"Things get about, don't they?"

A small, dry chuckle rustled in the earpiece. "Even before the newspapers print them."

"*Touché,*" I said. "If it matters."

"Your head matters."

"It's all right," I reassured him. "A small cut."

"Well," he said, hesitating. "Let me know if there is anything."

I felt slightly ashamed. "Thanks, Frank." I tried to put some warmth in it. "I will."

We hung up then and I was alone again. The Brahms had stopped and I didn't turn the record over for the last two movements. I was tired of listening to music by myself. I picked up the whisky bottle, uncorked it, and then put it back in the cupboard. I had a feeling it was the wrong sort of night to have more than one snort. I cleaned my teeth and went to bed. And when I was lying in the darkness, with my head tilted sideways so I could see the spangle of stars out through my window, I got that feeling of splendid insignificance that only the stars can give. It helped me, and after a while I went to sleep on the conviction that my deal with Colonel Tucker was going to turn out all right. For the Austins, and for myself.

Harry Wells came to work early next day, somewhere around half-past eight. I was piling my two breakfast dishes in the sink, feeling good, when he shuffled in with his teapot, and his sad blue eyes ran over me as though they were reading braille. I could feel their pressure.

"They tell me you got into some strife," he said.

"Who tells you?"

"About coupla hundred people," he grunted. "The whole town's hummin' with it."

"You surprise me."

Harry ignored the irony. He plugged in the water jug. "You gonna write somethin' about it?"

"No."

"Biggest news of the week."

"It can stay that way," I said. "I'm not going to spoil it with the facts."

Harry's eyebrows went up. "No story?"

"No story," I said evenly.

He made his tea and set the pot aside to let it draw. He liked it strong. Like beetle's blood, he used to say. He turned and leaned against the sink, sliding his big skinny hands beneath his leather braces, looking at me with eyes so melancholy that he reminded me of an emaciated bloodhound.

"You running a newspaper or not?" he demanded. "Or ain't it news when everyone's talking about somethin'?"

"There's not going to be any story," I said patiently.

"All right," Harry said, disgustedly. "But don't ever let me hear you moanin' about censorship again. Not ever."

I grinned, which was what I always ended up doing in conversation with Harry Wells. He got so damn lugubrious he was funny. Harry was good for me in that way. He picked up his teapot and headed for the door, the heels of his slippers making soft slapping noises on the floor. I could feel his disapproval of my veto and, for a moment, I nearly stopped him to explain that I had made a deal with Colonel Tucker. But I stopped myself. Harry was a good friend, but a talker. Tucker wouldn't want it to get around. Then I remembered something.

"And where were you," I asked, "when I wanted you?"

Harry turned. "Me?"

"I wanted you to bail me out. You didn't turn up."

He opened his mouth. "First I heard of it. Honest, Wade. I was home all—"

"Forget it," I said. "It doesn't matter now."

I didn't tell him why he hadn't heard. There was a lot of pertinacity about Harry. I needed to have something on him, or he would keep niggling for days about my refusal to publish the story.

A great squashed rectangle of sunlight was showing up the worn spots of my office floor when I went in to work. Whispers of early day were coming through the window. I went across and looked out, stretching my arms and quaffing air, and by some miracle of translucent light I'm damned if even the new wharf and the bridge across the Clay didn't have a sparkle, a touch, almost of poetry or of art. It was a benison of a day. My head, apart from a local soreness around the cut, was clear. I caught myself whistling as I turned away, stopped in surprise as I recognized what the subconscious had turned on. An air from the Brahms Second I'd been playing the night before. Somehow it didn't seem lonely any more.

I got cracking on some bread-and-butter work then, gathering the minutiae of Clayville for my readers. All done on the telephone. God only knows how journalists don't get bakelite ear as an occupational disease. The District Clerk announced that council was going to regrade the road between Clayville and Catfish Springs before winter. Mrs. Bernie Hartford, of Downey Fleece Station, coyly admitted to planning a débutante ball for her daughter Marilyn in the Institute Hall, featuring a three-piece orchestra, a pasty supper and three eighteen-gallon kegs of beer.

The new week's issue of the Clayville *Herald* was under way. I typed the stories, wrote headings for them, and took them out to Harry. It was much warmer there than in my office, and the whiff of heat from around his linotype, the smell of ink and dust, reminded me of my homecoming the night before. And as I went out I had a sudden emotional relapse. My mind filled again with worry for Clara and Belle Austin, and with hatred for William Stinking Clark. I started to think that maybe Tucker was just playing me for a sucker. But I stifled the thought. Tucker was a stuffed shirt, what another generation would have called an officer and a gentleman. I could not imagine, or would not allow myself to imagine, that he would let me down.

That simple exercise in doubt and faith made me feel better, and when I got back to the office I felt better still. Poldi was there, beating the keys off her old typewriter as though she had three minutes, instead of three days, to press time.

"Don't overheat," I said.

She turned in her chair, smiling at me as though she really meant it. She looked wonderful.

"I am not the one who overheats," she said.

I grinned. What I wanted to do was go over to her and put my hands on her smooth, bare, golden arms. But I grinned —and went behind my desk. "I didn't try to climb the fence," I said. "You didn't warn me about the guards."

She got up and came over to me, stood in front of my desk and searched me with her eyes. I did not resist. Her eyes were like deep oceans, and I had the feeling I could drown in them. "Were they very bad?" she asked softly.

"No." I shook my head. "I suppose, really, they were very reasonable."

"They hit you on the head."

"I asked for that."

"They put you in jail."

"And they let me out."

She put her head on one side, considering me gravely for a moment. Then she smiled. "It seems to have done you good."

"Check," I said. "Any time you're feeling poorly, just go and punch one of those guards on the nose."

"I was not meaning to be funny," she said. "I was meaning

you seem happier . . . as though everything is much better now."

"I know." I reached out quickly, involuntarily, and touched her hand. "Everything *is* much better." Then I added, knowing I could trust her. "I had my talk with Colonel Tucker. We made a deal."

"I am so glad," she said.

She spoke gravely, and yet somehow there was an infinite expression of pleasure in her voice. Her face glowed with it. You would have thought I had given her some magnificent present. She was wearing a white blouse, straight-tailored and plain, with a little lacey collar. She looked like Spring to me. You know, like an almond tree dressed in thick white blossom, with a blush of deep pink in the centre of the flowers.

"What work have you got to do?" I asked, and my voice was not quite even.

"I have this story about the Italian whose family—his wife and four children—arrive here from Italy on Friday morning. I am writing it in advance."

"Nothing else?"

She shook her head.

"Then let's have a swim," I said.

She hesitated.

"You don't have to be at Frank's until two o'clock."

"It is not that," she said.

"Then what?"

She smiled quietly, slanting her eyes at me. "You know how Harry gets if copy is late."

"Poldi," I said gravely. "When Harry was my age he didn't give a damn about late copy."

13

ABOUT TWO MILES SOUTH OF CLAYVILLE IS THE LITTLE BEACH OF Blowhole Cove, named for the great rock chimney that pierces its northern spur. It is shaped like the semicircle formed by holding out the thumb and bent forefinger of the right hand. The blowhole is at the end of the thumb, and the rocky coast runs away south again from the tip of the finger.

Just before you reach the cove the land humps up, so when you get there the white crescent beach is far below and, standing on the cliff edge, you can look down through the water to the bottom. The water is very clear, banded in deepening shades of green because the bottom changes from sand to limestone rock and then to some dark, igneous type as it falls away. From the cliff top, on a calm, sunny day, you can see fish swimming and, halfway down the stepped path leading to the beach, even see the waving sand plumes sent up by digging crabs.

That late Tuesday morning when Poldi and I went there it was calm and sunny, and deserted. The citizens of Clay- ville mostly used the bay. We stopped on the cliff top for a while, enjoying the sensation of being on the brink of space, letting serenity float up towards us, breathing it with the delicacy of connoisseurs. Two motor launches were anchored near the southern spur, their white paint dazzling against the deep green of the water. They were owned by sheep station people who used them occasionally for fishing trips. But from where we stood, some two hundred feet above the cove, they looked like white brush strokes on a seascape canvas—something by Dufy in his happiest mood.

"It is so beautiful," Poldi whispered.

"I used to come here as a kid," I said. "Father used to belt me, but it never stopped me coming."

She turned her head to look at me, and the spirit of the place was on her. She was one of those people who absorb things, transmuting them to enrich the mind and body. I dare say biologists would make nonsense of my claim, but I have seen tropical flowers, in New Guinea, that open their faces to the sun and follow it and will dull their colours if a shadow falls on them, and shrink back bruised if touched. Poldi was like that in a positive way. She didn't shrink from anything. She responded.

"I cannot believe it," she said softly. "No one would ever want to prevent a boy from coming to a place like this."

I grinned at her. "He didn't until one day I got scared halfway up the blowhole. They had to haul me out with ropes."

She smiled, and standing there with her head thrown back, sunlight on the warm, smooth column of her neck and her blue eyes touching mine, she was so beautiful I had trouble with my arms. They kept wanting to reach out for her.

"Could we climb down it to the beach?" she asked. "I would not get scared."

I shook my head. "I'm older now."

She laughed. "You are not that old."

"Too old for senseless risks," I said. "Look." I swept my arm around the outline of the cove, like a Biblical farmer sowing wheat, trailing my fingers above the flat planes of the placid sea.

138

"It looks asleep. But sometimes you get a ground swell. The wave just lifts itself up from the sea. And when that happens, a great spout goes whooshing up the blowhole. You don't need a storm. All you need is a decent swell."

Poldi gave a little shudder. She reached out and took my arm. "I will use the path," she said. "I am also too old."

We went down the cliff close together, keeping our eyes on the path the way I imagine sensible flies keep their eyes on a wall when they're sneaking along it. The rock had been eaten by erosion, and our feet started little cascades of dirt and pebbles. It was hot, and by the time we were down on the beach, beads of sweat had formed along my forehead. I wiped them off with the back of my hand.

"Let's swim," I said. "We've got two hours. We can go in now, lie about in the sun, and then swim again before we have to leave."

"Race you," Poldi said, and started to whip off her clothes.

She emerged in a yellow bathing suit, two-piece, with a halter top. She was a golden brown. She was smooth, rounded, exquisite, from her short blonde hair to her toes. Her legs were long and tapered, the thighs firm, and the hips above them neat without being athletic. Her shoulders, shown off by the halter top, were a flowing line. And I could see the tender swell that began her breasts. I watched it with a sense of wonder. Excitement began churning in my stomach, then an emptiness came, then nervousness. . . . And then I looked into Poldi's eyes, for I could feel them watching me. There was a strangeness in them, part curiosity, part challenge, and what else I didn't know.

"You have not even started to undress," she said, and her voice that was always so well modulated, was suddenly uneven. She must have noticed it, because she forced a laugh. "You were the one in such a hurry. And now you are unready."

I stripped down to my bathing trunks, folded my clothes and put them next to Poldi's on the shade side of a rock. My hands were not quite steady. And when I stood up she was sauntering down towards the water, waiting for me to catch up. I didn't hurry. There is something about watching a woman walk bare-footed when you've been used only to seeing her tap high heels across an office floor. The walk is more erect, back on the heels, and her legs are softer. And if it's someone you've got any feeling for, there's an intimacy, too. I didn't know how it was I had never gone swimming with Poldi before.

We swam out to the launches, taking it easy. The water was cold at first, then cool, then like a tonic. I used a free-for-all trudgeon stroke that served me pretty well. Poldi glided in an effortless Australian crawl, her arms in perfect rhythm and a little froth of white around her beating feet. It suited me to take it easy. If we had been racing, she would have been there and back before I'd got halfway.

We had a few dives from a launch, swam under it, played porpoises around its bow and stern like schoolkids on a hookey spree. After ten minutes or so we climbed inboard, puffing slightly, feeling the sun-heat of the planks comforting our chilled bodies. Then I noticed the cabin door was on the latch. I peeked inside, idly, the way one does in pointless curiosity. It stopped being pointless straight away. I became all newshound. The tiny cabin was stacked with provisions. There were four cases of canned food along the forward wall, six cans of petrol, three on each side, one of oil and, on the padded bench seat, a heavily greased .22 calibre automatic rifle, two fishing rods and a stack of canned bait. I closed the door.

"Here's something funny," I said, turning to Poldi. She was propped on her elbows in the stern seat, spraddled to the sun. "There's a whole grocer's shop aboard."

She looked at me lazily. "How is that funny? The owner is probably going to have a fishing holiday down the coast."

"The owner," I said, "is Mark Cousins. He's having a holiday already—in England. His whole family is with him."

Poldi inclined her head to one side, and slowly crossed her

outstretched legs. "There is a manager caring for their sheep. Doubtless he is using the boat, too."

"Not Brad Harris." I shook my head. "He's strictly a horse and jeep man." I lifted the planking above the petrol tank. The gauge showed full.

"Well, he has friends," Poldi said. "Probably he is lending it to them. Or perhaps he is making some extra money by hiring it out to people."

"Aha," I cried. "The woman's angle. Cherchez la bank account." I grinned at her and she made a face. "That's it, though. Of course. Brad's picking up a little on the side." I dropped the planking back and went to sit with Poldi. "But whoever's hired this tub is going on a lulu of a trip. With the rifle for rabbits, the fishing rods, the food and the fuel, there's enough to run the first leg of a trip clear around Australia."

"Let us go, then," Poldi murmured lazily. "Pull up the anchor, and away we go. Do you think Mr. Brad Harris would really mind?"

"Not Brad." Then I chuckled as another thought came into my mind. "Poldi, we're wrong. You know what this is?" I sat forward. "Someone's using this boat, or is going to use it, without Brad's knowledge. They've stowed this stuff aboard all at once, probably at night, so they don't attract attention by carting gear each time they come to the cove. They've got enough here now for a dozen or more fishing trips."

Poldi turned her head. "Should we not, then, inform the police?"

"Yes and no," I said and laughed. "Yes, if it were anyone else but Bert Thompson. No, because Cousins is a lousy skinflint anyway.'"

"You are a wicked, lawless man," Poldi said gravely, wriggling her toes. "It is a thing in you that I like."

After that we just sat, letting the sun warm us and the salt dry on our skins. We didn't talk much. What is there to talk about when you have a ring of cliffs, a white curve of beach, cool green water, and a blue sky sitting like a skull cap on your heads? Actually, there was a lot to talk about, the way I was feeling, the way she knew I was feeling, but both of us were keeping it in the background. I, because it worried me, because I knew that if anything happened it would be more than just some ecstatic frenzy for a season. It would be for keeps, and I had an unclean name. I couldn't play for keeps. I couldn't embroil a girl like Poldi in the mess I had made for myself. Her head was turned away and I could see the long unbroken line of her cheek, her chin and neck . . . like the tender sweep you see in some of those "woman resting" drawings of Augustus John.

I was sitting close to her, and I saw a pulse start beating in her neck. Softly. Steadily. Then she turned her head and opened her mouth to say something, but her dark-blue eyes were talking to me, and she was in my arms. She was soft and wonderful, sweet smelling of salt and sun-warmth.

The decking of the launch was hard, and hot against my thighs. We lay there together, side by side, turned to each other, and my hand was on her breast under the top that had somehow come loose but I didn't think about it. Her face, so close to mine, was soft with surrender. Her eyes were closed and the long lashes lay on her cheeks. Her lips were slightly open, shaped in a little smile. I kissed her, felt myself sinking, melting into her body. . . . Then I broke away. Abruptly and roughly.

"Poldi. There is something I must tell you—"

She reached for me. "Do not talk. Come here and hold me."

Her arms touched mine and she slid her hands behind my back, up to my shoulders, and tried to pull me down. I don't know how I resisted, but I did. Perhaps it was because she was so beautiful, not just physically beautiful, but through and through. She tried to pull me down again, but when I still resisted she dropped her hands away.

She was not embarrassed. She sat up slowly, pulling the halter top over her breasts, looking into my eyes with a quiet intensity. I did not look away, or try to shield what she was reading in my eyes. This was a moment of truth, one of those moments that occur at rare summits in a lifetime.

"You are in love with me," she said softly. "And you are afraid."

There was no sound but the music in her words. There was nothing for my eyes but the sight of her.

"I am not in love with you," I lied, making myself look her in the face and knowing she could see the lie. "It is just as well for both of us, because I've got a dirty name."

"That does not matter," she said quietly. She put a hand on my knee. "I know all about that, and it is nothing."

I shook my head. "You've seen too much trouble already in your life. I'm not going to add to it."

"Trouble is something you learn to live with when it is inescapable," she said. "Trouble does not mean anything once you get used to it."

I stared at her. She was deadly serious, and it made sense in a crazy way. "Poldi," I said harshly, "You're talking nonsense. It's time we were getting back."

The water was icy cold after the sun, and near the rocky bottom where my dive carried me, I frightened a school of rainbow fish. They were shaded red to pink, and I thought, savagely, that they were probably hiding there from William Bloody Clark. Then I kicked up to the surface, and Poldi was way ahead, making like a speed boat for the shore.

14 ——————————————

I WENT TO SEE FRANK BARBER AFTER DINNER THAT NIGHT AS HE
had suggested. I was feeling something like one of those fields
you see in a war, when a squadron of tanks has been playing
catch-as-catch-can. But there was a warm singing somewhere
in me, too. It didn't make sense, unless you remembered things
like that First World War poem about skylarks singing over
Flanders fields. Perhaps it had something to do with the fact
that Poldi lived with the Barbers, and I was certain to see her
after I'd finished talking with Frank about Clara and Belle
Austin.

People are like that, but it was the first time it had really happened to me. I was anxious for the health of Clara and Belle
Austin, snarled up with hatred for William Clark, bitter about
Lucy Austin, frustrated because I loved Poldi Lorenz and
couldn't do anything about it without being a skunk, but I
still got a lift from expecting to see her and felt, in unguarded
moments, like whistling some sort of song. Not Brahms.

Frank was in his office. It was the same room my father had
used, in front of the house, with a big window opening on to
the garden and filled with a glass-topped desk, a table of surgical

oddments, and three fat leather chairs. It had a faint smell of antiseptic and Frank, in shirt sleeves at the desk, had a scrubbed-up look as though ready to dash into the operating theatre. He nearly always looked like that.

His blue eyes peered at me through his thick, rimless glasses. He smiled faintly. "Before we talk there is a message I must give you. Mary commands that you shall stay for supper."

"Why, thanks."

His smile became as near a grin as Frank would ever get. "Poldi, too."

I felt a stupid schoolboy blush spread on my face. There was an element of coyness about the way he mentioned her name, and it ruffled me.

"So you reckon you know everything," I said.

"No." He lifted his heavy shoulders in the sort of shrug that only Francis Barbasiewicz could achieve, never Frank Barber. "I am only a doctor. But Mary is a woman. *She* knows everything."

There was nothing I could say to that. Women *do* know everything. It's only when they take university degrees that they start to become ignorant. But I was glad Mary Barber knew what was between Poldi and me, because she was a comfortable woman and somehow I felt a little less alone, a little closer to a family circle. Bachelors spend a lot of time looking in through lighted windows.

"You want me to tell you about the Austins?" Frank asked quietly. His white fingers were pushing a pencil delicately about his desk. He was watching it.

"When can I see them?"

He picked up the pencil and bounced it on the point. "It depends on what sort of a night they have. Clara, of course, is the worst. But I should imagine tomorrow . . . I have placed them both on tranquillizing drugs. These new drugs are very good."

I sank back, more easily, in my chair. "What, exactly, would you say was the trouble?"

"Exactly, I wouldn't say," Frank said deliberately. He was always deliberate. "But they are both obviously in an acute state of nervous tension. Maybe brought on through overwork with the children . . . children can affect anyone that way."

"Frank," I said gently. "Have you ever seen them with the children?"

He looked at me reflectively, and rubbed his chin with the tips of his fingers, as though looking for a beard. "Tension is a funny thing. Sometimes you never know where it is until it breaks through the surface."

"Frank," I said, still gently. "Come clean. You know it's not the kids."

He got up and paced about with short, urgent strides. He was beginning to assume the familiar pearshape of the over-fifties. It made him appear to jerk around the room. His round, white face was serious as he pursued some silent debate. Then he stopped, turned and perched himself on the edge of the desk, facing me. The brown circles that rimmed his blue eyes seemed to contract to a finer focus. He pinched his nose between the thumb and forefinger of his right hand. It was all, I knew, part of his medical training. Never make any pronouncement without first going through all the preliminaries.

"Wade," he said carefully. "I have had to think about what I can tell you. You are not a member of the Austin family, but you are such an old friend, and your father, that I believe now it is quite ethical to tell you just what is the position."

He slid off the desk and went around behind it to some shelves. He took down a folder and flipped through it, then shut it up and pushed it away. He sat down, folded his hands and looked across the desk at me.

"I am quite convinced the illness in both sisters has an organic cause," he said. "When they are a little quieter I will put them in hospital for a complete check-up."

He couldn't have surprised me more if he had jabbed me with a hypodermic. I stared. "Organic?"

"Why, yes," he said patiently. "Often, even generally, these mental . . . or rather nervous . . . upsets have their roots in some physical disorder. An overactive gland. Or an underactive one. An appendix that is playing up. Even tonsils. . . . There are many things."

"But Frank," I said. "They are both affected. Even though in different degrees."

"Quite true." He nodded thoughtfully. "And that suggests to me the presence of some dietary deficiency. They are, if you will pardon me saying so, strange old ladies. It is quite possible that they do not eat properly. That is, they do not perhaps have a well-balanced diet."

All this was well reasoned, but it didn't make any sense for me. And I was sure it wouldn't have made any sense for Frank Barber, either, if he had been present in that room when Lucy had hurled the name of Thomas Patrick Moody.

"I don't want to appear argumentative, Frank—"

"But you will be," he smiled.

I grinned back, tightly. "When you first saw Aunt Clara you said she'd had a severe shock."

"Quite true," he agreed quietly. "I did say that. I still say it. The point is that anyone in good health would have recovered from the worst effects by now. The shock, you see, is not the illness, but the thing that has disclosed it."

There is nothing quite so frustrating as listening to a doctor talk scientific nonsense. Frustrating because you can't combat it. They can give you all the answers, with illustrations of the body's functions, simplified to confuse the layman and bluff him into agreement, or self-confessed stupidity. I knew, beyond all doubt, that the sisters' illness was caused by Clark and Lucy and, somehow, by the evoked memory of Thomas Patrick Moody.

I was tempted to tell Frank about it, but turned the idea down.

Maybe he already knew, anyhow, and was being ethical with me. Clara may well have told him everything. If so, Frank would never so much as suggest a syllable of it, even to me. And if he didn't know, there was no point in involving him as yet. I had spiked Clark's guns; and without him for support I didn't think Lucy would cause much trouble. The tranquillizing drugs and a few days in hospital would do the Austins no harm. If they failed to respond I could always then seek to fill in the gaps for Frank.

"Frank," I said. "Forgive me for being difficult. I'm worried. That's all."

He came across the room and punched me lightly on the shoulder. "The whole world is worried," he said. "There is nothing for me to forgive."

So we went down through the house talking about things I can't remember, they were so unremarkable. And down in the kitchen were Mary Barber, with her big low homely bosom, and big high slavic cheekbones, and that matronly look of shrewd summation as her eyes took me in; and Poldi, looking just like that girl in the launch at Blowhole Cove. And straightaway I forgot about the world and myself being worried.

15 ⎯⎯⎯⎯ ⤳ ⎯⎯⎯⎯⎯⎯⎯

"WARMING UP," JOE PORTER SAID.

He was still spreading his fat bottom on the bench outside
Peltzer's hardware store as I walked down Main Street next
afternoon, on my way to visit the Austins.

"Hiya, Joe," I said, and kept walking.

Joe Porter was probably the greatest bench-sitter and button-
holer in Clayville. And that's saying something. He was like
it even at school. If you wanted to get anywhere, or didn't
want to get sucked dry, you kept walking when Joe called out.

So this afternoon I kept walking, but Joe came after me. I
hadn't thought he would have had enough speed. He came up
fast, puffing and sweating mightily, his fat gut wobbling, his
big hands working like paddles to push him along.

"Jesus, it's hot," he wheezed.

It was hot all right. The strip of bitumen down the centre
of Main Street was full of shiny patches where the bitumen
had melted. The red-brown earth of each side of it was covered
with inches of fine dust, and the lightest wind would have been
sufficient to create a first-rate dust storm. It was flat calm. The

heat burst up from the ground and cannoned off the shop fronts. The few cars parked along the street were covered with a fine film of dust, and you could smell the unpleasant blend of oil and petrol vapour as you passed them. It was a dry, desiccating heat. I could feel it striking right through my sparse flesh to my bones. Joe Porter, with all his fat, must have felt like a panful of French fries.

"Wassamatter with the Austins, Wade?" he panted. "Hear they're crook."

"Just tuckered out," I told him. "Frank Barber says they'll be all right."

"He did?" Joe's right hand stripped sweat, like water, from his face. "Thas good. He's a good man, Doc Barber. Wouldn't think he was a foreigner, would ya?"

"No," I said gravely. "He even uses the toilet."

Joe gave me a quick look. He knew I was ribbing, but he didn't mind. Joe was one of those fat men who rarely minded anything. It's not true what they say about fat men being easy-going; generally they're as senstive as stinging nettles. But not Joe Porter.

"How's about this fight you got into, Wade?"

I gave him my blank face. Now he was coming to the matter that had got him off his bottom in the midafternoon heat. "What fight?"

"Out at the wire."

"That was no fight," I said. "They slugged me with a gun butt."

"The bastards," Joe said.

"I hit 'em first."

"The hell you did," Joe said admiringly.

"So that's all it was."

"Hmm," Joe said.

We were then opposite Wilberforce Sunter's nostrum cave. I could see the old gnome himself, peering at us from the interior gloom. And I made a promise that I would press more questions on him on my way back from the Austins. It didn't matter now if he reported me. Clark wouldn't dare to spread his calumnies against my father's memory in defiance of Colonel Tucker. I still wanted to know the truth about Thomas Moody. I was certain that Sunter knew exactly where he fitted in. I had to know. It could be vital later on if Frank Barber's diagnosis of organic cause failed to restore the Austin sisters' health.

"I been hearin' the word about you, Wade," Joe said. "It's all over town."

Joe's panting seeped into my thoughts with gentle insistence. I paced along with it for a space of seconds, faintly surprised to find myself calm and relatively untouched by his fingering the spot that had been so sore, and now scarcely hurt at all. It wasn't because of the heat, and it wasn't because Joe Porter had once raided orchards with me. Or because he mattered less than other gossipmongers. It wasn't anything like that.

"Your old friends don't take no notice, of course," Joe said, feelingly. "Yore still Wade Scotter to us. Fancy labels don't mean nuthin', and don't you start thinkin' they do."

"Thanks, Joe," I said. "I'm still Wade Scotter to me, too. I feel and act just like Wade Scotter."

"Sure you do," Joe said. "Like I tole all the boys. I tole 'em: Lissen. Wade's regular. I know for a fact he's going out with a dame."

I stopped, hard and jarringly. My right hand jumped out and grabbed Joe by the shirt. "Let's get this straight," I snapped. "What's this word you've been hearing?"

Joe's face was pink and wet, like a badly made strawberry blancmange. His black eyes beseeched me. He was breathing through his mouth. "Now, Wade. I tole you I don't believe it. I tole you that. . . ."

"All right," I said and let him go. "I'm sorry, Joe. But what is it you don't believe?"

"Why?" Joe's eyes went round. ""Doncha know? They're saying' you got beat up because you propositioned the soldiers."

"Who said it first, Joe." I speared him firmly with my right forefinger. "Don't stall. You'll know."

"That flatfoot Clark," Joe said. "Who else?"

"Who else, indeed?" I was not surprised. I was not even annoyed. "Clark doesn't like me, Joe."

"I know that, too," Joe said. "He reckons you're a Commie."

"And you?"

"I reckon you're not," Joe said. "But some of the folk hereabout think different. Where there's smoke there's fire, they reckon."

"There's been a helluva lot of smoke," I said. "And I can't do much about it. But if any of the boys want to find out for sure about the other thing, tell 'em to come around. Any time. I'll take 'em with gloves, or bare fists . . . and for good measure I'll even give a prize . . . the Malthusian belt . . . to be won three times."

Joe looked puzzled. "What's that?"

"Like the Lonsdale," I said. "Only more fun."

I left him then. We were opposite the Austin home. Dust puffed up around my shoes as I stepped off the footpath, the hot bitumen made little sucking noises under my soles, then the soft, noiseless dust again. I looked back down Main Street at the gate, and Joe was hurrying away with the bursting energy of a man with news to spread. Doubtless he believed I was both homosexual and Communist. I grinned, wryly perhaps, but with more humour than bitterness. And I realized, with a faint wonderment, that I was learning to live with the label that society had slapped on me. The philosophy that Poldi had propounded at Blowhole Cove was beginning to sink in. Or perhaps it was the memory and influence of her embrace. I set my feet crunching up the driveway to the house.

"Ah," Lucy said. "The faithful one."

She was sitting in the schoolroom, behind a book. Some of the kids were in the room, others were outside raising Cain around the garden. She placed a hand on the book to mark her place, staring at me without welcome.

"How are they?" I asked.

"In the middle of a monster barbiturate party," she said. "You're just in time. They're really whooping it up."

Anger moved in me. "That's not funny."

"Nothing's funny," she said. "It's just the way you look at it."

"The way you're looking at things isn't funny," I snapped.

She put her head on one side and looked at me mockingly down her long, dark eyelashes. She was wearing a yellow cotton frock with a low neckline. She gave her bosom a forward and sideways thrust. It seemed incredibly lewd there in that classroom with the children looking on. "Don't you ever get tired of playing old friend of the family?"

"They're all the family I have," I said steadily. "They're all you've got."

"Stop drooling," she jeered. "It's spilling on your tie."

The children were gawking at us. Children have an instinct for scenes. I glanced around their expectant faces, then turned to Lucy. "Why don't you send these kids home? Their noise can't be helping your aunts."

"I'll do that." She sighed, theatrically. "Dear, thoughtful Wade. And where shall I wait for you? In the sand pit? Or do you prefer seduction amid the bushes?"

For a quick, hot moment I wanted to shake her, like trying to clean something that had been dropped in the mud. But I didn't move a finger. There was a strange defensivness back of the mockery in here eyes. I hadn't noticed it before. She was subtly different from the taunting, aggressive Lucy of our last encounter. She seemed in some way keyed to the general atmosphere of the house, the brooding unreality that overlaid the illness of her aunts.

"Tell me what's wrong Lucy," I said quietly.

"There's nothing wrong," she said.

"We've known each other a long time. We've been good friends."

"Bring out the family album, why don't you?" she said. "You in your short pants. Me in my pigtails."

"It mightn't be a bad idea at that." I paused, then added. "There's some interesting details tucked away."

Her eyes flicked disinterest at me. "Such as?"

"Thomas Moody," I flung the name at her.

Her expression changed, like curdling, as though I had dropped some acid into her mind. "What d'you know about Thomas Moody?"

"Enough," I said. It was the oldest trick in the world; the bluff technique. "I know enough to understand."

"Blast him," she said.

There was an incredible bitterness in the way she spat the words. There was a vast hurt, too. And I had a sudden intuition.

"He died too soon," I said.

Lucy's eyes were bleak. They hated me. "Go away." Her voice was thin and brittle. "Take your dirty, sniggering little mind away."

I went upstairs, trying to force the unbelievable intuition from my mind. But it fitted too neatly into the Austin puzzle to be easily dislodged. It stuck there like an ugly grit, smarting and bedevilling, so that when I slipped in through the door of the sitting room I was on edge, awkward, and self-conscious. It was a great relief to find Aunt Belle and Aunt Clara seated at the window, conning the view with their binoculars. I stood quietly for a moment, watching them in cowardice, sorting myself out.

They were partially in silhouette against the brightness of the day. They sat in firm uprightness on their straight-backed chairs, as I had seen them countless times. Nothing seemed to have changed, and if I hadn't seen them broken, I would never have guessed that anything had ever happened to cause the slightest fracture in their calm. They were wearing their uniforms of long, ankle-length grey dresses, with white lace collars. And they had on their hats, those wonderful reminders of the age when artificial fruit was chic, and hats were worn not as a flippancy, but as a declaration that society was solid, unchanging and unchangeable. The cedar furniture of the room glowed richly sombre. The very air was still, neither warm nor cool. Everything made an absurity of the intuition that I had carried up the stairs. I told myself I was a fool, and more, a dirty-minded fool, for ever imagining that Thomas Moody could have been a lover to either of these women. The thought now seemed obscene. But what else could he have been that the mere mention of his name should be so potently explosive?

"It's too early for rabbits," I said quietly.

They did not turn. Sunlight leaped from the lime juice drinking set on the sideboard as I moved across the room.

"It isn't the time for rabbits," I said.

Aunt Clara turned slowly, with all the dignity of manipulated corsetry, like someone turning inside a spring. Her large, weather-beaten face was stern. But her eyes were kindly, soft and large and grey.

"Wade, don't be a tiresome little boy," she said, with mock severity. "Any time is the time for rabbits."

"I'll go stand in the corner," I said, and bent to kiss her on the proffered cheek.

Aunt Belle put out a hand and touched me on the arm. She had the power of gentleness. Her white hair was a nimbus above her raw and lined face. "Wade," she whispered. "How nice to see you, boy."

I kissed her, too, and she smiled that sweet fey smile that made you wonder where she really was—with you or away? They were both looking extremely well, both back on that high plateau from which they surveyed the world with opiate detachment. It was hard to believe they'd been distraught so recently, so shocked, so almost broken. Frank Barber had been right when he'd said they were restored again, but at that moment I was prepared to bet it was their serenity more than his drugs that had achieved the result.

"Bring up a chair, my dear," Aunt Clara said, waving her hand towards the interior of the room. "Sit between us. You're always running away somewhere."

"Press tycoons can't sit still," I said, making the old joke that they could never see. "We've got ants in our pants."

Aunt Belle said "Ooh," or rather her mouth made the motions. One thin, brown spotted hand fluttered to her face.

"You work far too hard on that paper," Aunt Clara scolded.

"I'll get the chair," I said.

I went back from the window for the chair. The big, old spring rocker that I always used. It was too awkward to carry, with its floppy base, and I had just started to drag it across the carpet when I heard Aunt Belle make a funny noise. Something between a whimper and a shout. I swung around, quickly. She was crouched, half-standing, out of her chair. The binoculars were clamped to her eyes, and she was trembling violently.

"I saw one, Clara. I really did." Her voice, louder than it had ever been, was shaky with emotion. "There . . . there by the bush. . . ."

Aunt Clara picked it up then in her glasses. Her big, square body became arrested in the act of movement, poised in angularity like some piece of statuary draped with cloth.

"The rabbits are back," she said in a hushed, awed voice, saying it to herself, saying it almost like a prayer, or rather, like announcing the fulfillment of a prayer. "They are back, Belle. It must surely be a sign."

"It is a sign," Aunt Belle whispered, and the artificial fruit on her hat brim rattled softly.

I stood behind them, looking out over the shaven lawn that ran down to the river, and across the flat silver of the river to the yellow grassland that rose gently on the other side. I saw no rabbits, only the weathered grass, and that hot, pulsating fence, striding along the bank. And I remembered that other afternoon when Clark had been in the room, and we had seen the guard with his man-hunting dog and I had heard the name of Thomas Patrick Moody for the first time.

"The dear things," Aunt Belle murmured, and sighed ecstatically.

"So innocent, so gay," Aunt Clara said. She turned to me and her big, plain face was soft and almost young with happiness. She handed me her binoculars. "Look, Wade. See the little dears. Go to the animals and the birds, my dear, if you would learn how to live. Watch them, Wade. . . ."

There was nothing across the river but the yellow midsummer grass, dry, inflammable, and useless except to hold the soil together and save it from being scattered by the wind. I scanned each foot from the river bank to the skyline, and the only living things I saw were a few topknot pigeons pecking grass seeds. I knew then that Frank Barber had been wrong. And so had I been wrong. The Austin sisters were as sick as anyone could be.

I handed Aunt Clara back her glasses, but held on when she tried to take them. Her eyes met mine. They were misty and without depth. Her face had a strange, remote composure.

"Aunt Clara, what is it?" I clasped my free hand over hers. "Tell me what is wrong?"

"Dearest boy," she said. "You look so like your father when you are worried."

"Dearest Alec," Aunt Belle whispered, smiling quietly, as though touching the name with her lips.

"Your father," Aunt Clara said softly, "was the kindest man in the world."

"Life was a kind thing then," I said. I folded my height down until I was squatting on the window sill, facing them, and hoping that my eyes weren't giving too much away. I was beginning to get scared. "Tell me what is wrong."

"Life does not change, Wade," Aunt Clara said. Her hands were folded in her lap. She held them so tightly that the skin across the thickened knuckles was a parchment white. "Life is about people, and they do not change in a few years. . . . Not in a hundred years. . . . On the surface maybe, but only maybe. . . . Certainly not underneath, where it really counts."

"Tell me what is wrong," I said patiently.

"There is more good than evil in the world, Wade dear," Aunt Belle said, smiling and nodding as though I were not in the room, but standing bare-kneed and untidy-haired before her in some dream. "You must always believe in goodness. You must look for it. . . . Seek and ye shall find. . . ."

A glance passed between them, held for an instant, and expired. It was a message of affirmation of some agreed line. They were heading me off with their vagueness, deliberately refusing to take up my question. It was a strange feeling, coming up against this precocity of purpose in them. And, remembering the rabbits, I wondered if they were quite sane. I wasn't thinking about it in the broad sense, but in the harsh, narrow confines of everyday. The rule-of-thumb judgment that says insanity is being different from other people.

I watched them for a long moment, worrying about them, wanting desperately to help some way, but loath to break into their retreat. Then Aunt Belle put out her hand and Clara took it. They sat there, staring past me out the window and holding hands. They were seeking comfort from each other, courage maybe . . . I knew I had to do something. And I had to do it before the lump in my throat got any bigger and strangled me.

"What about this Dr. Moody?" I asked gently. "Did he believe in goodness? Was he a good man, too?"

There was a deep silence. So deep and intense it was like a vacuum, and I could hear my words go rolling through the room, booming in my head. I saw their hands tighten and was afraid that I had gone too far. Aunt Clara's face was pale, and Belle's grey eyes were watching her with a pitiful uncertainty. And I resolved that if they didn't answer, I would ask no more questions. But Aunt Clara drew her hand away, smoothed some invisible wrinkles in her dress, and looked me in the face. Her eyes were calm.

"Yes, Thomas Moody was a good man," she said quietly. "He believed in goodness." Then she added, "He has been dead a long time now."

"I know," I said. "I'm sorry."

"He died of scrub typhus in northern Queensland," she said. "That is the sort of good man he was. He went there looking for a cure for a dreadful disease, but found death instead."

There was pain behind her quietness and dignity. I felt ashamed. "Aunt Clara, I'm sorry. I shouldn't have asked."

She shook her head. "It is all right, Wade."

"But you are sick." I touched her shoulder. "There is something wrong . . . and you won't let me help."

"There is nothing wrong, Wade dear," she said gently. "We are not so old and foolish that we cannot help ourselves."

"Often it helps to confide in someone else," I said.

"I do not know that it does," Aunt Clara said, and Aunt Belle's artificial fruit rustled gently once again as she nodded her agreement. "One's conscience is the only worthwhile guide in anything, Wade. One should not try to supplant it with neighbours, or with friends, no matter how kind they are."

I knew that was the end. There was finality in her voice, and I recognized that what she had said was the principle by which they had both lived. There was nothing left for me. Aunt Belle picked up her binoculars and forgot that I existed. I stood up slowly and moved away.

"Call me if there is anything. Won't you."

Aunt Clara smiled. "I will, Wade dear."

She stood up, placed both her hands on my shoulders, and kissed me on the lips. She stood back smiling at me, and there was such an expression on her face that I was not surprised that the touch of her lips had been the touch of a young girl. "Wade dear," she murmured. "Marry that nice Poldi girl. Stop Worrying about the world and about Clayville and about us. Marry her soon. Do not waste your life in bitterness and argument."

"You were in love with Thomas Moody," I said softly. "Weren't you?"

"Very much, Wade dear."

I slid my arms around her. My eyes were smarting.

"Ask her soon, my dear," she said.

I turned away, not knowing how to answer. Somehow I found the door. My hand fumbled with the knob, and then I heard Aunt Belle cry out. I turned and she was coming towards me, with that funny little swooping run in which only her feet seemed to move.

"Wade, I have not kissed you." She gave me a quick peck on the right cheek, patted my face with both her hands, and smiled into my eyes. "Run along now, darling boy."

Then Clara called "rabbits" from the window and Aunt Belle turned away. They didn't see me leave. I trod heavily downstairs, leaving them to exult in their imaginary rabbits, to shelter behind the defence works they had thrown up against the encroaching, brutal world. The intuition that I had taken upstairs with me had hardened to conviction. I knew, and understood, what had shocked them so when Lucy had flung the name of Moody in their faces. I understood, too, what William Clark must have made of it.

16

LUCY WAS STILL DOWNSTAIRS, SITTING BEHIND HER BARE teacher's desk, propped on her folded arms and pretending to read. She was alone. She had sent the children home, but I didn't notice the quietness at first because there was so much noise inside my head.

She looked up as I went towards her, lifting her head slowly. A shaft of sunlight from the window gradually slid across it until, when she was sitting upright, all her face was in the light. It emphasized the drag of discontent around her mouth. It took some of the colour from her dark-brown eyes, but it didn't penetrate beyond the surface.

"Lucy," I said quietly. "How did you find out that Thomas Moody was your father?"

Her eyes considered me with steady hostility. "Go to hell," she said deliberately. "Go now."

"How did you find out?"

She closed her book, not marking the place, closing it in such a way as to declare it no longer mattered. She pushed the book away. Her face was set and hard. "I tried to get a job in

Sydney just before you came back. They wanted a birth certificate."

"And Clark?"

"What d'you mean 'And Clark?' "

"How did he find out?"

"Why don't you go to hell, like I suggested?"

"Too busy," I said steadily. "Right now there's something else. Did you tell Clark?"

"What's it matter?" she snapped.

"I'm curious."

Her lips tightened, then twisted in derision. "If you must know, he found out for himself. The same way he found out your sainted father got drunk and killed a man."

I lit a cigarette, busying myself with the small ritual movements, using them to cover the spurt of anger her jibe had aroused. "Sunter," I said.

"Your dad's old pal," she jeered. "Why don't you go and beat him up? He's just about your size."

"There's someone else I'd like to beat up first."

She smiled thinly. "Good. Just stick around. I'm expecting him to call."

I took a long, hard pull on my cigarette. I was shocked to think that Clark was coming into that house where he had already done so much harm. Tucker had promised that he would be warned off, but then, there had been nothing in our argument to say he would be banned from calling on Lucy.

"He will not be seeing your aunts?"

"My mother, you mean," she said. "I wouldn't know."

"Lucy," I said tersely. "They are very ill. They must not be worried. By Clark or anyone else."

Her lips curled. She dropped her eyes and spread her fingers wide on the surface of the desk, almost as though she were about to spring at me. "Bill Clark's done nothing but his duty. It's their fault if his questioning has hurt their consciences."

"What sort of questioning, Lucy?"

"Legitimate," she said, and laughed. "It's their turn to do some suffering."

"Suffering isn't going to help anyone," I said. "Surely you know that."

"Surely you don't know anything," she sneered. "It's helped me to see them suffer. They've kept me as a poor relation for thirty years. . . . Ashamed of me. . . ."

"Lucy." I stamped out my half-smoked cigarette on the schoolroom floor. "It's not like that. You know how they are. . . . . Withdrawn, gentle, shy. . . ."

She made an abrupt, cutting gesture with her right hand. "I'm a bastard," she snapped. "And I don't like it. I'm her bastard, and she doesn't like it." She stood up, pushing her body out in that exaggerated lewdness that I now realized was an expression of her self-contempt. "You think they're wonderful and you hate Bill Clark. With me it's the other way round. They've done me nothing but harm. He's helped me. He wants me. And wanting me, he has helped to punish them."

Her lips trembled slightly, and I saw pain burst through the patina of hardness she wore across her eyes. I thought for a moment she was going to break, but the crisis passed, passed so quickly I would probably never have seen it had I not been watching her intently. I paced slowly across to the window, torn with conflicting emotions, needing to look out of that room, away from Lucy, to find some new, considered basis for my position. When I had petitioned Colonel Tucker I had been supremely sure of myself. Clark was a detestable bully, Lucy his ally, and the Austin sisters their innocent victims. Now, these things were roughly the same, but in my mind there was some revision. The degree of culpability had changed. I didn't know by how much. It left me floundering.

I was, of course, suffering from reaction. I had come downstairs from Clara and Belle Austin in a state of stunned complaisance, accepting the fact that Clara had lain with Thomas Moody, and slipped, as a more or less normal thing. The sort of thing that could happen to any girl or woman in the unlucky season. But now, having talked with Lucy, my feet were back on the ground, and suddenly it all became incredible. Clara Austin was an unwed mother. I had thought myself worldly, but I wasn't sophisticated enough to take that much in my stride.

Sex, of course, belongs to the very young and the present day. Everyone feels faintly disgusted at the mention of grandmother begetting children in her four-poster bed. The thought of Aunt Clara Austin, that vague, unworldly symbol of the better life, lying with Thomas Moody was a profanation. And yet, even as I protested, I knew that I was being unfair. Grossly unfair. No one can know the compulsions of another's love affairs. No explanations, no amount of searching, can reveal the mood, the intangible spark of communion that can lift a man and a woman out of themselves, that can make their actions either noble or ignoble, that can represent the difference between lust and love.

The empty swings, and the see-saws and the monkey bars in the garden, all accused me of corruption. Clara Austin had loved Thomas Moody and had paid the price of love without legality. Maybe she should have told Lucy the truth . . . maybe that would have been only to make things worse. Who could tell? The only answer, the true one, was bound up in the personality of Clara Austin, and that conformed only with its own fey rules. One thing alone was crystal clear. She must have lived all these years in fearful desperation, sharing her secret alone with Belle, weaving it into their lives until it was almost forgotten; its discovery by Lucy and her paramour must have sounded to the sisters louder than the trump of doom. And right then I gave Thomas Moody, that man whom Clara Austin still loved and described as good and kind, the accolade for bumship, with star-and-garter clasp.

"Shocks you, doesn't it?" Lucy said. "Vice in the vicarage. . . . The wages of sin is Lucy."

Her voice sliced through my thoughts, astringent and bitter, dragging me back into the room to grapple with something about which I was no longer confident. She was standing at my left shoulder, contemptuous and self-possessed.

"Lucy," I said. "Why don't you get out? Go to Sydney. . . . Melbourne, anywhere. Start your own life afresh, and leave Clara, and Belle, to get on with theirs. Give them a chance to readjust themselves."

She tilted her head back and gave a short, hard rap of laughter. "I've stayed this long, I'll hang on a bit longer," she said harshly. "There's a lot of money coming to Clara Austin's only child when the old girl dies. I want to be around to collect."

She had said something like it only a few days before, and it had angered me. But now it was different, more urgent, more applicable. I was shocked, not angered. My eyes narrowed and I could feel the muscles ridge along my jaw. "Lucy," I said steadily, "I'm trying to understand. I've said a lot of things . . . some that I shouldn't. But now I know how it is, I'm trying to understand. . . ."

"Don't bother." She turned away, swinging one leg and swirling her skirt like a dancer. She looked back at me over her shoulder, and I swear she was enjoying herself. "No one can understand anyone else. You ought to know that. You've been around."

She crossed the room to the open French windows, and stood to one side, tapping a foot and holding herself with something of the spurious hauteur of a demi-mondaine dismissing an un-wanted lover. In the recent past I would have been annoyed, even affronted, at her calculated rudeness. Now I saw it differently. It was pathetic, a façade thrown up desperately to hide hurt and bewilderment. It was almost sad. Even remembering what she was doing to Clara Austin, and to Belle, I could still think of it as sad. She was hurting because she was hurt. And as I walked towards her, past the little chairs and tables of the room, I felt a sudden rush of sympathy. God, she was in a mess. I had lifted a hand to touch her shoulder, summoned a trite phrase of comfort that would comfort no one but would represent a try, when I heard a heavy, padding step and the big frame of William Clark filled the windows.

He stepped back into the garden and stood aside. Lucy smiled her bitter mockery at me, and I knew she must have glimpsed him coming and stage-managed our meeting. My sympathy evaporated with a hiss, like water falling on a red-hot spit. Her innate bitchery could comfort her. She didn't need anything from me.

Clark made a little bow. "Mr. Stanley, I presume."

"What d'you want here?" My voice was strained and thin. My body felt like one huge spring, pressed down, and held only by some lever that the slightest move would trip.

"My dear chap." He looked blank. "I have every right. This is a democracy. It's free for everyone. I've got your authority for that."

He was laughing at me, with his handsome blasted filmstar face. He was wearing a lightweight grey suit, with a white shirt and blue tie. His dark hair glistened in the sun. I watched him for a long moment, thinking how it would feel to drive a fist into his belly, to bring another up from the ground to smash his face as he doubled over. His presence meant no good; neither for Lucy nor her . . . Christ . . . I didn't know what to call them any more . . . her mother and her aunt. . . . Somewhere in my brain a gear engaged, a message ran down to my hands. I made the first movement, a shift of weight, when I remembered Colonel Tucker and my promise to play along. I remembered it just in time.

Clark said, "What a pity you have to go. I've always so enjoyed our little chats."

"Tell me," I said tautly. "Have you seen any good sewers lately?"

He grinned, widely, with that infuriating assurance of a man holding all the aces and a couple up his sleeve. "That's what I like about you, Scotter," he said. "Nothing ever gets you down."

I walked away with Lucy's giggling in my ears. I tramped down Main Street in a cloud of emotion and groping thought. I didn't see anyone, and by the time I'd reached the *Herald* there were two things uppermost in my mind. Firstly, I had to tell Frank Barber what I had discovered about Clara and Lucy Austin so he could readjust his treatment. Secondly, I was going to ask Colonel Tucker to remove William Sewer Clark entirely from the district. The situation at the Austin home was altogether too favourable for his malignant talents.

My office was cool after the blinding street, and dark. I paused inside the door to let my eyes adjust themselves. Harry Wells was lounging in my chair, slippered feet up on my desk. He was looking at me sadly, pale-blue eyes and lined face filled with resignation. He lifted his brown china teapot from my desk blotter, tilted back his head and poured himself a gullet full of tea. He put the teapot down. Very carefully.

"If you've finished fartin' around the town," he said. "D'you reckon we could do something about putting out a paper?"

17

THE REST OF THAT DAY I WORKED. REALLY WORKED. I WAS columns behind schedule; some eight of our weekly twelve pages were yet to fill. I might as well be frank. The *Herald* was a rag; but filling twelve broadsheet pages of a rag was still a lot of work. Hack work, scissors and paste where possible, a quick rewrite where the crib would look too obvious. We always cribbed a lot of stuff from the city dailies. All country papers do. It's quite honourable in a shifty sort of way. What I mean is that all the city papers know it goes on, and so long as it isn't too blatant, that special feature stuff is left alone, they turn a blind eye.

My first job was ripping through a condensation of the week's overseas news. I sorted clippings from one of the Sydney dailies, shuffled them around, welded them together and sent them out to Harry for our cable page that old Neil Townley had so proudly headed, "Behold The World." Then I pasted up a selection of current and juicy court cases from Melbourne and bunged them out.

The copy began to bank up on the old fruit case alongside

Harry's linotype, and every time I laid so much as a two-paragraph story on the pile, Harry grunted like a camel getting the last straw on its back. I have yet to meet the head printer who doesn't bleed piteously from the mouth approaching press time, but I had to admit that Harry was shipping it green.

"Sorry about all this," I told him. "I've been pretty well tied up with other things."

Harry pushed down his type-metal lever and leaned back in his chair. "Serves me damn well right f'working for a playboy."

His lined old face was blank, but his eyes gave the words their true meaning. I cuffed him lightly on the head. "I'll make you a pot of tea."

"Strong," he said. "Like beetle's blood. And get somethin' f'yourself.'"

"I'm all right," I said, which wasn't altogether true. "I want to get well ahead, fill her up, in case I get caught with something tomorrow."

Harry snapped his braces against his scrawny chest. "Sure you're all right," he drawled. "You're the liveliest lookin' corpse I ever seen."

I made him his pot of tea, poured myself a cup and took it and a slice of bread and cheese back to my desk. I shovelled trash into that typewriter for the better part of three hours, rewriting here and there, expanding a few simple telephoned facts from the Town Clerk into two columns, complete with speculation, reporting verbatim a long-winded statement from Mayor Hazelgrove that really merited the wastepaper basket. . . .

I didn't even go to the can until well after seven o'clock. And when I looked at myself in the mirror, washing my hands, I saw what Harry had meant. Only I wasn't such a lively looking corpse. Being thin, I always started off behind scratch when it came to looking good. My face, with its high cheekbones, seemed gaunt, and the deep shadow of beard around my chin gave it a sort of dark-green look, like those sickly portraits war artists used to turn out of prisoners and men with battle fever. There was a lot of nervous tension, and I could see faint stress lines running criss-cross, stretching the skin over the cheekbones and jaw. My mouth was tight and my eyes had shadows under them. It made them look too dark.

It wasn't the rush of work. I could have done that on my ear with one hand tied behind my back. The tragic tangle of the Austin household was fretting in my mind, frustrating me because I was now beginning to realize there was so little I could do.

It didn't matter to me that Aunt Clara was an unmarried mother, or Lucy illegitimate. It didn't make me feel any different towards them. In fact, after the first shock of discovering human frailty—or was it human strength?—in Aunt Clara after all the years of rectitude, if anything I had more regard for her. But there was no way of conveying that. Clara and Belle Austin were not the sort of people with whom you could discuss illegitimacy as an accidental commonplace of society. I couldn't go to them and say I knew all about their secret, and it didn't matter. That such things weren't so serious in the world today. They didn't live in my world. They didn't live in anyone's but their own.

So I was left with a deep frustration of anxiety and sympathy that couldn't be resolved. It hurt. It really hurt. And it wasn't helped by having met William Keyhole Clark at the kindergarten door. Nothing was ever going to be smoothed out while he was on the scene. I went back into the office and hammered out the remainder of copy needed to fill the columns. I took it out to Harry and dropped it on his box.

"That's the lot." I lit a cigarette. "Make up all the pages, but leave me two columns for a lead story. We might pick up something from Sydney or Melbourne tomorrow. If nothing breaks worth while, slap in the piece about that South American revolution."

"You were born about three hundred years too late," Harry

snarled. "You would've looked fine runnin' up and down a slave galley with a wire whip."

"Set the rest of it tomorrow," I grinned. "We don't go to press until five o'clock."

"Bugger you," Harry said. "I'll stay all night if needs be."

"Go home and be sensible," I said.

"Like hell," Harry said. "I'd rather have the grudge."

Night was settling in when I picked up the phone again. Pinpoint lights were blinking at me through the window. There was no wind and it was really hot. It was invariably like that in Clayville at the end of a summer's day. The day's heat stored itself in the earth and buildings ready for the next day's start. Even when the night breeze came in from the sea, the earth and buildings retained much of their warmth. In Main Street of a morning you saw dozens of squashed bobtail lizards that had crept out on the warm bitumen to sleep. And there wasn't a summer but someone drove into town with a dead snake wrapped around his wheels.

"Colonel Tucker, please," I said. "Wade Scotter speaking."

"Just a moment, please." The sing-song voice of the switchboard girl faded momentarily, then came back again. "I'm connecting you."

I smiled grimly to myself. At least Tucker was playing ball so far. He had told them to put me through.

"Hullo, Scotter." The colonel's precise, clipped words marched in and I could picture him sitting squared up to his desk, no lounging back, no crouching, but erect, with the phone held at some regulation number of degrees. "What can I do for you?—Don't mention any names."

"That man I spoke about."

"Trouble again?"

"Yes. When can I talk with you?"

A slight pause. Then, "Tomorrow?"

"Why not tonight?"

"Impossible, I'm afraid. Set any time tomorrow, and I'll be there."

"Nine o'clock," I said. "Here."

"Check," he said. "Oh-nine-hundred hours."

I put up the phone and thought, so far, so good. He had sounded as friendly as a ramrod ever could be. I squashed a flying ant on the back of my neck, and rolled him off with my fingers. I dropped him in my desk ashtray, that elegant accessory to graceful living made by denting a cigarette tin with a chair leg. William Clark, of the gold cigarette case and lighter, had been appalled at it. I felt a little happier then, remembering his distaste, because that was in the time when he was crowding me. Tomorrow, I was going to start hitting back.

Food hunger rumbled emptily around inside me. I lit a cigarette to stave it off, and dialled Frank Barber. He wouldn't keep me long. Frank was too professional to talk secrets on the phone, and I had had too much experience of Clayville's switch-board to dream of saying what I knew.

"Frank, I want to see you," I said. "Tonight."

"What is it, Wade?"

"I can't tell you here."

"Of course, it is about your aunts," he said, in that pedantic grammar book way that betrayed his foreignness. "They are very much better tonight. I have been to see them. Do not worry."

I jetted a stream of cigarette smoke at the ceiling, watched it streak upwards then dissipate and begin to roll as it lost momentum in the hot, steamy air. I liked Frank Barber, but his bland professionalism always irritated me. He wore his bedside manner like a second skin.

"Frank," I said carefully. "They are all right on the surface. They're sick as hell beneath."

"I am going to admit them to hospital for investigation," he said, his voice as cold as evaporated ether on the skin. "I, too, know they are not well."

I rubbed my cigarette out, dusted ash from my fingertips and took a deep, deep breath. "Frank. I'm not trying to tell you your business."

"Of course not, Wade. I understand. You are worried."

His voice was warmer, but still cool around the edges. I had to take him gently. "Frank, can I come down tonight and talk with you?"

"I have a great deal of work tonight," he said. "I am sorry. But perhaps you would like to come tomorrow . . . in the afternoon maybe?"

"All right," I said. That's fine."

"Good night, Wade."

"Good night."

I could have thrown the phone across the room. And don't tell me it wouldn't have done me any good. I knew that even tomorrow afternoon I was going to have a struggle to persuade Frank Barber that Lucy's illegitimacy was the sum of the Austins' trouble. He had his theory of a physical disorder, and would staunchly defend it against all suggestions from a layman. As I have said before, if Frank Barber had a fault it was that he took his position as a medico too seriously. And right then I began to wonder, did I like him for himself, or for what he had achieved? It wasn't easy in Australia for an immigrant doctor to buck the home-grown doctors' union. Or perhaps I liked him because of Mary and because a blonde named Poldi lived with them. I'm damned if I could tell. And maybe I would have thrown that phone, only Harry Wells poked his head around the door.

"I'm goin' home," he said.

I gave him the hard look because he was the only one around to whom I could hand it out. "What about your grudge?"

"That can keep," he grunted. "There's plenty of other things."

"Ah, go home to your wife," I threw my matchbox at him. "Hope she confiscates your liquor."

Harry grinned. "Se yu in th' mornin', son. An' don't forget to go and see young Poldi goin' through the hoops."

Good God! The naturalization ceremony. I had forgotten clean about it. I shaved and showered, put on a suit, and made it just in time. The welcome Poldi gave me, as I slipped in, far more than compensated for the famine in my stomach. She was standing, with the others, on a platform, each with a Bible, following Mayor Hazelgrove through the oath of citizenship. She didn't smile, or nod her head, or motion with a hand. She did nothing overt, nothing probably that anyone else in the hall could have seen. But she welcomed me. I felt it, warm and clean and strong. She looked up from her Bible and touched me with her eyes. I was more grateful in that moment to Harry Wells than I had ever been.

Next morning there was no sun. The sky was covered with a low, thick blanket of cloud. The heat came through it like something gone wrong with a Turkish bath. The harbour, seen from my window, had that grey-blue leaden look, giving the impression of a diorama in some war museum. All the colour of the town was muted. The roofs were just a little dirty, the trees too dark, the dry grass on the hill across the Clay was wet yellow, dull, instead of bright. Even the electric fence was subdued. A jet roar from the airfield spread deafeningly beneath the cloud, and when the aircraft hurtled seaward it seemed as though there was no buoyancy to help it fly.

I shaved and took a cold shower. It made me feel alive. But by the time I had got through iced grapefruit, toast, a boiled egg and reached for coffee, the stickiness was back. My shirt clung to my body when I moved. It was half-past eight, thirty minutes before Colonel Tucker was due to arrive. That's when I would really start to sweat.

Tucker, in defence of Clark, would not be easy going. I had nothing new, no positive evidence, to support my request for banishment. He was keeping company with Lucy Austin. So what? He was visiting the house to see her. Again so what? The old ladies nursed a guilty secret that tortured them, and Clark was privy to it. Again, and yet again, so what? So he would marry Lucy and become rich when she inherited the Austin money? For that too, so what? He broke no laws, apart from those that God laid down. And temporal authority had no truck with them.

And yet I knew, with a dreadful certainty, that Clark was at the very epicentre of the sisters' trouble. I was sure that he was pushing it along, probing it, exacerbating it, sadistically enjoying his power, as he had with me. I had to make Tucker see that. I had lost my former bargaining ploy of threatened publicity, so it would mean close reasoning, an appeal to his humanity. There was just a chance that I could make him understand.

A car stopped outside. It was nine o'clock. Colonel Tucker was on the dot, E.T.A., 0900 hours, rendezvous *Herald* office. I went into the office to meet him, stood there in the middle of the room, shuffling my points quickly into order. Then the outer door opened and Frank Barber walked in.

"Sit down," he said quietly. "I have to tell you something. It is very bad."

His face was so solemn it was almost lifeless. I felt the noise of something hitting the floor. It was my guts, or the fear that dropped through them. Whatever it was, I was left empty.

"Frank. What is it?"

"Sit down." He took me by an arm, firmly, and led me to the visitor's chair just by my desk. He leaned against the desk, arms folded, chin buried on his chest. His eyes assessed me, roving like a stethoscope. "Wade," he said. "Your aunts are dead."

I stared into his light-blue eyes, and the brown rings about the irises grew larger and larger until they seemed to leave the eyes and encircle his entire face.

"Their bodies were found in the bay early this morning. By the new wharf."

"Yes, of course," I said. "The current sweeps up that way."

It was a terrible, inconsequential thing to say. I heard my voice pronouncing it, and it brought me to my senses. I clamped down hard, imposing discipline, mastering the shock that had momentarily bowled me over.

"Tell me what you know," I said. "Everything."

Frank offered me a cigarette, bending forward without vacating his perch on the desk's edge. I waved it away. I didn't want any drugs to soothe me.

"Everything points to suicide," he said slowly. "It seems that they threw themselves into the River Clay at the bottom of their garden."

"You told me they were both better last night," I said bleakly.

Frank spread his white hands, palms uppermost, in the gesture of Francis Barbasiewicz that came out so often in his moments of emotional stress. "They were calm because they had made up their minds to end their lives." He dropped his hands. "I did not realize it then. I am sorry, Wade. I am deeply sorry."

A blind and hopeless anger began to rise in me. I sat stiffly upright in my chair, clutching the arm rests, wanting to shout accusations at him for refusing to see me when I could have told him what was wrong. . . . But he had been too busy. . . . Too busy doing what? What could have been more important than two peoples' lives? Then, just in time, reason took hold of me. What I had had to tell him could not have altered anything. It would have been too late. And memory came to shout accusations at my own head. I, too, had failed to realize their intention. They had said good-bye to me, kissed me good-bye, and I had been too busy sniffing out their secret to recognize the stench of death. A voice began spitting one name in my mind, like a machine gun in an ambush . . . Clark, Clark, Clark . . . rat-a-tat-tat . . . Clark, Clark, Clark . . .

"The police are at the house questioning Lucy," Frank said quietly. "They want to see you, Wade."

I stared without seeing him. "I'll get my car."

"No, come with me," he said. "They want to see me, also."

A small knot of people stood gawping at the Austins' gate, the righteous matrons of Clayville shopping for morbid thrills. I saw them only as blurred faces and amorphous figures. I didn't have to look to know them. I'd seen them all before . . . in Saigon enjoying the bloody scraps lying around a bombed café, in New York around the pulped bundle of a high building suicide, and at Beit Jirja, in southern Israel, after Arab commandos had struck and left twenty men castrated and with their genitals sewn into their mouths. . . . People. The human kind.

Sergeant Bert Thompson was in the schoolroom, big, red-faced, and certain with that pompous sort of majesty possessed by police sergeants on duty. A young constable sat at the desk with notebook and pencil. Lucy was slumped in an easy chair they had dragged in from another room. She looked up as Frank and I came in, face haggard, but eyes bitterly defiant. I stared through and past her. I hated her so much I couldn't trust myself to speak. I looked around for Clark, but of course he wasn't there. It was probably just as well, because I would never have been able to keep my hands away from his throat.

"This is a bad business, Wade," Bert Thompson said.

He offered his great ham fist. His gesture was assured, but there was a flicker of discomfort in his eyes. He was embarrassed at having to offer sympathy after what had passed between us. I took his hand, but with no enthusiasm. His sympathy was conventional with death. It had nothing to do with me.

"Yes, a bad business," I agreed, echoing his triteness because it meant I was giving nothing away.

"D'you know any reason why they should've drowned themselves?"

The only answer to that was the one I couldn't give. I slanted a glance at Lucy and she was watching me, challenging me, mocking me because she knew my lips were sealed. Tell Thompson the Austins' secret and it would be repeated in the

Coroner's Court to become the property of the whole town. There was nothing I could say.

"D'you know any reason?" Bert Thompson said again, and I saw his eyes rest thoughtfully on Lucy.

"They've been sick," I said.

He switched his eyes back to me. "Nervous trouble. That right, doctor?"

"Broadly speaking," Frank said. "But I had thought they were recovering."

"What caused their nervous trouble, Wade?"

"I don't know."

"You don't seem very surprised at their deaths."

Frank Barber interposed. "He is still shocked, Sergeant. You cannot base any conclusions on his reactions at this stage."

Bert Thompson turned slowly, hitching his bullock shoulders, displaying the sergeant's chevrons on his sleeve. "I'm asking Mr. Scotter some questions, doctor," he said heavily. "I want him to answer. Not you."

I sat down on one of the children's stools that stood around the room. It was only then that I recognized the dreadful emptiness of the place. Children's furniture always creates emptiness when adults are standing and sitting among it, making it seem like driftwood. Perhaps because it is always paint-chipped, bent, or sawn or cut or scribbled on. I stretched my long legs out and looked between them at the scrubbed and worn floor. Footprints were there for me to see, footprints in my mind, and for a moment I was almost overcome by the thought of two old women watching rabbits that were not there, resolved to kill themselves rather than face the scandal that they had buried, and that had been dug up again. I could hear, in fierce imagination, the sneers, the hateful innuendos, the threats that Clark must have plied them with. . . . "And wanting me," Lucy had said, "he has helped to punish them." My bitter hate for him was mixed with tenderness for his victims. I felt as though hate and compassion were pulling me apart, stretching my nerves to breaking point. . . .

"Where are they, Bert?" My voice was a whisper.

"Upstairs."

He had moved, was sitting beside the desk, near his young shorthand writer. He leaned slightly forward, hands on his knees to support his torso's weight. "One of you, you or Lucy, must have some idea what went wrong."

I didn't move, not even to look at Lucy. Bert Thompson's eyes, hard now, travelled from me to her and back again. He anchored them on me.

"No one suicides without a reason."

"You're certain it was suicide," I said.

"You've got something else in mind?"

His voice had hardened, like his eyes, and there was no longer any sign of sympathy. He had sensed the conflict between Lucy and I, if he had not already picked it up from town gossip. He knew we were both withholding something.

"It could have been an accident," I said evenly. "They often walked by the river in the evenings. One could have slipped in, and the other tried to save her."

Frank Barber nodded in agreement. He was standing by the window, leaning against it, and the moroseness on his face lifted slightly, as though my suggestion had relieved his mind. They were his patients and he had pronounced them out of danger. It was only natural that he should embrace my proffered out.

"That could have been so," he said, almost eagerly. He stood away from the window and his fingers were plucking at each other with nervous uncertainty. "Many people have been drowned in just such a way. One slips and—"

"Only it didn't happen that way," Bert Thompson snapped. "There'd be marks on the bank where they'd slipped in. There's none." He paused and looked at each one of us in turn, slowly, and with a sort of ponderous satisfaction. "But there's scratch marks on the old dead tree that overhangs the river. Marks two people would make crawling out on it and dropping off. There's even a piece of cloth torn from Miss Belle's dress— stuck on a broken spur."

Frank lifted his pale hands and let them drop slackly to his sides. I looked at Lucy and she was lighting a cigarette with an absorption that proclaimed all this was none of her affair. I wanted to leap across the room and slap her into tears. I balanced on the point of doing it for a long moment, then gradually drew back. For all her hatefulness, she was nothing but a pawn. Clark was my man, my target. William Clark, the guardian of the public's conscience, the bloodhound with its nostrils in a filthy rag. I heard Bert Thompson's chair scrape back. He stood in front of me, looming like a mountain of blue serge, spotted with silver buttons, wrapped in all the impeccable authority of the law.

"You got nothing to suggest? I'm askin' you for the last time, Scotter."

"Nothing," I said.

"It'd pay you to level," he said warningly. "You've gotta name that's not so clean."

I stared at him. "Thanks."

He turned away. "Lucy?"

She shook her head.

"All right," he said harshly. "You'll both appear in the Coroner's court. Tomorrow. Three o'clock."

I was right back where Clark had put me, on Bert Thompson's blackguard list. And I think he was almost glad. His thick face looked at ease for the first time since I had arrived. I had resolved his problem of equating the convention of sympathy for an old, though cast-off friend, with the necessity of disliking a subversive. Dislike, disapproval, hatred, were simple emotions that a man like Bert could handle without perplexity. They probably even gave him a warm feeling of virtue, of being so unmistakably on the right side of the fence. There were a lot of folk like Bert, I knew. I didn't blame him any more. I didn't even care about him. Poldi was right. It didn't pay to care about such things.

"May I go up and see them?"

"Help yourself," he said brutally. "Don't touch anything."

They were lying together on one bed, faces upturned, and arms crossed over their chests. Some people say they see serenity on the faces of the dead, the imprint of a call to higher things. I saw nothing. Nothing but death, the emptiness of bodies from which life had gone, and the pitiful dripping of their clothes. Someone had disposed them neatly. They lay as they had sat in those high-backed chairs before the window, stiff and angular, orderly and arranged. Their buttoned boots stuck out from beneath their sodden dresses. Those fantastic, fruited hats were resting on their stomachs. It was sight of them that finally unlocked my tears. I cried like I have seen soldiers cry, fiercely, making of the occasion a solemn promise of revenge.

Frank Barber was waiting downstairs. He took me by the arm. "Come home with me. You will need to take a rest."

I put his hand away. "Later," I said. "There are some things I've got to do."

We drove back down Main Street and I noticed the day's heat once more. The bitumen strip was tacky with it and the tires were making sharp slapping noises. My clothes were moist, lying against my skin, tugging a little every time I moved my legs or arms. The big red and pink hibiscus flowers in house gardens were unfurled and drooping. They needed brightness, not this sapping heat. Shadows under the high, thin-pillared shop verandas were little more than a deeper grey than the street they looked out on. Few people moved, and they slowly. But I knew the good citizens of Clayville, in front bars, in shops and private homes, would be pouring out their energies in minute discussion.

"I think you should take a sedative," Frank said. "Just something mild. Enough to settle the nervous tension I can see in your hands."

I glanced down quickly. My hands were clasped over one knee, white with pressure and curved like talons. I unclasped them. "No, Frank, but thanks. You're being very kind."

I looked out my window and could see the great arch of the new Clay bridge. The stutter of rivet guns, distorted in that soggy air, sounded like small-arms' fire. No pause there for gossip about the Austin sisters. No pause, either, in the guarded buildings beyond the hill. Apart, I thought, from one man who must surely be thinking of what his sadistic bullying had wrought. And this time I knew my hands had clenched. I pressed them tightly together in an effort to stop their shaking. I saw Frank throw a downward glance, but made no attempt to hide them. The anger that was shaking me had taken me beyond caring. I was utterly possessed.

Then we had turned around and braked in front of the *Herald*. The sight of familiar things, the shapes of doors and windows, the faded lettering of the façade, seemed to sober me. Or maybe I was still drunk with rage, but the *Herald* reminded me of work and shored me up, restoring my faculties by the mechanism of habit.

"Thanks, Frank." I climbed out of the car. I reached for and took his hand. His eyes waited for me to speak. "Don't blame yourself," I said. "You weren't to know. They had made up their minds. There was nothing anyone could do."

He shrugged, canting his shoulders, turning his body slightly in the confined space behind the driving wheel. His eyes, magnified by their glasses, were large and a gleam of curiosity showed deep below the surface. His pale face was impassive.

"Tell me, Wade." He let go my hand. "Tell me, have you really any idea why they did it?"

"No." The lie came naturally; the thought behind it followed. It was not his business any longer. They were not his patients now.

"Sergeant Thompson seemed certain that you knew."

"Sergeant Thompson is a bloody fool."

Frank nodded gravely, swung himself back behind the wheel. He pushed in his clutch and made first gear. Then he paused, as though in thought. "I wonder why they did it?" he murmured, not so much saying it as thinking it aloud. "As Sergeant Thompson said: 'No one commits suicide without a reason.'"

"I'll tell you why." I was suddenly irked by his persistence, although God only knows he'd have been a strange man not to have wondered about such a thing. "They did it because, somehow, they must have realized for the first time what a screaming, howling mess the world is in, and didn't want a part of it."

Then I turned abruptly, not wanting to debate the point, not wanting to be offered a sedative again, not wanting to do anything but shut a door behind me. There's a lot of comfort in the shutting of a solid door. I shut mine, locked it and took the phone off the hook. It was just after eleven, and there were two columns open on the front page, held in the hope of a better local story than the South American revolution of several weeks, or maybe months, before.

I slid some paper into my typewriter. The better local story had broken in my time. Sometimes the mechanics, and the morals, and the terminology of newspapers, make me want to throw up. A front-page local story. I began to tap it out.

"Two well-known Clayville spinster sisters kept a suicide pact last night . . ."

I wrote it right through to the bitter dregs.

18

POLDI TOOK A CIGARETTE FROM THE PACK LYING ON MY DESK, and lit it. She put her hands on the desk and leaned towards me. Her face was tense, not so much with impatience as with concern, but there was a touch of impatience below the surface. It showed in a slight furrowing of her forehead. The concern was in the wonderful, blue swimming depths of her eyes.

"And what will you achieve by hitting William Clark?" she demanded. "It will not help your aunts. It will not even help you in any permanent way."

I looked up at her without appreciation. I was tired from the emotional drainings of the day, and the clammy heat that even then, after six o'clock, was still oppressive. But the thought of Clark was a thorn, a burr, a festering sore that wouldn't leave my tiredness alone. Our old flatbed press was clanking dismally in the composing room next door. The *Herald* was going to press, with its front-page lead inside a black border, and I was free to attend to William Clark. I wanted to sink my hands into him, to tear at him, to hurt him physically in any way I could. I wanted to hear him bellow in pain. I wanted him to know fear, in the way Clara and Belle Austin must have known it when they had thrown themselves into the cold darkness of the river.

"You're wrong," I said at last. "It would help to beat Clark into pulp. Whether it'd be permanent, I don't care. I want it for now."

"You are tired," she said firmly. "You are not thinking in a straight line."

"I don't need to think about this."

"Everyone needs to think."

"When it's time to act the only excuse for thinking is indecision." I spoke brusquely, trying to cut off her argument. "My mind is quite made up. There's nothing left to think about."

Poldi watched me carefully for a space of seconds that seemed like minutes. She had a hard-to-describe expression in her eyes, as though she were weighing my determination against her own. Then she moved smoothly around the desk towards me. She was dressed in a dark blouse and black skirt. Her face was rather pale, possibly in contrast with the clothes, or maybe because she was worried. She stood close beside me, touching my shoulder with her soft, flat stomach. She slid one smooth, bare arm around my neck and pressed my head against her.

"Wade, darling," she said softly. "I do not want you to fight William Clark. I am afraid. He is so much bigger than you, and he is a fighter. If you attack him he will beat you cruelly."

"He's a bully," I said harshly. "Bullies don't fight worth a damn when cornered."

I spoke harshly because I knew well enough that Clark would deal out brutal punishment before I got him. But I was quite sure I would get him in the end. Even the most cynical of men and nations believe that right will triumph any time they've got it on their side.

"I am afraid," she said. "When fighting starts one never can tell how it will finish. Men sometimes are killed."

"I don't intend to kill him, or be killed.'"

She whispered. "I am still afraid."

"Listen, Poldi," I said flatly. "I owe this to myself . . . to my self-respect if you like. It's something I have to do."

She took away her arm and moved around me, back to the other side of the desk. "Remember you made a promise to Colonel Tucker. You said you would leave William Clark alone."

"He made a promise to me, too," I snapped. "And broke it. He was going to call Clark off."

"Speak to him again." Her voice was stressed. Her eyes implored me. "I also want to see William Clark punished. But I would want it done legally."

"Tucker won't do anything," I said stubbornly. "He came my way the other day because I threatened him with publicity. I can't threaten him any more."

"Tell him the whole story just as you have told me. About Thomas Moody, and Lucy . . . about William Clark and Lucy . . . how she boasted that Clark was making the Austins suffer—"

"And he'll excuse it all on the sacred grounds of duty," I said stonily. "I've been through that before."

She threw up her hands in a gesture of despair. "People had not died before. This time he will have to listen to you, Wade. It is the only way. If you fight William Clark you will only make trouble for yourself."

I pushed back in my ancient swivel chair. Now she had come to the very basis of her opposition. I should have guessed it before, but my mind was working in only one direction. "You don't want me to fight Clark because he represents authority?"

She folded her arms, and looked down at me with grave severity. "You will get into trouble, and achieve nothing. What punishment can you deal out with your fists that will hurt as William Clark has hurt? In a few hours he would be all right again, and you would be in prison." She shook her head slowly, from side to side. "Only Colonel Tucker has the power to hurt William Clark. You can only hurt yourself."

I thought that over, looking at it from all angles and always seeing it the same. I had to think about it because there was something in her face, a waiting, an unhappiness, that pierced me like a knife. She was too beautiful, not merely physically, but deeply beautiful, for me to plough on heedlessly. She was a part of me, and in the first bitterness of anger my senses had failed to remind me of it. And I felt then, as I suppose many men have felt before me and will do so after me, that she had to be right because nothing else really mattered.

"All right," I said. "I'll ring Tucker."

She smiled slightly with her lips, eyes grave, and pushed the phone across at me. But Tucker wasn't in. I asked for Clark, and he was out, too. I asked the switchboard girl if anyone was in and she told me, primly, "Personal information may not be given over the telephone." Then she cut me off.

"That leaves the other way," I said, putting up the phone, deliberately, like a man putting away a book before picking up a sword. "I'm going to find Clark, wherever he is, if I have to wait a year for him to come out from behind that electric fence. I'm going to hit him and keep on hitting him until he breaks down. Then I'm going to drag him before Colonel Godalmighty Tucker and make him tell how he hounded two old women to their deaths in the sacred name of security."

"You will not be swerved?"

I shook my head. "I must do it. He must be punished. He must be stopped."

"Very well," Poldi said crisply. "I will help you find him. At least you will take him to Colonel Tucker."

The sudden switch in her intentions left me floundering. I think my mouth was hanging open. It felt open, anyway.

"William Clark will not want to see you," she said. "But he will want to see Lucy because he hopes to marry her. Particularly does he hope to marry her now that her mother and her aunt are dead, and she will inherit a large fortune."

"So I watch Lucy."

"No," she said calmly. "There is a better way. I have many

friends among the immigrant workers. I will organize a chain of informants. The men on the bridge will watch for William Clark. Others, off duty, will follow him. He will not suspect them. Others again will keep watch on Lucy Austin, because she might meet Clark away from the house. They will telephone reports to you here when William Clark begins to move."

"I sit here and play spider?"

She wrinkled her brows for a moment. Sometimes idiom and allusion tricked her, but rarely for more than a moment. "A big, hairy one," she said. "You need a shave."

I rubbed a hand across my chin. It was scrubby, and yet I had shaved as usual that morning. I wondered if it were more sensory than actual, a reflection of my whole mental and physical condition. Everything was scrubby and on edge.

"When does the watching system start?" I asked. "Tonight?"

She stood away, the first move of departure. "I will go to see them now, before I return home."

"Good." I stood up. "Who will they be? Do I know them?"

"No names," she said quietly, and shook her head. "If there is any trouble it would be better that you do not know their names. It is a lot to ask of these people to spy on a security official."

"All right," I said. "No names."

She turned for the door and I followed. Her shoulders were very square and her head well back. There was a slight stiffness about her that I wanted to dispel. I thought to put my hands on her shoulders, turn her around and explain just why I had to do this thing. But what could I explain that I had not explained already? I did nothing. At the door she stopped, one foot in the dusk, and looked up into my face.

"You will not change your mind? You will not let the police, or the Security officials, find out for themselves and punish William Clark?"

"They won't find out," I said harshly. "And if they did,

they'd shield him. He's a protected bird, with the whole country for his sanctuary."

She went then without another word, with scarcely another look. Her only reaction was a slight tightening of soft lips. I watched until she was swallowed in the dusk. And it was only when she had disappeared that I remembered I hadn't even thanked her. She had set aside all her convictions to help me, and I had been too obsessed to be grateful. I went back into the office, wretched, and suddenly deflated. I rubbed a hand across my chin and I swear the beard had grown at least two inches.

Harry Wells said: "Any man who thinks a woman changes her mind for the fun of it, will wind up with the arse out of his pants."

He was lounging in the composing-room door, thumbs in his braces, and cynicism in every line of his cobwebbed face.

"Mind your own damned business," I snapped. "And stop listening-in to my conversations."

"You'd fall for the three-card trick," he said blandly. "I'll bet a week's pay her watchers don't see Clark. An' fer why? Because she don't want you to find him."

19

THERE WERE NO PHONE CALLS THAT NIGHT. NONE THE NEXT day. And just before three in the afternoon, when it was time to go down to the Town Hall for the Coroner's inquest, I had to ask Harry to sit by the phone for me. Friday was his easy day. The *Herald* was out for the week, and all he had to do was set up a few stock advertisements for the next edition. I left him sitting in my chair, slippered feet up on my desk, and a steaming fresh teapot at his right hand.

"Rest easy," he said. "There won't be no calls."

"Dip your eye," I said.

"Don't get me wrong," he smirked. "I don't *like* bein' right all the time."

It was stinking hot in the street. It had been hot enough inside, but outside it was about as bad as a day could be. A heavy overcast was keeping the heat down close to the earth, and the windless air was so heavy with moisture that you felt as though you were wading through it, instead of walking. There was a big bank of black cloud on the seaward horizon, and every now and then it gave out a belly rumble. But there was more threat in it than promise of relief.

Main Street was crowded, for Friday was market day. The farm and sheep-station families of the district were in on their weekly buying raids. The housewives of Clayville were stocking their larders for the week end. Cars crammed the pavements outside the stores; others cruised slowly about, putting in here and there, like dogs following a scent. And everywhere, among the cars, on the open pavements, beneath verandas and in the darker caves of shops, were ragged groups of gossipers. They always gossiped on market day, but this Friday they surpassed themselves. They had a tragedy, a topic for inexhaustible conjecture.

I stopped, appalled at the prospect of having to run the gauntlet of their questions and demands, went back behind the office and got out my car. I tooled it carefully along the tacky bitumen to the Town Hall, not looking anywhere but straight ahead. But from the corners of my eyes I could see the faces turning to watch me. The car, the people, myself, and all Main Street could have been turning on the one-geared wheel.

The inquest was over quickly. Lucy knew nothing, and neither did I. Frank Barber gave evidence of nervous tension, and Sergeant Bert Thompson made a report of his investigations, punctuated by glowering looks at me. William Clark was not in the hall, nor was he mentioned by name, which reduced the whole proceedings to something below the level of a farce. Mayor Hazelgrove, who was also Clayville's coroner, returned the stock verdict of "Suicide while of unsound mind," and declared proceedings closed. As far as he was concerned, they were. The events about to burst were far beyond his scope.

Back in the office, Harry said, "Two calls. You spelt Thelma Daly's cat's name wrong in that pet show report. Tom Colquhoun reckons your gardening notes are punk . . . . you don't put pig manure on asters. It's too strong."

I frowned. I wasn't feeling funny. "Nothing else?"

"What more d'you want? A libel?"

I dropped into the easy chair. "Nothing on Clark?"

"Christ, no," Harry said disgustedly. "I told you. Poldi don't want to see you in trouble with the cops. She's betting you'll give in if she can hold you up for a few days."

"She offered to help," I said. "And I believe her."

Harry spat hard, and accurately, into the wastepaper basket. "Grow up, son," he growled. "Time you knew about women. They don't play our rules. They got their own."

"Meaning she'd lie to me?"

Even though I was used to Harry, I couldn't keep the stiffness out of my voice. He heard it, and his leathery old face wrinkled up with puckish joy. He shifted his false teeth with his tongue, and grinned at me.

"Depends on whose rules you're playin', son." He ran a skinny hand over the top of his head, rubbing his ragged hair into fresh disorder. "Lissen, son. I've been watchin' women all m'life. The last ten years I been watchin' 'em without the urge. And it's these last ten years I been seein' how they work. Yu don't see it when you've got the urge. Yu don't want to, then."

"Harry," I said. "I've just come from an inquest. I'm tired. I don't want to argue."

"They say anything?"

"No," I said. "Suicide while of unsound mind."

Harry got up and slopped around the room, hands in his braces, small head thrust forward on his skinny neck, and his face drawn down. He stared out the window for a while, then came back slowly towards me, like a man with his mind all set.

"Lissen, son. You've gotta lissen to me. I know everything that's happened."

"You surprise me," I said. "Didn't think you'd stoop to eaves-drop."

He stood in front of me, looking down, his pale-blue eyes direct, and harder than I had ever known them. "I liked the Austin sisters. They've been good to me and mine. I hate that bastard Clark an' I want to see him slapped down fer what he's done."

"I'll get him," I said tersely.

"Yeah, I know," he said. "But look at it this way. Why bring Poldi into it? If somethin' goes wrong, she'll be in trouble. Why'nt yu do it on your own?"

"Tell me."

"He won't come out until dark," Harry said. "That's fer sure. You park your car near the Austin's, and watch Lucy. I'll hang around near the bridge and follow Clark. That way, one of us is sure to catch up with 'em if they've got a meet on."

I mopped sweat off my face and thought about it. And the more I thought the better it became. Harry's plan was simple, it was workable, and it would keep Poldi and her friends from possibly blotting their copy books with Security. Just the same, I had a feeling that Harry had got at me.

"You've got your own rules, too," I said ironically.

He grinned crookedly. "What you beefin' about? I don't say she's deceiving you. I'm just puttin' up a better idea. It'll work as good as her's, and she'll keep her nose clean."

I grinned back at him. The first time, I think, that I'd grinned all day and meant it. "All right," I said. "We'll do it your way. You cut off home now and get some sleep. Likely you'll be up all night."

"Sleep!" he snorted. "What d'you think I am? A bloody baby?"

We filled in time the rest of that afternoon. Harry set up some ads, and drank gallons of hot tea. I listened to Julius Katchen showing how good the Diabelli variations can sound, and drank a slow, slow whisky. I didn't really enjoy either of them. The Austin sisters whispered to me through the music —they loved Beethoven—and the whisky, taken slowly and but once, kept reminding me I was in training for something for which I wasn't built.

Clark was big, and though packing too much flesh, he was strong as a bull. He would be able to fight, too. You could see that in the way he moved, the way he held himself, the way he looked you in the eye and invited you to speak out of turn.

I was perhaps a fraction of an inch taller, but thin, and trained to punch a typewriter. The only fighting I had ever done was a couple of times at school, and on both occasions I had lost. But I had been fighting without purpose then. Now I had one, and it gave me confidence. I was pinning my faith on getting in the first hit followed, if possible, by a knee in his groin. I knew it would be dirty fighting, but it didn't worry me. Clark was a dirty man.

Harry and I had supper together in my kitchen, eating it straight from the refrigerator. Dusk had dropped softly around us, but we didn't use the lights. We were both feeling tense. The air was charged, too. The thunder that had been on the horizon all day had moved in close, and though it still did little more than grumble, you could feel it building up. Once, when I flicked a dry tea towel near my arm, the hairs stood up. Huge drops of rain thudded on the roof at intervals, sometimes singly, sometimes with a quick drumming rush that stopped almost the instant it began.

"Better ring Poldi before we go," Harry said. "Else she might ring here and find we've gone."

I threw down a pint of milk, lit a cigarette and went into my office to the phone.

"Don't tell her anything," Harry called. "Just not to ring up because yu want the line clear."

Her voice was warm and she was sorry she couldn't sit with me because she was still working on Frank Barber's books. Some women look wonderful, but sound lousy on the phone. Others sound wonderful on the phone, but look like bags. Poldi was none of these. She was wonderful all ways. I got an empty feeling just talking with her. I got a guilty feeling, too. I couldn't kid myself any longer that I had adopted Harry's plan purely to keep her free of implication.

"Poldi," I said quietly. "Have you got your people out?"

"Everything is arranged," she said.

I lowered my voice so Harry wouldn't hear. "You can call

them off. I don't need them. Harry's thought up a better plan."

A hushed silence, then she said, "Oh, Wade." And I knew from the sound that Harry had been right the first time.

"There's no one watching, is there?" I said.

"Wade," she whispered. "I love you. I do not want you hurt any more."

I looked across the darkened office to her desk, and I could see her there, twisting in her chair towards me smiling gently, and I remembered the look and the feel of her that day at Blowhole Cove.

"Darling," I said. "Stop worrying. I've got Harry Wells to help me. He's a terrific fighter."

"I do not mean that sort of hurt," she said, and her voice went suddenly off-key.

I touched the mouthpiece with my lips. "I know."

Harry was ready and impatient to go, so I didn't tell him anything about my conversation with Poldi. He would only have said, "I told you so." I wasn't in the mood for his cynicism. I switched on the office light as we left. Then I went back and lit up the toilet, thinking it might explain the empty office to a casual check. The big raindrops were still splashing down outside. The air was very still, like breath withheld. If thunder split those clouds the water was going to come down solid. It was no sort of night to be outdoors.

"I'll be at the end of their driveway, in the bushes, if you want me," I told Harry. "Walk on the edge of the driveway. There's no gravel."

I drove Harry home to get his rattlebang old car, then steered myself around back streets to the Austin place. The Main Street shops stayed open until nine o'clock on market days. I didn't want all Clayville to see me taking up position. I left the car in a side street running to the river, close in to the footpath and in a patch of shadow just out of streetlight range. I climbed the Austins' side fence and sneaked through the bushes to my watching post.

There were two lights in the house. Both of them in Lucy's rooms on the ground floor. She had a bedroom and lounge there, just off the schoolroom. I watched for an hour without seeing anything, and was just beginning to wonder if she could have used my trick of leaving lights on for the benefit of snoopers, when she moved in silhouette across the curtained window of the lounge. I nodded to myself, grimly satisfied to know the decoy was in position, changed rumps and settled down for as long a wait as William Clark imposed. A flash of lightning lit up the house, etching two black and silent windows on the upper floor. They looked out on the garden like sightless eyes. Someone had hung them with black drapes. Poor Clara . . . . Poor Belle . . . A lump came in my throat.

Then sentiment was struck aside, shattered by a blast of thunder. Instinctively I hugged the ground, feeling as though the breath had been driven from my body. Then the rain came. Or perhaps, more accurately, the water. It was too heavy for rain. The clouds must have split from top to bottom. At one moment I was dry. The next I was sodden, and Lucy's windows were a yellow blur on the far side of an aquarium tank.

It lasted twenty minutes, then stopped as suddenly as it had begun. The sound of running water was everywhere. The leaves above me rained droplets heavier than many a winter's shower. I was kneeling in mud and I stayed right where I was. There was nowhere else to go. Forked lightning stabbed the sky, and thunder cracked and grumbled close at hand. This was in the pattern of our summer storms, and I knew there was more to follow. I didn't like being in trees with forked lightning about, but I needed their concealment. I had to take the risk. At least it was not cold.

Another half-hour of waiting and my moulded shirt and pants were beginning to dry out a little, unsticking from my body. I wanted a cigarette. Lucy was walking about a lot, passing from room to room. I hoped, savagely, that she was frightened. But her movements suggested, rather, that she was packing. I toyed with the idea of sneaking up for a closer look, but put the thought away. It didn't matter where, or when, she went, so long as she gave me Clark.

I had settled down again when I heard the squelch of footsteps down the drive, coming down the side where the gravel had been pushed away. The footsteps of a man in a hurry, and not caring greatly about his noise. I rose quickly to my feet, tense with a sudden, fierce animal elation. It could be Clark, and I knew what I was going to do. I was going to step out of the trees, call his name once and then hit him with everything I'd got. It was my only chance. The footsteps were on me then, and I could make out the dim figure of a man. I started to move and he stopped.

"Wade," he hissed. "Wade. It's me. Harry."

I heard him, but my fists would not unclench. I stood unanswering for a moment. Then my mind engaged. "Here. Just ahead of you."

"I got Clark for yu," he panted. "Gone in Frank Barber's place. Back gate."

I grabbed his arm. "You're sure?"

"Course I'm sure," he snapped.

"Good man." I punched him on the shoulder with a short, exultant right. "Harry. Here's what we do. You stay here and keep an eye on Lucy. I'll go and nail Clark."

I turned to go, but Harry stopped me. "There's somethin' screwy—"

"Some other time," I rapped. "Clark's all I want right now."

"He'll keep," Harry said grimly. "Don't worry about him gettin' back inside the fence too soon. I pulled up half a dozen planks in the pontoon bridge . . . chucked 'em in the river."

I stared at him through the darkness, and laughter jumped up inside of me. Shades of the partisans. "You old villain. Tell me what's so screwy."

"First, goin' to Frank Barber's place instead of here."

"That's not so odd," I said. "Probably guessed I'd be watching, and gone there to ring Lucy."

"Don't kid yourself," Harry said. "Since when's Clark been scared of you?"

That jolted me. "It's different now," I said, defensively. "He's in the wrong."

"All right," Harry said. "But here's somethin' else . . . somethin' real screwy. I snuck up that side lane and watched him go right in. Y'know what happened? He musta knocked or called out real soft. I couldn't hear. Then the lights went out, an' when they come on again, Clark was inside."

I took a good, long look at that, turning it over in my mind. Harry was right about it. It was screwy.

"Maybe the bastard's got somethin' on the doc," Harry said. "Or he's got the pox, and gettin' treatment on the quiet."

"The former, I'm afraid."

I was too preoccupied to grin. I was remembering that other day when I had taken a beer with Frank Barber, in his kitchen, and Mary had talked about democracy and been hushed to silence. Clark had cropped up in my mind then to explain their consternation. Now I was certain of it. He had them on his list.

"Okay, Harry," I said at last. "You watch Lucy. I'll sniff around the Barbers' and nab Clark on his way out."

I went up the driveway at a run. Noise didn't matter any more. I walked across Main Street, looking neither right nor left, and then sprinted up the dirt lane that ran alongside Frank's place. It wasn't lighted, but that didn't slow me. I knew every inch of it.

There were some loose palings on the fence. I found them, pushed them quietly aside, and slipped into the bottom of the garden. There were lights all over the house, but no noise. It was like a silent party. I edged forward, up behind a clump of tall sunflowers, to the sitting-room window. I had seen a chink of light coming from one corner of the drawn blind, but all it afforded was a view of a blank wall and a slice of ceiling. There was another window on the other side, so I decided to try it for better luck.

I was just stepping back when I heard a noise behind me. I wheeled, but not quickly enough. Something hard jabbed into my ribs and stayed there. A gun. I stopped my wheel and a harsh voice said: "All right, pussyfoot. Suppose you join the party."

I didn't know who it was, couldn't even guess, but you don't argue with a gun. Certainly not when it's backed up by a voice like gravel and an arm strong enough to push it halfway through your body. I went in the kitchen door with the gun's snout on my spine, marched up the hall and into the sitting room. The gun was withdrawn and the door closed behind me. I didn't catch so much as a glimpse of the man who had brought me in. But I knew what he was, instantly, from the people in the room.

Colonel Tucker sat to attention at the big round table. The extension phone stood in front of him, and he was obviously waiting for it to ring. Frank and Mary Barber sat near him, close together, white-faced and stiff. Poldi was sitting forward, tensely, in an armchair, watching me. Bert Thompson stood straddle-legged before a window, and three tough-looking young men were disposed around the walls. One at each of the two doors and the third just behind the Barbers. There was no sign of Clark.

Tucker looked at me coldly. "Sit down, Scotter."

"Where's Clark?"

"Sit down." He gestured sharply. "I thought I'd asked you to leave Clark alone?"

"And you promised to hobble him," I snapped back. "Instead of that, you let him kill the Austin sisters."

"Suicide," Tucker said flatly. "Let's keep our terms right."

He was dressed in sports clothes, fawn trousers and a darker jacket. The jacket was open, and I could see the butt of a pistol in a shoulder holster. I made a quick check around the room. No one had moved.

"Where's Clark now?"

Tucker motioned towards the phone, a precise, spare gesture based on the one, two, three of drill. "I am waiting to find out."

"And when you find him," I said. "What then? D'you present him with a medal?"

Tucker frowned, looking at his hands, spread out on the table. "You're not making things any easier for us, Scotter."

"How foolish of you, Wade," Frank Barber said, in a steely, mocking tone. "You should put all your faith in the colonel. He is your guardian angel, your conscience, your watchdog, and your jailer . . . . all in one."

"Shut up," Tucker flared.

"What the hell?" I started up from my chair in protest. Then I saw the manacles and fell back. Frank and Mary Barber were handcuffed together. I turned to Tucker, numbed, feeling as though I had been kicked brutally in the stomach. "What's this?"

"Espionage," he said shortly.

"I don't believe it." My voice sounded far away. Hollow. Booming in my head.

"You will, though," Tucker said. "We've caught them with the goods. Formulae. Nicely faked for the occasion." Then he added grimly, looking me straight in the eye. "And if some idiot hadn't removed a section of decking from the pontoon bridge and held up our cars, we'd have caught Clark with them."

"Clark?"

"The fall guy," he snapped.

It was more than I could take in quickly. I sat uncertainly, groping about my mind, looking for something that would explain this thing to me, some clue that would prove it either right or wrong. . . . Then the phone shrilled. Tucker listened without speaking for perhaps thirty seconds. Then he said "Right," and put the phone back.

"Clark," he said. He got up swiftly, but without haste, perfectly in command. He gestured towards Frank and Mary Barber. "Take these two out to headquarters, and lock them up. Separately. Under close guard."

Frank stood up, pale lips sneering and eyes glitter sharp behind their thick glasses. Mary rose, too, her pleasant face unpleasant, staring at Tucker with such malevolence as I had never seen before. And it was then that I lost any remaining doubts as to what they were. There was fanaticism in their faces, in the tense, spitting contempt they projected into every corner of the room. I watched them leave in silence, shepherded by two of Tucker's men, conscious of Poldi's eyes on me, of the stressed tightness of her lips, but unable to give her any sign of recognition. Then I heard Tucker, on the phone again, giving orders in a hard, dry voice.

"Radio all cars to head for the southern road block. Clark left his car there five minutes ago. He's in the paddocks somewhere, on foot. Deploy spotlights along the line of scrub. That'll keep him in the open, along the coast. Keep the cars weaving to pin him down. A detailed sweep will commence at first light."

It sounded like a first-rate plan, the way he laid it out. Operation Manhunt. A wall of light along the sheltering inland scrub where a fugitive might run to hide, prowl cars scouring the mile-wide open strip of land between the scrub and coast, forcing the fugitive to hole up. And then, in the grey of first light, a line of dogs and armed men beating the cover until they flushed their quarry. It was straight out of the tactical training handbook, officers only, field rank and above. Operation Fine-tooth Comb, raking through and blocking off all rat holes. And yet something kept telling me it was all a waste of time. Some memory that was snagged way back, an inspired instinct that could guide but was not strong enough to lead. It was like a signal, in unbroken code, bleeping in my mind. It clamoured in a frenzy as Tucker strode across the room, with Bert Thompson rolling after him like a blind, escorting tank. Then, as Tucker yanked the door, the memory burst alive.

"Wait," I shouted.

Tucker stopped, turned sharply. "Be quick."

His voice barked impatience at me. His face was hard. Bert Thompson stared with dull, antagonistic eyes. I went across to Tucker.

"Where's this road block?"

"Two miles out. Why?"

"Near Blowhole Cove?"

"Just before it," Tucker snapped. His eyes bored into me. "All right?"

He turned to go, but I grabbed his arm and pulled him back. Roughly. "You're losing him."

Tucker snatched his arm away, bristling with indignation. I grabbed it again and hung on. "Listen . . . don't be a damn fool . . . listen to me. . . ."

Then I told him, gabble fast, about the launch in Blowhole Cove, with its fuel supplies and provisions, its rifle and fishing rods—and its owner 12,000 miles away. What had seemed odd that day was odd no longer. William Clark had prepared his line of retreat in case his plans misfired. Once down into that wild southern coast territory, with its thrusting inlets and the tangled scrub that came right down to the water's edge, he would be as hard to find as a separate grain of sand. And later, he could slip quietly away.

"Seal off the cove or you're buying trouble," I told Tucker. "If he gets down south you'll probably never catch him."

Tucker stood quite motionless for a space of seconds, as though he hadn't heard. Then he erupted clear across the room, snatched up the phone. "Tucker," he barked. "Get this and no mistakes. Clark is making for Blowhole Cove. He's got a boat. Race two men across there, with tommyguns. Post them on the path. One at the entrance. One halfway down. Concentrate all cars in the area. I'll be right out." He slammed up the phone and looked at me. "Good work. You like to come along?"

I glanced across to Poldi. She was still hunched tautly in her chair, face white, and hands clenched together.

"Poldi," I stepped towards her and she met me with a faint, but warming, smile.

"Snap to it," Tucker barked. "Come now, or stay behind."

20

THE STORM BROKE AGAIN AS OUR CAR MOVED OFF. LIGHTNING
tore great fissures in the black sky, and the rain poured through
them. The beams of the headlights were lost in the water
curtain. We had to drive dead slow. The thunder was vicious,
deafening, trying to crush us with sheer sound. But the wind
was the worst of all. When it had rained before there had been
none. Now it came rushing furiously from the sea, trying to
batter the car off course.

Tucker, Bert Thompson and I were in the back seat; Tucker
was in the middle. One of Tucker's young men was in front
with the driver. They were calm and silent, and their stolidity
heightened the unreality for me. I was still bemused by the
turn and rapidity of events . . . Frank Barber and Mary arrested
. . . Clark a fugitive. . . . My head ached with it, and my
reason floundered far behind the car. But though I was still far
from comprehension, a high, cruel excitement was beating in
me . . . something I did not need to think about, or understand.
It drove everything else from my mind. I had no thought for
Frank and Mary Barber. They were spies who had been friends.

Just that, at that moment . . . nothing more. . . . We were hunting William Clark.

We swung south out of the town and in ten minutes, miraculously, were free of the rain. The road ahead was bone dry. But we still had the wind. I could feel the car swaying under its side pressure. The south road was about half a mile from the coast, but even with the windows closed, the taste and smell of salt spray was so strong we could have been on a ship.

"Let's hope there's no more rain," Tucker said.

"We'll catch him sooner or later," Bert Thompson said.

"Sooner," said Tucker coolly, "is the operative word."

He turned to me. I couldn't see him very well, but his dry, clipped accent was unchanged. If there was any excitement in him it was under lock and key. "I haven't brought you along to give you a front-page story, Scotter," he said. "I've brought you because, in a way, I owe you some proof of our sincerity. Clark is one of our men. He went wrong, and we're going to get him. I know how it's been between you and Clark."

I said, deliberately, "I hate his guts."

"You'll probably hate mine, too," Tucker said, "after what I've got to tell you."

"It isn't possible," I said. "I haven't got anything left over."

Tucker cleared his throat. "I'll put you in the picture while there's time. Clark was blackmailing your Austin sisters—"

"Blackmail. . . ." The word clanged out, shuddered and hurt. Blackmail. An ugly, shocking word, but even as I echoed it, I wondered how I hadn't guessed it for myself. Or, at least, suspected it. It explained so many things.

"I knew he was doing it," Tucker said. "That why I asked you to go quietly. Why I made that deal with you."

"You knew?" My voice was suddenly thin and whispering. Incredulous. "You knew, and you let it go on?"

Tucker put a hand on my knee. "I never once thought they would take their own lives. I should have known, I suppose.

Such people as they were. Now I can see it was inevitable. But not then."

Bert Thompson said, "You should've reported that to us, y'know. Blackmail's a police matter. Nuthin' to do with the Security Service."

No one answered him. The car lurched around a clutter of fallen branches on the roadway. We were going fast. I stared past the silhouetted heads of the security men in front, along the tunnel of light that bored ahead of us, and listened to the whisperings of fear in my mind that were two old women's fears, the jeering threats that were Clark's vileness, the promises of help in return for help that were Colonel Tucker's final contribution to the callous inhumanity that enwrapped their precious, rotten, gut-stinking nuclear society. I felt sick. Not just physically sick, but sick right down to where my soul must have shrivelled. And out of that there grew in me an understanding of murder, a clear and instinctive understanding of why some men killed. Not expecting to right anything by their killing, or to be upheld by their fellows, or to escape the hangman. But merely to fulfil a terrible conviction of rightness, of nomination, that filled every corner of their being until nothing else existed in the world.

"Listen to me, Scotter," Tucker said. "Listen and think before you blow your top. Think. Put yourself in my position. What I did, I had to do. There was, on the face of it, no other way to act."

His voice was hard. Urgent and controlled. There was an impelling force about Tucker, the force of credo, of belief. I had to listen.

"We discovered a long time ago that Clark was a weak link. He was digging up too much dirt that didn't matter, that we didn't want. He was working too hard at things outside our compass. Personal things."

"You don't have to tell me that."

"We also knew that one of our scientists was suspect," Tucker went on. "We also knew, from past experience, that there has to be an outside man for the inside one to be effective. Our job was to find him. . . ."

"You thought it was me?"

"No," Tucker said. "We checked everyone in sight, without Clark's knowledge. We decided you were all right. A bit cranky about the big, bad world. But all right."

"Thanks," I said.

Bert Thompson, in his far corner, leaned towards us slightly, the better to hear. I felt the seat move as he shifted his vast bulk.

"We really started to get hot when Clark turned to the Austins," Tucker said. "We knew all about Lucy, and the Austins were rich. We watched him hobbling you with that old scandal about your father. He had to tie you up because you were close to the Austins. Clark was obviously working himself into a spot. We had to let him have his head. . . ."

The man in front screwed around. "Road block coming up, sir."

A cluster of red lights spanned the road about half a mile ahead. Four cars were crawling across the open country to the left, making towards the coast, their headlights swinging as they zigzagged. I judged them to be somewhere about Blowhole Cove. The land was smooth there. They were zigzagging not to pick their way, but to use their headlights to search for Clark. He was out there in the darkness somewhere. Running. My senses quickened. I edged forward.

Tucker said: "Clark became a goat tethered to attract the tiger. When he first put the finger on the old ladies, we knew that, sooner or later, he'd lead us home. The double blackmail is standard technique for spies. Their favourite ploy. They sniff around until they find someone they can put pressure on, and then they're in. We were waiting for someone to put the pressure on William Clark."

"And you let him torture two old women."

"We were playing for high stakes, Scotter. There's more at issue than two lives. There's a whole system of civilization."

"You make it sound heroic."

"Scotter, you must forget Saint George," Tucker said. His voice turned harsh. "The old heroism is dead. But the reasons are still alive. These things we are doing are as important as any major battle in any war that you can mention. You've been in wars. You've seen the ideologies in action. You ought to know."

"Two frail old women promoted to the front line," I said bitterly.

"For God's sake, man," Tucker barked. "Innocence is no protection. It never was against the sword. It's even less so against the hydrogen bomb. The innocent and the guilty are now lumped together, Scotter. Get that firmly in your mind. Realize it. Grapple with it. There's no place left to hide."

I turned my head and tried to read his face. But it was too dark for me to discover what expression there might have been on that well-drilled, regimental mask. There was both shape and substance to what he had said, though. My mood was not so dark as to obscure that. In Korea, in Indo-China, in Malaya, I had seen the putrid innocent lying slaughtered in the cause of peace. Their own cause, although probably none of them had known it. But they had been strangers. Cipher figures I could evaluate dispassionately. Old men and women, boys, and young girls who provoked the tears of compassion, but not of loss. Now I had known the tears of loss, and they had confused my evaluations. I came to accept, in time-suspended, sobering moments, that it was just as Tucker said.

Clara and Belle Austin had fallen, too, in the labyrinthine cause of peace. Pathetically. Uselessly. Their innocence of war and ideologies had been no protection. It never would be for anyone any more. The world, which had been shrinking ever since the first creature had killed another, was now no bigger than the area covered by one man's feet. There was, as Tucker said, no place left to hide. There was something for me in that, too, for I had come back to Clayville looking for a hiding place. I should have known better. I held my hand out to Tucker and he must have sensed my mind. He grasped it instantly.

"There was nothing else you could have done," I said, and felt the dry, hard pressure of his hand.

"Thanks," he said simply. "Thanks."

"That leaves Clark," I said thinly. "There's no place left for him to hide, either."

Tucker nodded, an almost impreceptible movement in the darkness. "I thought you'd come back to him."

Then we were braking hard and the road block came up fast. It was formed by a car parked in the middle of the road, flanked by piled boughs and stones. Red lanterns glowed in line along the ground. A security man with a tommy-gun stood to one side. Another kept a spotlight on us. We stopped sideways on to the block and piled out.

The wind was savage. It hit me in the chest and all but knocked me off balance. It was cold, with teeth in it. But the sky was clear again. The storm had raced inland, sucking this wind in its wake. The dry grass in the paddocks whistled. The sea, across the paddocks, was so loud it sounded like continuous thunder. And as we went around the car towards the road-block guards, I heard the whoosh and then the dreadful, sucking sigh of the blowhole. I hoped that Clark had got his boat, if that had been his purpose. He would go to hell the hard way.

"Bring me up to date," Tucker barked at the tommy-gunner.

The man thumbed on his safety catch. "He's out by the cove, sir. Lawson and Collins are on the path. He won't get past them."

"The other cars?" Tucker said. "How many men? What have they got in arms?"

"Sixteen . . . no, seventeen," the man said. "Four tommies, I think. The rest rifles and pistols. They've got two dogs."

"Good," Tucker snapped. "We're going over. Watch yourself. I'll have your skin if you let him double back and grab your car."

The man grinned wryly. "You wouldn't have to take it, sir. I'd strip it off myself."

We climbed back into the car and started for the cove. The other cars were cruising up and down along the coast. One of them had a shooting spotlight on the side. It roved like a great white finger, methodically, stopping now and then to probe deeper at some rock, some thicker patch of grass. Then the wind carried the blare of horns. I saw the spotlight stop and the car's headlights swing around. The other cars closed in. They were concentrated on the northern headland of the cove, a place of stunted undergrowth and rocks. The blood beat in my head. They had him. Cornered like a rat, with nowhere to go but two hundred feet down into the raging sea. There was emptiness where my belly should have been. I crouched far forward over the front seat, trying to catch a glimpse of Clark, but we were still too far away. I saw the four cars edging forward again, slowly, the spotlight tracking, not searching any more.

I swung around on Tucker. "Have you got a spare gun?"

Bert Thompson said. "You keep right out of this. You're not sworn in."

"Balls," I snapped. "Colonel Tucker, have you got a gun?"

"Yes," he said, "but not for you. The idea is to take him alive." He reached out and tapped the driver. "Faster. Get up with 'em."

We closed the distance quickly then. The car bucked and shuddered on stones and small hillocks, but I knew there was little risk. The country was comparatively smooth, and then we swung into the tracks of one of the other cars, deeply cut through the long, dry grass. The cars had stopped again. Only the spotlight still moved, and suddenly, at the end of its beam I saw Clark run, stumbling from behind a rock to disappear behind another. My hatred boiled over. I sat there, tense and rigid, hating the man with such a hate that I felt twelve feet tall and twice as wide. My hands clenched and I was killing him.

As we came up with the cars, the blowhole spouted, throwing a great column of water fifty feet in the air. Its roar outroared the sea. Then the water fell back, all that wasn't spray, and I shuddered at the fearful noise of suction as it went down that jagged chimney. It wasn't more than fifty yards behind the point where I'd seen Clark. He had run clean out of space.

The wind was so strong on the cliff top that I had to lean against it. The sea was deafening. So no one heard the first shot, or the second. Only, suddenly, a great star opened on a windscreen. Then a headlamp shattered.

Tucker ran to the spotlight car, and I followed. I knew what he was going to do. The dogs were there. And as I turned around the far side of the car, I saw the dogs rush forward into the spotlight's beam. A grey Alsatian and a big, black Doberman. God, they were fast. And deadly. A vice of dread took hold of me. It was Clark out there. William Bloody Murdering Clark. But he had the body of a man. Even a soul, in some misshapen way. I was watching a man being hunted like an animal by dogs. There was an awful, chilling eagerness about them.

Then I saw Clark leap up from behind his cover. He turned and ran, wildly, with his coat flying open in the wind. Probably he was screaming. I didn't know. The spotlight followed him. The dogs stretched out, low to the ground, like greyhounds coursing a hare. Tucker and his men started forward, spread out, their weapons at the ready, and the end was close at hand.

It happened in a split-second. An instant of time so horrible that it was like a lightning flash that comes blindingly and goes, leaving its glare fused in the eyes and brain. The Doberman closed first on Clark. Then the Alsatian. He turned to fight them off. He didn't have a chance. The Doberman grabbed his arm in its huge jaws, and he pulled it right off the ground in a desperate effort to get free. It swung there for a moment, scratching and kicking until it fell off, and turned back for another charge. Then the Alsatian leaped for his throat. It hit him in the chest and he staggered back. At that instant, in the moment of being overwhelmed by the snarling fury of dogs, the blowhole roared. A vast column of water shot up, and I saw Clark topple back into it. A noiseless shout died in my throat. The column held upright, then collapsed with its awesome sucking noise. And when it had gone there was no Clark. Only two dogs, charging about like crazy things, sniffing the ground, pawing it in frustrated fury.

"Christ," the man on the spotlight said.

I put a hand over my eyes.

"Poor, stupid bastard," the man said. "He wasn't a bad sorta bloke."

I went around in the darkness behind the car and retched. All the hatred and bitterness had gone out of me.

It was quiet going back. No one spoke. Even Bert Thompson could think of nothing stupid to announce. We dropped him at his police station and went on up Main Street. It was just past ten o'clock. The shops were shut, and the street deserted. The whole town seemed deserted. The night was clear and blameless. There was not even the slightest aftermath of storm. We pulled up outside Frank Barber's front gate.

We climbed out, and Tucker said: "There's just a spot of tidying up to do. It won't take long."

I followed him inside.

21

THEY WERE IN THE SITTING ROOM, POLDI AND TWO YOUNG
Security men whom Tucker had left behind. They were having supper. Poldi was in a big, high-winged chair, balancing
a cup and saucer on her lap. The two young men were going
through a stack of papers on the table, munching biscuits. It
was so normal, so other world, after what we had just been
through, that a crazy laugh climbed up my throat. I choked it
off. Poldi was watching me.

"He's dead," Tucker said.

Poldi's deep-blue eyes opened wider for a moment, flicked
from me to Tucker, and back to me again. I crossed the room
and took the chair beside her, reached out and grasped her
hand. It was cold. The two young men were standing, watching Tucker like well-trained bird dogs, expectant, waiting for
him to go on.

"The damned fool tried to fight," Tucker said. He sat down
at the table, drummed his square fingers on the polished top,
and frowned. His lean face was set and stern. There was
tightness around his mouth. "We cornered him at the cove.

He opened fire. We set the dogs on him and he ran. And once a man starts running he just can't stop." He lit a cigarette, drew on it as though he needed comfort. "He went down the blowhole," he said harshly. "Probably the best thing that could have happened . . . for him and all of us. He was rotten. Right through. Rotten to the core."

I realized then, from his depth of bitterness, how badly Tucker had been hurt. Not by the death of Clark. Death to him was a thing inevitable, a part of living. But by the fact that one of his men had let the service down. The knowledge added to my respect. Tucker might have been stiff-necked, but he held his head up straight. If he hurt you, it would be according to the rules and not of his own desires.

One of his young men pushed and envelope across the table. "Maybe you ought to read this now, sir."

Tucker read the letter slowly, without a sign of expression on his face. It was overdone. It made me feel uneasy. My eyes dropped to the envelope, lying before him on the table. It was upside-down, but I could read the inscription like a printer reading type. It was addressed to me. The writing was Clara Austin's. No one in the world wrote that way any more, in big fat letters, with heavy downstrokes and light upstrokes, like the examples in old-time school copybooks.

"This is for you," Tucker said at last, stretching half out of his chair to hand the letter across. His face was still impassive, but there was a touch of warmth in his steady eyes. "You will excuse me for having read it first. It was unavoidable."

The letter was not long. A little more than a page of Clara's big, space-taking script. But before I had reached the end I couldn't see the words. I handed it to Poldi without saying anything. I was fighting hard to stop myself bawling like a kid.

"It is part of our evidence," Tucker said quietly. "Against Clark and against Barber. But you can have it. It is yours to do with as you wish. I guess we owe you something."

Poldi pressed the letter back into my hands. "Oh, Wade," she whispered. She stood beside me, one hand on my shoulder, and I could feel her strength flowing through it into me. I read the letter again, very slowly, and this time got right through with Poldi's silent help.

Dearest Wade

By the time you read this note, Belle and I will have returned to our Maker, if He can find it in the goodness of His heart to forgive us the sin of taking our own lives. I had intended making the journey alone, but Belle, my dear sister and life's companion, insists on accompanying me.

As I think you have suspected in these last few days, Thomas Moody and I loved deeply. Lucy was our child, born out of wedlock, and all these years I have lived a lie, afraid to tell her the truth, repeating the lie until I came almost to believe it myself.

But now I have been brought to reckoning. Mr. William Clark and Lucy have forced me to give them money. They threaten me with scandal which I cannot bear to contemplate. I do not blame them; the blame lies on me for what I have done to Lucy.

But I do enjoin you, as your dear father's son, as our own dear boy, to make up your quarrel with Lucy. She has been deeply, desperately wronged. She is blameless, and yet she has been made to suffer. Cherish her, Wade, and forgive your aunts for what they are about to do.

Your loving aunt,
Clara Austin.

I folded the letter back into its envelope, marvelling at my hand's steadiness. A sick anger was at work inside me, and perhaps it was that which steadied me. I looked up at Tucker and my eyes were hard and gritty hot.

"And you claim you didn't know they were going to kill themselves?" I didn't recognize my own voice, it was so strained.

"I read this for the first time tonight," Tucker said steadily. "You saw me."

"I saw you," I repeated. "You weren't surprised."

He turned across the table. "Cummings. Tell Mr. Scotter everything about the letter."

Cummings cleared his throat softly. A broad-shouldered, keen-faced man who could have been a musician, or a wrestler. He looked uncomfortable. This was something outside the training manual, disclosing information to a civilian.

"We found this letter in Dr. Barber's safe after you had gone," he said stiffly. "It had been steamed open. An expert job."

"Obviously, this was to be his final, complete hold over Clark," Tucker said. "Your aunt must have given it to him on his last visit. Probably he guessed its character from her disturbed condition, and steamed it open just in case it was important. And it was . . . to him."

"The good Doctor Barber," I said bleakly. "So ethical. So professional . . . so utterly—"

"He is a dedicated man," Tucker said. "The most dangerous animal in the world."

The room became very still. No one spoke, or if they were speaking I did not hear them. Frank Barber had killed the Austins as surely as though he had pushed them into the Clay, or loaded his healing hypodermic with some deadly poison. He was more the real murderer than vain, stupid Clark. The realization shocked me beyond measure, to the point of trauma, or perhaps beyond. I was in no condition to assess myself. I had hated Clark, and his villainy was no surprise. But I had liked Frank Barber, liked Mary, too. And this is what they were.

I understood, then, Barber's insistence on trying to prove to me a physical basis for Clara and Belle Austin's illness. He had wanted, at all costs, to keep me away from the truth in case I should hobble Clark. And I had once worried for him, and for Mary, felt compassion when I fancied Clark had bullied them.

"What makes people go like that?" I wondered aloud. "Everyone's been good to them here. They've had friends."

"They didn't go like anything," Tucker said quietly. "They came like that. They came as spies, not immigrants, or I miss my guess."

I moved my eyes around the room, not seeing it so much as feeling it, feeling the dark woodwork, the ornamental stonework of the fireplace, the winged plaster cherubs on the ceiling, that round table and these straight-backed chairs. . . . All these things that had formerly recalled to me the sanity of those other days, when I was a boy and my father a bearded hero. The things that had brought me back to Clayville because I had wanted to touch them, like a pilgrim touching footmarks on some holy stairs in Jerusalem or Rome, because he believed, or wanted to believe, they held the power to build again whatever it was that had fallen to ruins within him.

And now I felt as the pilgrim would feel if someone had plastered the stairs with filth and carved dirty words deep in their stone. First Clayville had rejected all my efforts to find peace. Now Francis Barbasiewicz had spewed obscenity throughout my father's house. And I remembered, without summoning the memory, Tucker's words on that windswept road on our way to superintend Clark's death. "The innocent and the guilty are lumped together now. There's no place left to hide."

Then I began to feel something pressing hard on my left shoulder, pushing down through the nightmarish dream that had taken hold of me. Slowly, like a man awaking, I recognized it for the pressure of a hand, the dig of fingers. I turned my head slightly, and it was Poldi's hand, slender, capable and firm. I looked up and she was watching me, her blue eyes dark with worry, white teeth biting on her bottom lip.

"God," I said. "I'm tired."

Some of the worry left her eyes. "You have had great strain." She slid her hand around my back to grip my other shoulder. "If Colonel Tucker has finished, I think you should go at once to bed."

Tucker stood up instantly, in sections, the way he always did, like assembling a Bren-gun mounting. "Certainly," he said. "You look all in. We can go through our formalities some other time."

I still had Aunt Clara's letter in my hand. I held it up to Tucker. "You really mean this is mine?"

"If you want it," he said steadily. "If you don't, your friend Thompson will be interested. It contains the essence of a blackmail case against Lucy Austin."

I tore the letter into small pieces and piled them in an ash-tray. "Make up your quarrel with Lucy . . . she has been deeply, desperately wronged," it said. I knew I could never make up my quarrel with her, but this at least I could do. Aunt Clara would have wanted it. I struck a match and burned the pieces.

Tucker leaned over and broke up the ashes with his fore-finger, squashing them to powder. "Lesson number one," he said. "Always pulverize your ashes." He moved towards the door, and his junior sleuths went swiftly around the table to go with him. Cummings opened the door and held it for his chief but, in the act of passing through, Tucker turned back.

"By the way," he said. "None of tonight's happenings are to go in your paper. And I must ask both of you not to talk about them to anyone."

"For how long?" I asked.

Tucker frowned. "Maybe never. I can't say off-hand."

His answer wiped my tiredness away. I stood up. "So Clark's name remains pure, and mine stays mud."

"What can I do?" Tucker gave that military shrug, but it

seemed this time as though he were trying to make his shoulders more comfortable. "We have to protect the Service."

"To hell with the Service," I snapped. "I'm thinking of myself. Clark gave me a dirty name right through this town . . . through the entire district."

"I know," Tucker said softly. "Don't think I'm unaware of it. Perhaps one day, when all this has simmered down . . . perhaps then it can be divulged. But that would be a matter for higher authority. I don't make policy. I merely carry it out."

"Oh, fine," I said bitterly. "That's really fine. That's really stinking, rotten fine."

Poldi came up and took my arm, not just in her hand, but hugging it all to herself. "It does not matter, Wade," she said. "Good names do not matter. Only good people."

I looked down into her eyes, and they were imploring me. I looked away, quickly, before I changed my mind. "Good names *do* matter," I said, my voice a strangled noise. "The whole world works by names . . . labels . . . grades. . . ."

"I do not," she said. "The world, as you should know, is a very silly place."

"Poldi," I gripped her arm with my free hand. It felt soft and warm and wonderful. "Poldi, you've had enough trouble in your life—"

"I have learnt to live with trouble," she said. "It is only a state of atmosphere . . . like . . . like air-conditioning. You control it . . . get used to it . . . you settle down."

There was such a sincerity, such an outpouring of warmth in what she was saying, how she was saying it, her face sweetly fierce with conviction and with argument that, if Tucker had not been standing by, I know I would have taken her in my arms and said all the things I had told myself I had no right to say. But there was Colonel Godalmighty Tucker, watching us with his all-observant, microscopic eyes. Examining. Assessing. I freed myself from Poldi and stood away.

219

"No," I said. "No. The kind of mud I'm wearing sticks. You don't get used to it. People don't let you."

"Wade," Poldi said softly. "Sometimes you are so intelligent. But mostly you are a great big fool."

"Listen, Scotter." Tucker's voice rasped like a saw. He marched three paces forward, and stood at ease, legs wide, hands locked behind his back. His lips were twisted in a wry smile. "Your personal affairs are not my business. But if it's any help to you, I invite you to consider the fact that Miss Lorenz has been living in the same house with two spies."

He pole-axed me. He stood before me like a cut-out soldier figure, in metal, immovable, not human any more.

"For Christ's sake—"

"I don't suspect her any more than you do," he said harshly. "Any more than I suspect you. We've checked her right through. But being innocent isn't enough these days. You have to *appear* innocent in all things, too. You had a visa cancelled. She's been living with spies. You're both on the query list, officially."

Poldi turned to face me, squarely, smiling right to the bottom of her eyes. "You see," she said. "It is as I have told you. Good names do not matter. Particularly they do not matter when both our names are bad."

I suppose I should have been appalled. Only a short space of words ago I had been shocked and angered at Tucker's branding her as suspect. But now, by some virtue of cadship or, more probably, by a vague realization that the inevitable was beyond assault, I was conscious only of a feeling of relief, of a problem, if not solved, at least equated. It was as much as any man could expect of a major problem in a tangled world.

Poldi moved a little closer. "You cannot escape me now," she whispered. "We are, as you say, eggs in the same basket."

"Bad eggs," I said, and I was grinning like a fool. A warmth that wasn't of the summer was working up in me. I looked away from her because she was tempting me, or I was tempting me, or we were tempting both of us. Cummings and the other sleuth at the door were watching us expectantly. Tucker was smiling, really smiling, like an austere uncle thawed by a good dinner and a stomach full of port.

"I want both of you to stay in town for a day or two," Tucker said. "I'll need statements from you for my report."

"We'll be around," I said. "For a while, at least."

"Good night, then," he said. He gave Poldi a smile and a little bow, me a nod, and executed a smart about-turn. "Cummings, you stay here the night. Forder, take all that stuff on the table and come with me."

He went, and Cummings stayed. Poldi looked at me.

"Have you a spare bed?"

"Yes," I said. "But—"

She smiled impishly. "If I am to be compromised, I would rather it be you."

Outside, the wind had softened to a breeze. The stars were out and near enough to touch. We crossed Main Street, walking arm in arm, hip to hip, and step by step. We breathed, I think, in unison. My car was still there in the side street, and as we got in we saw a light in the Austins' house, filtering through the trees.

"Poor Lucy," Poldi said. "I feel we should go in to her."

"We should," I said. "But no. I'm not all that Christian. I'd probably hit her in the face. Clara and Belle are in there with her, too."

"Of course." Poldi touched my hand. "Just let us go home."

Night air is kind to engines. We flowed down Main Street, silently and smooth as a royal barge. We passed one car. The houses slept, dark, and curtained against the spacious freshness of the night. And I thought, this was the Clayville I had come seeking. The town I had imperfectly remembered and idealized as some psychiatric spa, somnolent, protected by its very yawns from the world's perplexities.

But out to the left, floodlights showed where men were still working on the river bridge. Farther out, over the brow of the limestone hill, and above the buildings of the Atomic Research Authority, a glare of light suffused the sky. Beneath it, doubtless, Frank and Mary Barber were being questioned. And scientists, ignorant of hours, were tirelessly at work, coaxing and shaping their material into the new patterns that had transformed the world. And I thought again, this was Clayville now. The world was here. . . .

But then I stopped. Had it ever been so very far away? Had I not come back in search of a dream that had no substance? I had known Clayville only as a boy, and remembered it as that. But while I was a boy, obsessed with birds' nests and pirates' caves and swimming, what had been the Clayville of adults? The past few days had supplied my answer. The world had been close to my father, and to the Austin sisters. A more graceful world, perhaps, not so insistent, but basically the same. The hydrogen bomb, the rival ideologies, the security screens, were no more than sophistications of an ancient problem. Man had always had to search for ways to live with man.

"When you have finished making growing noises," Poldi said, "perhaps we could go in."

I stretched awake. We had stopped behind the *Herald* office. I had driven there by the same instinct that takes old horses home. We climbed out and walked slowly, arm in arm, around to the front door.

"Poldi," I said. "What d'you think about Clayville now?"

"For whom?" she said.

"Stop being so grammatical," I said. "For me. For both of us."

"For you it is not good," she said quietly. "For me it does not matter. But you waste your talents here. It is time you went back to the cities and faced the big things that a man must do."

"And what are they?"

"The things you want to do. All the little things that, added up, become big things. Doing what your conscience says is right to do, saying the things you know are right, so that while you live and after you die, your friends will know that you have been alive. That you have been you."

I stopped and turned, and she moved in towards me. Her face lifted, and we kissed. There was conviction in the kiss, a conviction and assurance that together we could face anything. It made me feel whole, complete as only a man can feel who has sought completeness, been thwarted, and been found in time.

We went inside, juggling through the door, arms linked together, and Harry Wells' pale-blue eyes were saucers of surprise. He was sitting, feet up, at my desk, his brown teapot at his right hand.

"Harry." I clasped my head. "I clean forgot. . . ."

He waved me off. "I saw you go harin' off with Tucker, so I come back here. I reckoned watchin' Lucy didn't matter any more."

"You did right," I said, and could feel myself grinning to my ears. "She doesn't matter any more."

Poldi said, "Wade, you have not yet kissed me since we came in through that door."

We kissed again then, in the middle of that blotchy little office, with its smell of grease and printer's ink, its naked light bulbs—and its audience of one. And if the first kiss had made me feel complete, this one overflowed. I was lost in it. There was no thinking, no wonderment. Only giving and accepting, the most perfect trade balance in the world.

"For Gawsake," Harry said. "What happened?"

We broke away then, turned to face him, laughing at his bewilderment.

"Why everything," I said. "Poldi and I are going to get married."

"Married!" Harry said.

Poldi giggled. "Is that all you have to say?"

Harry stared at us in slack-jawed incredulity. Then he picked up his teapot, held it at arm's length above his head, opened his mouth and poured. The stream of tea hit him fair between the eyes. He dropped the pot and yelled blue murder. He wiped the tea from his face with the back of a muddy hand.

"Jesus," he said. "M'nerves."